CAST IN HELLFIRE

THE MAGE CRAFT SERIES

SM REINE

CAST IN HELLFIRE

The Mage Craft Series
Book Two

SM REINE

In tuo adventu suscipiant te martyres,
et perducant te in civitatem sanctam Duat

ONE

November whispered cool air over the Mojave Desert, sending dust devils swirling through the sagebrush to blast into Seth Wilder's face. He was lying atop a ridge under a veil of gaean magic, hiding from surveillance, but he couldn't help coughing.

"There," said Brianna Dimaria. "Beyond the Joshua trees." She handed the binoculars down to Seth. She had brought a lawn chair to the stakeout, refusing to get in the dirt like Seth did. The tie-dyed canvas was plastered with so many illusion spells that it seemed to vanish every few seconds, even from within the magic circle.

He looked in the direction the witch had indicated. She'd spotted another pile of rocks that was too uniform to be natural, stacked into a symmetrical, three-sided pyramid. Its unnatural evenness would be obvious from the air, assuming that one was flying low enough to see such a small formation; Brianna had managed to spot it from half a mile away on the ground. She had good eyes for stakeouts, if not the temperament.

The fact that they needed to have a stakeout was ridiculous. The target that Seth intended to rescue never should have been moved to the detention center in the first place. If she'd been given a trial, any judge would have happily released her.

But no matter how much time passed or how many government regulations were forced upon the Office of Preternatural Affairs, they still had a nasty habit of imprisoning people without due process.

On the bright side, it meant Seth felt no guilt about breaking the law to free said prisoner.

Seth set the binoculars down. The sun was dropping low. It was almost nighttime, which meant that shifts would be changing soon. He needed to move in. "You can head out."

"How will you escape without my help?" Brianna asked.

"Not your problem," he said.

Seth jumped over the edge of the rocks. He slid down the steep slope, knees bent, arms stretched out to balance himself like a surfer in the desert. Pebbles sprayed behind him.

The messiness of his entrance blew the secrecy of the illusion spells, which was exactly what he'd intended to do.

Men appeared in a desert that had, until that moment, appeared empty. They stepped from behind the trees, stood behind sagebrush. They were dressed to be as obvious as Seth in their own way. Their black clothes leaped out against harsh yellow desert painted violet by sunset.

Much like the signs that had warned Seth that he was entering a restricted zone, the agents were meant to send an obvious message.

Turn back or be shot.

Seth drew his gun. Three agents closed in. Their chests, heads, and shins were protected by body armor, so he fired three gunshots aimed for their unprotected thighs.

He hit with every single bullet.

They weren't killing blows, but they hurt. It would take people trained better than American government employees to absorb that kind of gunfire without falling.

These guys fell.

When they tumbled, there were others behind them. Another three—no, five. Several more than Seth had expected to find at the facility. He only had so much ammunition, and only so much time.

Seth aimed again but didn't get a chance to shoot.

Magic sizzled over the desert, reeking of burned hair. Brianna whipped a dust storm through the valley that froze the sweat on Seth's skin.

Her magic caught the agents up, lobbed them into the air. Random gunshots thunder-cracked high above and echoed off of the hills.

Seth had to trust that she caught them on the way down. He didn't have time to watch.

When he reached the unnatural cairn of rocks, the door at its rear was still open. It was only open for fifteen minutes a day in five-minute spurts, allowing changing shifts to enter and exit. The door, ordinarily cloaked by magic similar to Brianna's, was clad in steel and lit by red warning bulbs that flashed every second. They reminded Seth of the lights along runways that guided airplanes to takeoff.

He leaped through the door and plunged into cool darkness while the agents were still screaming in a dust storm five hundred feet above the desert.

Seth landed at the bottom of stairs with his gun raised.

It didn't take much time to get his bearings, even though he'd never been in that particular place before. Once you'd visited one building designed by the Office of Preternatural Affairs, you'd visited them all. They were hideously uniform in their narrow lobbies and sterile furnishings. White walls, blue carpet, furniture from Office Outlet. The government agency with most of the defense budget should have been able to hire better interior decorators.

Two agents leaped to their feet at Seth's entrance. They must not have seen much action at an OPA installation in the middle of the Mojave— they weren't ready to be attacked. They didn't even have sidearms. With all the agents guarding the surface, they shouldn't have needed them.

Both had security badges with their surnames and photos on them. The man on the left was named Stalwart. The man on the right was Hanes.

Seth was on the guy on the right in a heartbeat, arm locked around his throat, Beretta pressed to his temple. He wouldn't shoot, not ever, but they didn't know that.

"Open the cells," Seth said.

"Do what he says," whimpered Hanes, his captive.

Stalwart backed away, looking bewildered. "But the revenant isn't drugged yet and—"

"I'm not making a request." Seth shoved the gun hard enough into Hanes's temple that his neck bent. "Open the cells."

Stalwart bolted for the stairs.

If he thought he'd be able to escape like that, he was probably right. As soon as he hit the surface, he was going to enjoy a flight courtesy of Air Brianna.

"Damn it," Seth said. He stared at the control panel behind the desk. It was a mess of runes, switches, buttons, and security monitors. If there was an easy way to let himself into the cells, he didn't see one. "How do I get in back?"

Hanes answered by kicking out. His heel caught the control panel, flipping a switch.

The door behind the desk unlocked.

Seth tossed the agent back into his chair. "Stay here." He plucked the security badge off of Hanes's lapel.

"No," the agent protested weakly. He didn't care all that much, or else he would have surely tried to fight back, rather than remaining limp in his chair like Seth had sucked all the energy out of him.

It wasn't Seth who had weakened him like that.

His heart was laboring to beat.

Seth stopped by the door behind the desk, gripping the handle, as he stared at Hanes. It was like a black cloud was descending on the man. He was sick, his arteries clogged with plaque, inadequate oxygen reaching his organs.

Special Agent Hanes was dying. He needed prompt intervention.

It seemed unlikely that he knew.

"What are you waiting for?" Hanes asked nervously when Seth didn't move.

That was a great question.

Seth wasn't working as a doctor at the moment, and he wouldn't have been treating OPA agents at the facility if he were. There was someone nearby in much more dire need of help.

Seth pushed the door open and faced a hall so long it might have been endless.

"If I were an OPA paper-pusher, where would I hide a revenant?" he muttered to himself.

There were steel doors on either side of the hallway, each of them equidistant, none of them labeled. It was a prison, of a sort; a simple prison, and one that looked unremarkable despite its insidious purpose. Those doors led into rooms where the OPA intended for people to vanish without due process.

Five years had elapsed since the OPA's habit of detaining people without observing their constitutional rights had been revealed in an expos?, but the wheels of justice were slow. Preternaturals who got arrested still had too good a chance of disappearing down hallways like these, never to be seen again.

Seth propped the door open with his foot. The lock clicked repeatedly, unable to secure itself while he was in the way. "Where's the revenant?"

"I don't know." Agent Hanes was sweating so hard that it dripped down his neck. His heart thumped unsteadily in his chest. "I don't assign the rooms."

Rooms. It was a nice thing to call the caskets of this veritable mausoleum.

Thumping echoed from upstairs. More agents were heading into the facility, which meant that they'd escaped Brianna.

Seth needed to find that revenant.

He let the door fall shut behind him. The lock clicked.

With the door closed, it was eerily silent. The only sound that followed Seth deeper into the hallway was the beat of his footsteps against carpet. It was only once he was a dozen doors down that he realized the hallway was dipping lower, slowly dropping deeper into the desert.

It could have been endless for all Seth knew.

How many preternatural prisoners was the OPA detaining under the Mojave Desert? The revenant had been arrested less than a week earlier. New prisoners could have been miles deep.

"Damn," Seth muttered.

But he heard a thudding when he passed one room—a fierce banging like claws against metal.

He stopped, backtracked. Returned to that door.

It was only two-dozen, maybe three, doors away from the lobby entrance. Too close to the surface to have recently confined anyone there.

Agent Stalwart had said that the revenant hadn't been drugged yet, unlike the other prisoners.

"Charity?" Seth asked, pressing his hand to the door.

A distant lock clicked.

The door to the lobby opened again. At least two agents were on the other side—probably more, but Seth couldn't see them. It was a narrow entrance.

He swiped Agent Hanes's badge and pushed the door open.

The room on the other side was too dark for Seth to distinguish anything beyond the first few inches of concrete floor. It wasn't carpeted for sure. No bland office decorations for detainees.

A tall, slender figure emerged from the darkness, shimmering with rage.

The revenant.

Seth backpedaled. It felt wrong going deeper into the hall, like he was headed in the wrong direction. He should have been escaping. Going toward the surface. But now the revenant was between him and the guards, so there was no way to escape.

The revenant studied him with unrecognizing eyes like sunken pits. She was a lanky creature with pallid skin, bony joints, and a black tongue so long that it dangled from the gash of her mouth.

Seth tried not to lift the gun. He had to rail against every instinct that told him to flee or attack or *something* because his life was in danger.

He pointed a finger. The revenant turned to see what he was indicating. Those hollow eyes fixed on the agents. Her mouth opened to release a furious hissing.

Seth leaped back as the revenant launched at the agents.

He'd been reading up on the species in the last few days. Revenants were similar to vampires: creatures who had been human until death, then resurrected as something else. What was unique about revenants was that it wasn't the body that returned. It was the soul. So they weren't exactly tangible in the way that vampires were, nor were they as vulnerable to flame or wood.

In short, revenants were big, angry, and difficult to kill.

And he'd just released one that was especially vengeful from her cell.

She moved in a flash of colorless flesh and smoke. Her foggy form obscured the agents, so Seth could only hear the screaming.

He hadn't meant for them to die.

"Wait!" he yelled.

By the time he raced up behind the revenant, she was done. She stood, hunched, over a pile of bleeding agents.

The revenant had gone easy on them.

When Seth had first seen her attack, she'd decapitated a man with her bare hands, wrenched his jaw out, and scraped the meat of his tongue off with her teeth. So the fact that only one agent was little more than a collection of limbs and a crushed skull... Well, it could have been worse for them. Most looked to have died instantaneously.

A ragged gasp drew his attention into the lobby again.

Agent Hanes had fallen from his chair. He gripped his left arm, cheeks reddening, sweat pouring from his forehead.

Seth elbowed past the revenant. He kneeled over Hanes, rolled him onto his back, tipped his chin back to open the airway.

Dying.

The revenant hissed again behind Seth. Bodies crunched wetly.

She was feeding.

Agent Hanes's panicked eyes were fixed on Seth's face. His mouth open and closed wordlessly.

The scent of blood was thick in the air. It sent Seth's heart pounding, being trapped within such narrow confines with that stench. He caught himself staring at the spread of murky black blood through blue office carpet.

It slurped under the revenant's feet when she shifted her weight, trickling into the shallow gouges left by her toenails. Every motion seemed to waft more of that coppery odor toward Seth.

So much blood.

If Agent Hanes was having a heart attack, what was Seth supposed to do?

He'd been a doctor for a decade. Saved thousands of patients. Spent thousands more shifts working in the emergency department.

The medical knowledge had fled from him.

Seth's entire awareness had narrowed down to the pinpoint flickering of Agent Hanes's fading life.

"Charity," he said. "Nurse, help me." His tongue was thick in his mouth. He was salivating, becoming nauseous.

The revenant's hands trapped another man on the floor behind Seth. It was Agent Stalwart again. His coworkers must have dragged him back into the facility, and he hadn't died yet.

He emptied his gun into her body, but he must have been armed with something like iron or silver: excellent for taking down the common preternatural species, but useless against vampiric breeds. The bullets punched through Charity's revenant body, shredding flesh to tattered ribbons, exposing dusty-dry bones. Holes exploded in the drywall.

Even being so close to gunshots wasn't quite enough to clear Seth's head.

Agent Hanes wasn't struggling to breathe anymore. As Seth held him, his heart stopped beating, and the blood stopped flowing. The life faded out of him.

It was sweet—so sweet, a perfect moment.

Charity wrenched Agent Stalwart's arm off. Seth snapped out of his reverie. He pitched to his feet, leaving Agent Hanes on the floor. Seth's head was ringing and his fingers tingled.

"Hey! Charity, stop that!" Seth's fingers brushed her shoulder.

The revenant spun, backhanding him. He bounced off the wall.

Pain rushed through him.

Now he tasted blood on his tongue. It came out of his body, so it was human blood, intoxicating and richer than chocolate cake.

The taste coupled with the smell of so much death was too much, even for him. Good intentions could only take a man so far.

When Seth bounced off the wall, he landed on hands and knees. His fingers were in the spreading puddle of blood. He was slick with it. The whole world seemed to vibrate around that blood, like gravity sucking him toward it.

He should have been trying to restrain the revenant he'd released.

Instead, he sat back on his heels, lifting his blood-slicked hands to stare at them. Focused on his own extremities, Agent Hanes's recently dead body was little more than a blur, though Seth was acutely aware of his cooling corpse.

So much death.

Seth licked his fingers.

It was like he'd been thirsty for years—for his entire life, ever since he'd woken up after Genesis

—and for the first time, he had gotten a sip of water.

He'd never tasted anything so good.

Seth rubbed his hand in the sodden carpet and licked again, and again.

The death of the agents nearby was little more than a distant, hollow throbbing, softer than the pounding of his heart. The blood nourished him, flushed him with heat, made his muscles burn strong.

He was growing.

Filling.

In that blood, Seth tasted mortality: the way that life could break in an instant, a rubber band snapping into fragments.

Legs appeared in front of him.

He forced himself to look up, gaze tracking from the knobs of Charity's ankles to her jutting hips and hollow belly—not quite so hollow now that she was glutted on the flesh of OPA agents. The bullet holes were already sealing, but her shriveled organs still peeked through the holes.

When he finally met her gaze, he noticed the ghost of recognition in her.

He got to his feet, simultaneously leaden with the desire to drink more blood and exhilarated by the strength it had given him. The revenant had killed all the agents. Every last one of them, aside from Agent Hanes, who had died all on his own while Seth did nothing to help.

Charity's hands flexed at her sides. Blood drizzled from her shiny black fingernails. Her head fell to the side as she studied Seth thoughtfully, questioningly.

Seth extracted a pair of thick-framed glasses from his breast pocket and lifted them toward the revenant.

"I recovered these for you from evidence," Seth said. He'd accidentally smeared blood on the lenses.

Charity's mouth puckered with surprise. She took the glasses. Her blunt thumbs pressed to the gems inside the arms and she slipped them onto her face.

Reality folded in on itself around her.

Seth blinked.

When his eyes opened again, Charity Ballard looked the way she had when Seth had first met her—back when he had been known as Dr. Lucas Flynn, and Charity had been a nurse. She was petite and mousy. Her hair was tangled. Her pointed chin was dotted with blood, though not as much as had been on her face as a revenant.

The glamour was good enough to affect a physical change. She didn't just *look* different. She *was* different. A lot of the carnage had been stripped away when her physical form changed.

She also looked shocked at the sight of Seth drenched in blood. He could feel it caked on his chin and hands, much like it had been on her.

"What's wrong with you?" She hadn't been distracted by the killing enough that she hadn't seen what Seth had done. She knew the blood on his body didn't belong to him.

It must have been bad when a murderous revenant was the one asking him what was wrong with him.

"If only I knew," Seth said.

TWO

Many hundreds of miles away in the United Nations, Marion Garin gripped a pen so hard that it snapped.

Black ink oozed across the table. She bit the inside of her cheek and tried to mop it up with a piece of official stationary before anyone noticed.

"What's wrong with you?" muttered the vampire on Marion's left. Her name was Jolene Chang, and she was representing the American Gaean Commission. Jolene was an asanbosam—a weak breed with knives for teeth, long fingernails, and insignificant social power. Yet Marion was forced to sit beside her.

What was wrong with *her*? Marion wasn't seated at the head of the table—that was what was wrong with her.

She was among a dozen preternaturals who

had been selected as speakers for their various factions, which meant that she was ranked equally among them in this particular context. But in every context—including this one—she was still the Voice of God, and she should have been in charge.

Instead, she was seated at the far end of the table beside Jolene, a great big nobody, and another vampire delegate, Lucifer, who was just as much a nobody.

Being surrounded by speakers from insignificant factions spoke volumes about the organizers' respect for Marion.

On the other hand, Prince ErlKonig of the Autumn Court was seated near the head of the table. When he caught her looking at him, he winked. Marion reluctantly smiled.

"Cast your votes," said Rylie Gresham, Alpha of the North American Union shapeshifters.

She was the one in charge, so she had been seated at the place of honor at the head of the table. It was her logo on everything. Her blond-haired, apple-cheeked face on the posters ringing the room. Her guards, from both the Summer Court and the shifter sanctuary, protecting the doors and watching the delegates to make sure that they couldn't cheat while voting.

Rylie Gresham was all over *everything*.

Marion couldn't cast her vote with a broken pen. She gestured to her assistant for help. Jibril was an angel who looked as pleased to be her assistant as he would have been to scrape dog crap off of the bottom of his designer shoes.

Everyone else around the table had already marked off their vote, folded their papers, and passed them to Rylie.

That was how they were voting. They were writing "yes" or "no" on a paper, and then Rylie would count them. It was irritatingly low-tech for a summit of such importance.

Konig had said that Marion had originally been slated to cast some kind of voting spell. Unfortunately, Marion's oeuvre at the moment was more along the lines of breaking pens, irritating the angels, and making people hate her, and not so much with the politically oriented magic.

So they were casting votes manually.

Marion glanced at Konig again. He was sitting back in his chair, hands folded behind his head. The decision had been easy for him.

Marion moved to mark her vote, but the tip of her new pen hovered over a clean sheet of paper... and she didn't know what to write.

It felt like everyone was looking at her.

Jolene certainly was. So was Jibril. Marion didn't want to look at anyone else in case they really were, too.

What is wrong with you?

A question that applied perfectly to so many situations.

Marion wrote quickly. She folded her paper. And then she passed it to Rylie Gresham.

Rylie's eyes were warm but worried when she smiled at Marion. Their hands brushed, and Rylie's fingers lingered in a fashion that was most likely meant to be comforting. "It will only take a moment to add these up," Rylie said, returning to her seat.

The Alpha sorted them by yes and no votes. She counted them, and then had her Alpha mate count them as well. Abel seemed to take longer to count. He probably struggled to get above numbers like five or six. Abel was a stupid idiot moron who had only become important because the skanky Alpha female was sleeping with him.

Marion was so busy glaring at Abel and thinking mean things that she forgot to be anxious about the outcome of the vote.

"No," Rylie finally said. "Nine votes say no. Four say yes."

There were no cheers, no groans. Not a sound in the entire room.

Quite the anticlimax.

"Thanks for your time," Rylie added.

Chairs were pushed back. Bodies shifted.

Then the whispers started.

Marion watched the others without getting up. She was getting better at picking up on their thoughts. That was apparently part of her oeuvre too—part of the oeuvre of anyone who had angel blood, which Marion did, though hers was watered down more than that of the others. She was only half-angel. Half seemed to be more than enough.

Elation radiated from the seelie sidhe serving as speaker for the Summer Court. Storm must have voted no.

His elation was tinged with anxiety, though. He

knew what his "no" meant.

Ad?n Pedregon, speaker for *Los Cambiaformas Internacional*, was angry as he stormed past Marion. He'd likely voted yes, as getting the angels out of the Ethereal Levant would mean more room for his gaeans to expand—or perhaps an easy route to move down into Africa.

She didn't need to reach into Konig's mind to know how he'd voted. He had told Marion how he wanted things to go, and she had ultimately agreed with him.

"What did you write?" Jibril asked.

Marion stood, smoothing her dress. It was a flashy thing that day: a red dress with a fitted bodice and ridiculous number of skirt layers, more akin to something sidhe might wear than an angel, half-blood or otherwise.

"Votes are private," she said, stepping into the hallway behind the other speakers. Marion glanced over her shoulder at Rylie and Abel, who were still seated at the head of the table, discussing the votes in whispers.

"Votes aren't private within the factions." Jibril grabbed Marion's arm the instant that the door swung shut behind her. "Did you vote for angels to get control of the Winter Court?"

The Winter Court was in the Middle Worlds: one of the four courts that were meant to be occupied by the sidhe. Specifically, it should have been occupied by the unseelie sidhe.

There had been a coup five years earlier that had resulted in the queen's assassination. The rebels hadn't managed to maintain power either, and since then, the Winter Court had been in anarchy.

The angels wanted that Middle World for themselves.

The gods had commanded that Marion should take stewardship of it until the unseelie could resume leadership.

The vote of nine against four meant that an overwhelming majority agreed with the gods.

"Hands off, angel." Konig had been waiting for Marion outside the boardroom, leaning nonchalantly against the wall. Now he hovered beside them and he radiated danger.

Jibril released his grip on Marion instantly. He knew better than to pick a fight with Marion's boyfriend.

"Are you okay?" Marion asked. She couldn't imagine that Konig was thrilled about the outcome of the meeting.

"Of course I am. It's over! Now we can deal with the next thing." Konig was immediately pleasant again once he'd been obeyed. It was shocking how quickly he swung between intimidation and charm. "I thought I'd die of boredom during all the final speeches leading up to the vote." He planted a kiss on Marion's lips, wrapping a firm arm around her waist.

"Me too," she said. "And they seated me so far away from you."

"Precious thing," Konig said. He seemed to think that Marion was offended that they didn't get to sit together, not that she had been seated with a couple of vampires.

Jibril made an impatient noise when they continued to kiss.

"Time to turn this loss into a victory," Konig said. "Good thing I had my knights getting everything packed this week, just in case. Now you and I can get to our home. Our *new* home."

Her heart fluttered. "Already?"

"The sooner we move in, the sooner we can get the refugees somewhere safe." He beamed at her, excitement glowing from the violet gemstones of his eyes. Sidhe weren't subtle about any of their emotions, whether it was anger, lust, or happiness. He was shining brighter than the sun. "And the sooner we can get comfortable in Niflheimr."

Marion wasn't shining along with him. She had been trying not to think too hard about what the "no" vote would mean personally.

War with the angels was bad enough.

Becoming steward of the Winter Court—a Middle World frozen in eternal darkness—meant that Marion had to leave her comfortable home on Vancouver Island to live in Niflheimr.

Marion found the idea of such a leadership position appealing. The climate...not quite so much.

At least Konig had agreed to go with her if such a thing happened. He wasn't from the Winter Court, but his unseelie power meant he'd be able to engage most of the wards around Niflheimr, and he was more familiar with the local culture.

Together, they would cooperate to gather refugees and start the court anew.

It was like buying their first house together. Except that house happened to come with vassals, enemies, and an entire kingdom.

As a prince, Konig had spent his life prepared for such responsibility, and he got to do it with his girlfriend at his side. Of course he was excited.

"I should see Jibril off," Marion said, twining her arms around Konig's neck. "Will you wait for me?"

"Afraid not, princess. Have to give the order to start moving my belongings into the Winter Court. I'll have Nori pick you up in a couple hours. Don't be surprised if you get waylaid in the Autumn Court—my mother will want your feedback on her decisions about redecorating Niflheimr." He rolled his eyes.

"*Her* decisions?" Marion asked.

"Don't start with me." Konig kissed her again, hard enough to take her breath away and scramble her thoughts.

He released her, and Marion staggered, hand pressed to her beating heart.

The look he gave her... It almost made Marion forget about how queasy she felt about the outcome of the vote.

How could Konig be "business as usual" when that decision was going to piss off the angels so thoroughly?

He was already striding away with his entourage, leaving Marion with Jibril. The hall had otherwise emptied. Everyone was in a rush to get home.

Get home, and probably batten down the hatches.

"Well, Marion?" Jibril demanded.

Marion swallowed the knot in her throat and got into the next elevator. An empty one. "It doesn't matter what I voted. We lost."

"We'll appeal," Jibril said, joining her in the elevator.

She pushed the button to take them to the zeppelin dock at the apex of the tower. "Appeals aren't possible." That vote had concluded the summit. There had been other, more minor issues debated in the last week—such as territory squabbles between independent shifter packs— but the fate of the Winter Court was the only issue everyone had cared about.

"What am I supposed to take back to the EL?" Jibril asked. "I can't tell them we've lost."

The lights flickered.

"Control yourself," Marion said. "You'll break the elevator." Angels could disable everything electrically powered within a mile if their power flared—say, during an emotional outburst. Jibril looked to be on the brink of an outburst that could fry all of New York City.

"Don't you know what Leliel will do?"

Marion could imagine. Leliel was the ruthless leader in the Ethereal Levant—an angel who had been de-winged shortly before Genesis and hadn't taken the amputation gracefully.

She'd tried to assassinate Marion in order to keep her from delivering a message from the gods. The one that had led to the vote.

Leliel was not a woman with an even temper.

Marion sighed, massaging her temples with her fingertips. "I'm sorry, Jibril." She lowered her voice. "If it makes you feel any better, I voted yes."

Jibril's eyes widened. "You did?"

"I'm the Voice of God, not the Mindless Obedient Zombie of God. I'm allowed to have my own opinions." At least Marion assumed she was allowed such things. Her memories didn't stretch far enough back to include her last conversation with the gods, presumably when they had told her they wanted the angels to stay out of the Middle Worlds.

"Why?" Jibril asked. "You want to run the Winter Court. You want to run *everything*."

Marion wasn't going to argue with that. "Believe it or not, I don't want to fight with you people, nor do I want angels to die out. If the Winter Court's the best place for all of you to nest, then you should have it."

"You've surprised me." Jibril drummed his fingers on his hip. "What would you think of negotiating some kind of compromise, now that you're steward?"

"I'd be thrilled to discuss it. I'd also be shocked if Leliel is willing to talk to me rationally."

"We'll see about that," Jibril said. "We can arrange something without her, though. I'll meet you and Prince ErlKonig tonight in the Winter

Court. There may be something we can do."

"Hopefully Leliel will come." After all, Leliel led the angels in Dilmun—they couldn't make a binding agreement without her. "I'll propose negotiations to her personally."

The angel had failed to kill Marion once already. She was reasonably certain she could handle another tantrum from that woman.

And Leliel probably wouldn't try to murder her now that the summit was over. Angels were, if nothing else, deeply logical creatures. The vote had ended, so killing Marion at that point would only be a waste of energy and a great way to piss off the Autumn Court.

The elevator chimed and its doors slid open. The dock was already occupied by the rest of the ethereal delegation, preparing to return to the EL after the summit.

Suzume stood on the left—an amusingly crass angel—with Leliel on her right. Marion had been planning to escort Jibril to the edge of the dock, but the sight of Leliel stopped her two feet in front of the elevator.

Leliel was beautiful. Curvaceous for an angel, statuesque, auburn-haired with skin in warm olive tones. Her body was draped in layers of peach that accentuated her large breasts and hips. She could have also probably hidden a few knives under that dress. Maybe even one of the flaming swords angels so often carried.

The instant that Marion saw her expression, Marion knew that Leliel had already heard of the vote.

"I have a message for you to deliver to your future in-laws," Leliel said. "Tell them that war is coming."

"Wait, Leliel. We should talk," Marion said.

"You've done enough, mage girl." Her enchanted wings whipped free of the tattoos on her back. The other angels unfurled their wings as well—genuine wings, feathers glowing with so much energy that all the lights immediately extinguished in the dock.

The wind caught them, and they were gone.

Marion stepped up to the edge to watch the three of them go. She had a foul taste in her mouth.

"I voted in your favor, dammit," she said into the foggy evening.

But it didn't matter.

Marion's fists were shaking, and she realized that her fingernails had cut neat half-moons into her palm because they'd been clenched so tightly.

Strangely, she wasn't angry that Leliel refused to listen. Marion never would have expected her offer to talk to go over well.

She felt queasy that she'd even voted in the favor of Leliel, her would-be killer, even though she and Konig had agreed that it would be the easiest way to prevent war.

What's wrong with you? Jolene had asked.

"If only I knew," she muttered.

THREE

Marion arrived in Niflheimr with no fanfare and only Nori at her side.

"Here we are," Nori said. "Home sweet home." Marion couldn't even make out her face because she was bundled in so many furs.

Like Marion, Nori Harper was half-human, half-angel Gray, and equally unexcited to move into the Winter Court. But she was capable of planeswalking like many of the sidhe, and Marion wasn't, so Marion couldn't travel between dimensions without Nori.

Nori had agreed to assist Marion in establishing the court, but only when Marion had promised a prestigious position as her advisor. And also a pound of very fine Belgian chocolate.

Marion couldn't respond at the moment because the coldness of the wind had sucked her breath away. She pulled the scarf up and her hood down until only her eyes were uncovered, allowing her to see her new kingdom.

And what a kingdom it was.

She'd known that the Winter Court was in trouble after its years of anarchy and infighting among the sidhe. Its population was estimated in the hundreds, and the survivors were spread out in camps in the forest where the warring Summer Court hadn't been able to kill them.

Even so, she hadn't imagined Niflheimr would be such an absolute wreck.

It was a castle of ice standing alone in a frozen ocean. Nori had taken her to the landing platform that Konig had indicated would be safest, but safest didn't seem to mean intact. They were on a balcony near the top of the only tower that didn't have any holes in its walls large enough to suggest imminent collapse. A couple of the other towers were swaying in the wind.

The balcony, however, had several large holes in it, and the door leading into the tower stood ajar, windows shattered.

Beyond the delicate railing edging the balcony, there was a vast ocean, bordered on one side by a frigid shore. A broken bridge crossed the space between the two.

Marion couldn't see a single hint of life.

This was what the gods had wanted her to take. She was steward of this—little more than a grave.

"Changed your mind? Want to go back?" Nori must have been smiling, because the corners of her eyes were tilted up.

Marion gathered herself, standing up straight and throwing her shoulders back. "Very funny."

Niflheimr didn't look like that much, but it meant that Marion's legacy would be so much more impressive once she restored it. She'd need to take pictures before she began repairs. Before-and-afters would make quite an impression on the front page of the newspapers.

"Princess, you're here!" Konig strode onto the balcony, unaffected by the cold and easily dodging the holes in the floor. He wore a long scarf over a snug t-shirt that hugged every line of his lean body.

He swept Marion up into a hug, spinning her in place. She choked back a squeal.

"There are *holes*," she said, trying to push away from him, closer to solid ground.

He laughed without releasing her. "Not afraid of falling, are you? You're an angel!"

Marion wasn't nearly as afraid of falling as she was striking the icy ocean many thousands of feet below. "Let's go inside. I'm cold."

Konig all but carried her inside. The Raven Knights milled around the landing, murmuring amongst themselves. They were dressed as lightly as their prince. Nobody who was loaned from the Autumn Court was going to care much about the climate.

Marion was finally set on her feet.

"I've been looking at bedrooms," Konig said, keeping his arm around her shoulders as he steered her downstairs. "The king's quarters are truly impressive. Cooper's taste really was something!"

"Cooper? The king was named Cooper?"

"And my father is named Rage." Konig rolled his eyes. "All the old guard kind of suck at names. But not at decorating! Wait until you see the ice sculptures above our bed."

Marion's cheeks would have gone hot if she hadn't been so cold underneath her scarf. "Our bed," she echoed.

Moving in together meant that they would finally get to share a bedroom. Konig had a drawer at Marion's house in Vancouver Island, and her quarters in the Autumn Court were adjacent to his, but they hadn't truly shared a living space yet.

In fact, Marion hadn't shared anything with him since waking up in Ransom Falls aside from a few kisses. Konig made passes at her. She had the kind of lingerie that had made it clear that they'd had a *very* active sex life. But she still didn't remember any of it, and she balked every time things got too intense between them.

Konig had been respectful of her boundaries. He was wonderful in every way.

Now they were going to share a bedroom.

"Konig..." Marion began.

She didn't need to finish. "There's another room behind the king and queen's," he said. "It looks like it belonged to a non-unseelie member of the court. It's enchanted to a somewhat more jungle-like climate. You might be more comfortable starting out there."

Marion rested her head against him. "Thank you. So much."

"Anything for my princess," he said. "I'll work on the perimeter wards with the knights so that you can join me in the king's bedroom—once you're ready."

Even Konig, patient as he was, couldn't mask the longing in his voice.

Sidhe were creatures who needed hedonism the way that most people needed air to breathe. Konig claimed that they would waste away without the staples of good food, good drink, and great sex —if not to the point of dying, then to the point where they could no longer cast magic.

Konig wasn't short on food and wine, but he'd gone weeks without sex, and Marion knew it was hurting him.

She didn't feel quite guilty enough to get over her trepidation. Her excuses for continuing to resist were rapidly dwindling, though.

They reached the throne room without falling through any holes in the floor. It was as pathetic a hall as the rest of the towers; one of the walls had been blasted away, and the icy thrones had melted into lumps. It must have been impressive at one time, though. There were giant cogs and chains of shining snow. The fact that those had survived when everything else degraded meant the magic that had erected them must have been impressive.

Marion circled the bump in the floor that had once been a throne.

"What happened here?" she asked.

"Not a clue," Konig said. "The knights will bring some real furniture to replace all of this stupid frozen crap, though. We'll get some proper décor in here and it'll be great!"

Marion eyed the rolled tapestries that some of the sidhe were carrying in. One of them was already hung, and it featured one of the forest nymphs typical of the Autumn Court. "Your mother's choice of décor?"

"It's easiest to just nod and smile when she gets opinionated," Konig said.

"What about my opinions?"

"You don't want to make the Onyx Queen angry, do you?"

Marion couldn't tell if he was joking or not. Truthfully, she had little urge to pick fights with Violet, even less than she wanted to pick fights with the angels.

On that note... "What do you think of trying to negotiate a compromise with the angels? I was talking to Jibril and he's interested."

"It's not Jibril we need to interest," Konig said. He whirled his hands through the air, and magic splayed over the hole in the wall, blocking the harshness of the wind.

"Oh, thank the gods," Nori sighed, finally dropping her hood. She'd followed them downstairs silently, and in the few stories they'd descended together, her eyebrows had frozen.

Marion hooked a finger in her scarf and tugged it down to expose her face. The temperature wasn't as chilly as it had been on the balcony, but her breath still came out in foggy plumes. "Jibril seems to think we can work something out without Leliel. He wants to discuss it tonight."

"Look at you, getting back to your old manipulative self, with all those darling little back-room deals of which you're so fond," Konig said. "Be practical, though. Where would we even put the angels? The mere presence of sidhe in the dimension makes the magic too intense to grow a nest."

"The Wilds," Marion said. It was an uninhabited swath of forest on the edge of the world. "Once we've moved refugees into Niflheimr, there should be enough distance to safely isolate the angels there."

"Hmm." He rubbed his jaw thoughtfully. "We won't be able to repopulate the old villages."

"We'll also have to regrow the Wilds so that they're less hostile," Marion said. They had been hit hardest in the invasion by the Summer Court, and the Wilds were somewhat barren at the moment.

"How do you know that? Have you remembered?"

"I've been reading everything I can find on the civil war this week."

"Cute. Very cute. Yes, we can talk to Jibril and offer the Wilds. You should let me take the lead, though." One of his knights dropped a chair near a mirror in the back corner, and Konig hurried over. "Be careful with that! It's an authentic looking glass!"

Marion followed him, unwilling to drop the subject. "I can lead discussions with the angels. I've been working with them all week at the summit."

"Which is why it'll be easier for me to play hardball," Konig said. He ran his hands over the looking glass, as if searching for cracks.

Marion frowned. "I guess."

"Do you need my help?" Nori interrupted. She'd already pulled her hood over her head again.

"I'd appreciate it if you could get some clothes from my house for me," Marion said. Her warm house on Earth that was not a ridiculous ice castle.

Nori gave her a look of gratitude. "Of course." She ran upstairs for the ley line, rubbing her hands together.

Konig watched her go, mouth twisting with something that resembled disapproval. "You angel types are so cold-blooded."

"Hence why smart angels hang out in the Ethereal Levant," Marion said.

"If they're smart, what does that make you?"

"Steward of the Winter Court," she said, which seemed increasingly like it was synonymous for stupid.

Konig laughed, sweeping her into his arms again. Now that her face was exposed, there was nothing to keep him from kissing her all over. He considered them to be as good as alone when they were in the company of his guard. He got very handsy.

Marion couldn't help but laugh along with him, even though she wasn't nearly as comfortable. His joy was infectious.

Niflheimr may have been miserable, but it was *theirs*.

"When did you say Jibril would be here?" he murmured, tangling his hands in her hair, lips trailing along her jaw.

Marion's head tipped back and she sighed. "Tonight."

"Then there's plenty of time for us to clear out Leiptr."

She pulled back, surprised. She'd been expecting him to make a pass at her. "The village on the shore?"

"I've already sent some of my parents' army with trucks to start gathering refugees," Konig said. "Would you like to help supervise bringing them to Niflheimr?" They'd agreed it would be safest to home the survivors of the Winter Court within the castle, but Marion had said that before seeing the condition of the castle.

Still, better the ruins of a castle than spread out in the frozen wasteland.

"Let me get another coat," Marion said.

The instant Ymir saw the army descend on Leiptr, he knew that he had to run. It had been months since he'd seen an attack from the Summer Court, and he had no clue why they'd have returned to attack again, but the reasons were irrelevant. The sidhe were relentless hunters.

The twisting alleys were narrow enough that only a child of Ymir's size would be able to fit within them, so they were his refuge. The sound of the approaching army echoed against the ice-encrusted walls, magnifying the sounds of descending sidhe a thousand-fold. The seelie invaders wouldn't need to fit into the alleys to kill Ymir; they had proven that they only needed to shoot bolts of magic down those narrow paths.

It was pointless for Ymir to run, yet he still tried. He would keep trying until the seelie collapsed a cave on him the way that they had his parents.

He squeezed behind the back wall of an inn—a space that offered perhaps twenty centimeters between building and the sheet of ice bordering the southern edge of Leiptr. The ice was so thick that no light could penetrate it, though it did glow faintly. Ymir's frightened face reflected back at him, distorted in the waves, fragmented by captive bubbles.

The army's motion was reflected on the ice as well.

They were coming.

Shouts followed him as he squirmed around the corner of the inn. He dropped into a window well, crouching down to hide behind the ground.

Moments later, seeking spells flitted past him like deadly little acid fireflies. Their mere proximity carved divots into the ice wall. The melt trickled a few inches before freezing again.

Ymir peered through the frosted window to the inn. There was an uninhabited storage room on the other side.

Were those boxes filled with food? Or instruments of war?

He was weak with need—too weak to pry the window open on the first try. But he kept wiggling his fingers in the cracks, pushing and pulling until ice snapped. The window opened. It was narrower even than the alley behind the inn, but he was very thin with hunger.

Ymir dropped inside the storage room. Light flashed outside as more seeking spells darted overhead, barely missing him.

The nearest of the crates was a big plastic red thing with black latches. It wasn't locked, but his cold fingers fumbled to throw the lid open.

There was no food or weapons inside.

It was filled with furs. Blankets. Coats. The sort of accouterments that an invading force unaccustomed to the cold would need to survive in the Winter Court.

Ymir couldn't hold back his sob.

Someone moved on the other side of the storage room door. The handle twisted.

He dropped to the floor behind the crate and peered around the edge to see a willowy woman slam the door, flattening her back to it as she let out a sigh.

She wasn't one of the sidhe warriors who had

ransacked villages throughout the Winter Court. Ymir had seen enough of them that he'd have recognized their cruel inner glow, far harsher than that of the seeking spells. This woman was olive-skinned and pale-eyed. Her body was wrapped in so many furs that it overwhelmed her form.

The woman felt around her pockets. Plastic crinkled.

A wrapper.

She had food.

A longing groan escaped Ymir before he could stop himself. Her gaze snapped up, pale eyes focusing on him in the shadows behind the box.

"Why, hello," she said.

He scrambled for the window. It was still open, gusting frigid wind into the basement.

"Wait!" the woman called.

Ymir jumped, trying to reach the window. He missed.

"I can share with you," she said.

He finally turned.

The woman was still hanging by the door, extending the food toward him with one hand. She pulled her furred hat off with the other hand, allowing mounds of chestnut curls to tumble free around her shoulders. She had a pleasant, open face.

"It's a granola bar," she added when he didn't move. "You can have it. I have another one."

"Yes *please*." Ymir edged toward her. She handed him the unwrapped bar, and their hands brushed. She was so warm that it hurt.

41

Leaping back toward the crate of furs, he scarfed the bar down too quickly, watching her out of the corner of his eye.

She shed her cloak. Underneath, she wore a long white blouse over slim-cut jeans and snow boots. She was human. A human in the Winter Court. It made no sense. But she wasn't sidhe, and it had been a long time since Ymir had seen anyone who was friendly.

"My name is Marion," she said. "Who are you?"

He swallowed down the last bite of granola bar. "Ymir."

"Ymir," Marion echoed. "What are you doing in here, Ymir?"

"Hiding from the army," he said.

"Funny, I am too," she said.

"You're hiding from the seelie? Why do the seelie want a human?"

She surprised Ymir by laughing. She sat on the floor to be closer to his level, using her furs to keep herself off of the dirty floor.

He started to edge away again.

"The seelie armies are nowhere near here," Marion said. "I'm hiding from the Autumn Court's army. They're moving survivors to Niflheimr for safety's sake. That's what I'm doing here. Helping the army. But they are asking a lot of questions of me, and it's very tiring, so I thought I'd take a break." She held out another granola bar. "Still hungry?"

Ymir sat next to her. He took the snack. "Thank you."

"Where's your family, Ymir?"

He broke the granola bar in half and swallowed one side. "Dead." They'd been gone for months, maybe years. He'd lost track of time.

"Who's been taking care of you since?"

Ymir gave her a blank look.

Sympathy creased her face. "I was going to save this for later, but you look like you need it more." She produced chocolate from her furs—real chocolate. He snatched it from her hands. The contrast between her olive and his blue flesh was even weirder than how warm she was. "Why haven't you joined one of the unseelie camps?"

"They don't want me 'cause I'm not unseelie," he said. "I'm a frost giant."

She laughed, and the sound was so much warmer than even her hands, flooding him with a sense of pleasure. "A giant, are you?"

Ymir went rigid with pride. He knew that he must not have looked like much, but he'd be ten feet tall as an adult, assuming he survived long enough. "I will be someday."

"You do seem to be exceptionally tall for your age." She ruffled his hair. "You don't have to hide from my army. We're here to help, not hurt."

"What's in Niflheimr?" he asked.

"Not much yet. My boyfriend—uh, Prince ErlKonig, he's from the Autumn Court—has been arranging a camp while we sort everyone out. We have food and beds right now." She watched him finish eating. Her smile was gone. She looked so sad. "There are convoys taking refugees right now.

Will you go with one?"

"Yeah, I guess so."

Too tired to stand, he remained limp as Marion gathered him into her arms. Ymir was tall, but she was taller. She easily put his weight on her hip. It was a relief to wrap his arms around her neck and rest his head on her shoulder.

Marion carried him through the inn. He tensed initially at the sight of the sidhe soldiers sitting around the dining room, but they were unseelie—creatures of the Autumn Court, judging by the brassy tones of their hair and skin. Marion had been telling the truth.

The Summer Court's invaders were gone.

A woman rushed through the crowd to meet them. "My lady!" She stopped short. "Who's this?"

"This is my new friend Ymir," Marion said, shifting his weight onto her other hip. "I'm going to take him with me to Niflheimr. And please, Nori, I've told you—don't call me that. It's weird."

"Sorry." Nori's attention had already shifted away from Ymir. "There's someone waiting for you at your home in Victoria."

"They'll have to wait. I'm meeting with the angels tonight in Niflheimr. Remember? And I have to get the refugees settled into their new homes."

Nori followed Marion and Ymir outside. The wind blasted over them, relentlessly cold. Marion shivered. "My *lady*," Nori said admonishingly, throwing furs over Marion.

"What did I just tell you?" Marion asked.

They bickered good-naturedly while Ymir stared over Marion's shoulder. The inn was at the top of the cornice under the frozen waterfall, which meant that Ymir could see all the way down into the village of Leiptr. It was under complete occupation by the Autumn Court now. In truth, it didn't look all that different having the streets crawling with unseelie rather than seelie; the power of their magic had the same distorting effect.

Yet the army of the Autumn Court—Marion's army—wasn't burning the city. They weren't slaughtering. They were loading survivors into trucks.

"But really, Marion," Nori said, her more serious tone catching Ymir's attention again, "I think you'll want to attend to this visitor." She lowered her voice until Ymir could barely hear her over the wind. "It's Luke."

Marion stiffened against Ymir. "Seth?"

"Seth, Luke, whatever. He's at your house. He wants to talk to you."

"I see," she said. Marion set Ymir in the back of the covered truck. Her cheeks had gone red with cold, the tips of her hair gathering snow, but she still smiled at him. "Ymir, it seems I have to take care of some things. I'm going to send you to Niflheimr ahead of me. My friends will take very good care of you, though."

"You're leaving me?" Ymir asked.

She ruffled his hair again. "I'll be back." Marion leaned around him and dragged a box toward the end of the pickup. "In the meantime, help yourself. Eat until you're sick."

It was filled with insulated bottles of water, tins of fish, and more granola bars. Ymir's eyes went so wide that it felt like they might pop out of his head.

Marion summoned an adult refugee to the truck. "Will you make sure Ymir is okay on the way to Niflheimr?"

The other refugee was a burly, opal-fleshed unseelie with teeth that were eerily white against the blackness of his lips. Ymir didn't think there was a chance that the man would willingly associate with a frost giant. He looked like one of the gentry—the highest caste of sidhe. The gentry would have nothing to do with those who were unlike them.

But to Ymir's surprise, the man said, "Yes, of course. I'd be happy to." That was when Ymir noticed two little girls waiting nearby. He had daughters who must have been Ymir's age, though significantly shorter, as they were not frost giants. "Hello, Ymir. I'm Cyprian," said the adult sidhe.

"Hi," Ymir said without looking at him. He scuffed the snow with his bare foot, which was only a few shades of blue darker than the surrounding world.

"Thanks. I'll owe you for this," Marion said, clasping Cyprian's hand in both of hers.

She started to step away. Fear seized Ymir.

"You will be back?" he asked.

Marion took Nori's hand, offering him a smile as bright as the starlight in the eternal evening of the Winter Court.

"I promise," she said.

Both women vanished.

FOUR

The first breath of Vancouver Island's air was a relief to Marion's system. It had been only hours since she'd left New York City behind for the Winter Court, but those hours had been enough that she felt like she'd never be warm again. Even the soggy sixteen-degree weather on the island in November was like sinking into a Jacuzzi by comparison.

The ley line nearest to her home was just offshore, within view of the lagoon upon which her house sat. Marion doubted it was a coincidence that she'd chosen to buy her home there, where Konig could easily visit from the Autumn Court.

Her house sprawled over the hill, with many wings and buildings and garages tucked in the trees. It was west of Victoria, the largest city on the island, and therefore a short drive to enjoy the urban center and its many delightful shopping options. But her home was vast enough that she hadn't felt the need to leave it for long over the last week. Familiarizing herself with its many empty bedrooms and cavernous bathrooms could have kept her entertained for weeks.

It was a veritable castle, and she lived alone in it.

"Do you want me to go back, or keep packing for you?" Nori asked, waiting outside the gate to the garden when Marion entered.

"Go back," Marion said. "Konig could use your help, I'm sure." And she didn't need anyone listening in when she talked to Seth.

Her heart fluttered.

Seth.

Marion hadn't expected to see him again so soon, if at all.

"He said he'd wait out that way." Nori jerked her chin toward the orchard.

"Thank you," Marion said, and she waited until Nori left to seek Seth out.

Her garden was as impressive as the rest of the house. That was where she'd spent most of her time during her visits that week.

Marion hadn't felt so lonely when she was in her private orchard among the buzzing bees and singing birds. She could easily imagine that there was family in the house, waiting for her to bring back enough apples to bake a pie, or entertaining themselves in her private indoor swimming pool while she got sweaty in the cool fall sunlight.

Unfortunately, she'd seen too little of the house or garden that week with all the work the summit had provided. And she'd see little of it in the months to come now that she was steward of the Winter Court.

Marion followed a spiraling path toward the sound of a fountain. Rain began drizzling as she sought Seth out, leaving a cool mist clinging to the leaves of her flowerbeds.

He was on the opposite side of the fountain, partially shrouded by the wall of rippling water.

She cleared her throat, swallowed hard. "Hi there."

Seth turned. He was wearing a black jacket, black jeans, hiking boots. He was dark-skinned with short hair and expressive lips, which were faintly marked by old scarring.

At the sight of her, one corner of his mouth lifted in a lopsided smile. "Hey, Marion."

"Luke." She caught herself and bit the inside of her cheek. "Or—I guess I should call you Seth, shouldn't I?"

He looked disappointed, as though he'd been hoping that somehow, through some stroke of bizarre luck, Marion wouldn't have learned the truth about him. "Yeah. I'm going by Seth again, for the moment."

The implications of that hung heavier than the humidity in the air.

He'd come to see her as Seth, but he was still planning to move on, become someone else.

"How did you get here?" Marion asked. "I didn't see a car when I came in through the ley line."

"We don't have a car with us."

"We?"

"Charity and me," Seth said. "She stayed back at the Empress Hotel, where we're staying. I wanted to talk to you...alone."

"Is this an apology for your elaborate deceit?" She hadn't meant to make it sound accusatory, but that was how it came out. *Oh well*. It had been an elaborate deceit, and there was no point dancing around it.

"Would an apology make you feel better?" Seth asked.

She wilted a little. "I guess not."

He stepped toward her, and she moved from around the fountain to meet him. He stopped a few feet back. He hadn't expected her to approach.

They still weren't touching.

"How'd the summit go?" Seth asked.

"I'm surprised that the ex-fianc?e of the Alpha werewolf wouldn't already know."

He didn't even blink, so he wasn't surprised by how much Marion had learned about Seth in the last week.

Rylie had been interested in hearing about Seth's exploits getting Marion to the summit—*very* interested—and she'd been free about responding with information, too.

The Alpha had explained that Seth had moved to Las Vegas after Genesis to work as a private investigator. During that time, he hadn't communicated much with Rylie. He'd had a fight with his brother, Abel, so Rylie had thought it best to give Seth space.

They hadn't talked for almost six months when he abruptly vanished without a trace. None of their mutual friends had admitted to knowing his whereabouts.

After all that time, Rylie had assumed that Seth was dead.

In Marion's opinion, that was perfectly fair. Rylie was the one who had cheated on Seth with his brother. Seth had always been loyal. She was the heartbreaker, the slutty Alpha, a total jerk. Seth owed her nothing, least of all updates on his location.

"I don't talk to Rylie anymore," he said.

"She wasn't pleased to see that you came to the United Nations without talking to her. I think she's angry at me too."

"I don't care if Rylie's pleased or not, and neither should you. What could she do to you? You've got an intimidating resume, even compared to the Alpha. You were the speaker for the ethereal delegation. The Voice of God. Steward of the Winter Court." That last job description lingered.

"You forgot one other thing," Marion said. "Patient of Luke Flynn."

"Luke Flynn doesn't exist anymore," Seth said.

She rested a hand on the rim of the fountain to steady herself. The roughness of the stone grounded her, even more than the stable soil under her feet, so unlike the slippery halls of Niflheimr. "Who will you be next?"

"I haven't looked at the paperwork Brianna put together for me, but I've arranged for a new identity. A new life. Everything's in place. It's just—before I go, I needed to talk to you." He took a deep breath. "I need your help."

"Okay," Marion said. "What do you want?"

He gave a short laugh. "Just like that?"

"Just like that." She plucked an apple off of a low tree branch and rolled it between her fingers, savoring the solidness of the meat, the smooth flesh.

"You could make me work for it." His lips twitched with mirth. "Buy you something nice? Designer clothes?"

"Don't be silly. It's safe to say that you're the only reason I'm alive at this point, so tell me what you need and you'll have it." She grinned. "In any case, I don't know if you noticed, but I'm quite rich. I can buy all the nice things I want without your help."

"You seem like you do pretty good for a kid."

"*Excuse* me. I'm nineteen years old."

"Oh," he said. "Nineteen. So definitely not a kid."

"You're picking on me."

"Someone should," Seth said.

"I'm fairly confident that I have dungeons in the Winter Court. I could lock you away in prison for the rest of your life as easily as the Office of Preternatural Affairs."

His smile quickly faded. He cleared his throat. "Look, Marion, we have to get your memories back. Someone emptied your head of everything but the drive to seek me out, and the memories haven't returned even though the summit is over. The loss was either unintentional, or it wasn't related."

"I don't see how restoring my memories helps you."

"You still don't remember Elise and James, do you?"

Rylie had mentioned those names. Marion understood that they should have been meaningful, but she could only shake her head. "I don't remember anything since the last time we—when you helped me give that speech."

"Damn." He raked a hand over his hair. "You mean your mom didn't tell you?"

"My mother doesn't seem to be speaking to me," Marion said. She hadn't been able to get in touch with Ariane Kavanagh.

"Aw, jeez. I don't know how to tell you this."

"Tell me what? Who are Elise and James?"

"Elise is your sister," Seth said. "She's also God."

* * *

Marion was a little too sober to discuss having a deity for a sister.

It was a short walk through the orchard to

reach the house. Her kitchen was as lovely as her garden: decorated in marble, with platinum fixtures and white everywhere. A little slice of heaven with three different ovens stacked atop each other so she could bake multiple batches of cookies simultaneously.

She kept Seth in the corner of her eye to see if he was impressed. She *wanted* him to admire her home.

Seth barely seemed to notice it.

"Bottle opener is in the drawer to your left," Marion said. "I'll be right back." She stepped down into the wine cellar to pick out a bottle.

Yes, Marion had a wine cellar. It was almost as big as her closets, too, and equally well organized.

It turned out that being the one independent force that could essentially audit all factions—and the Voice of God—was a *very* profitable job.

Seth's amused expression when she returned with a bottle of zinfandel said that he was thinking the same thing. "A wine cellar."

"And everything in it is excellent, I assure you." Marion plucked two glasses from where they hung upside-down by the window. She set one in front of Seth. "Open the bottle."

"*You* open it." He tossed the bottle opener to her.

Her instinct was to argue with him simply because she hated being told what to do, but picking fights over a wine bottle was stupid.

She poured. "This Elise, my sister—you'll have to start from the beginning. Make it simple for me, please. I'm still overwhelmed by trying to piece my life together." Although saying she was overwhelmed might have been an understatement. "On the brink of emotional collapse" was a little closer. Ergo why her wine cellar was several bottles emptier than it had been before she returned home during the summit.

"This is as simple as it gets," Seth said. "I told you that there was a battle between old gods and new gods, and that's how Genesis happened. Right? Well, your sister wasn't a god at the time. She was the Godslayer. A weapon made by Metaraon—your father—to murder Adam, the previous God."

"My father made one of his daughters to murder God?"

"Elise has a different father than you." He picked up his glass once it was half-filled. "You guys share a mother."

"Ariane Kavanagh." There were pictures of the woman around her house, so their relationship must not have been terrible, even if Ariane was impossible to contact.

"Right," Seth said. "Anyway, Elise won. In order to kill the last gods, she entered this thing called the Origin, which basically mixes people up and spits them back out as gods. She took her husband with her. James."

"Elise and James. That's so boring. They should have taken notes from the Summer Court and renamed themselves," Marion said. "Think a little more about branding. Zeus and Hera, or something like that."

"They don't care about branding. They don't want anyone to know who they are, where they are, or what they're thinking." A hint of bitterness had entered Seth's tone. "That's why they only speak to you. Ever." He studied Marion's face closely. "Are you following me?"

"I think so," she said.

"Are you okay? Your sister and brother-in-law are gods. That's big news."

Marion chuckled into her glass. "Of all the news I've endured since waking up in your hospital, learning that my half-sister is God is one of the easier things to wrap my mind around." She could feel his eyes on her as she drank, perhaps a little too fast. "I have a formal sitting room. Let's relocate."

She took him to her sitting room the long way around, and this time, he examined things with more interest. Not unlike the way that Marion had examined his humble apartment.

Marion wondered what he saw in her decorative choices.

To be honest, she wasn't even certain she'd decorated everything herself. She had a cleaning staff. She'd probably hired an interior decorator, too.

Perhaps her surroundings said nothing about her at all.

The sitting room had large windows overlooking her front yard. The sight wasn't as impressive as the gardens of Myrkheimr, but it was well enough for a teenage girl living alone on some wet island. Nice trees, nice lawn. Her curtains were operated by remote control so she didn't even have to get up to open them.

Marion took a seat first, picking a fainting chair on one side of the coffee table. Seth chose a stool on the opposite side—as far from Marion as he could be without being rude. His elbows rested on his thighs, wine glass cradled in one hand as he studied the room, and Marion studied his face.

Nothing had changed about him. He still had that scar on his bottom lip and the graceful hands of a surgeon. Even at that distance, he smelled faintly of leather.

He didn't belong in Marion's pristine palace.

She wasn't sure she did, either.

Marion realized she was still carrying the apple from her back garden. She set it on the coffee table between them, where it glistened, ruby-black, in the cloud-filtered sunlight.

She refilled her glass. "What does my sister matter? To you, I mean?"

"We worked together for a little while. Partnered up on a couple of cases involving the werewolves. Once I got tangled up with Elise and James, I ended up dead—that was a year before Genesis."

That was news to Marion. "I thought that the only people who came back after Genesis were the ones directly killed by the void."

"And me," Seth said. "*They* chose to bring me back."

"Why? Did they feel guilty?"

"I doubt that's the reason. Lots of people died because of Elise and James, but they did special backflips to bring me back, while everyone else stayed dead. The only other person I know that they did that for is Rylie."

The mention of the werewolf Alpha stung Marion. She didn't like the way his expression changed when he mentioned her. "So Rylie is friends with them too."

"From what I heard, Elise and Rylie were tight in the end," Seth said. "They fought together, side by side. Not always friends, but a team. You don't come out of something like that without being changed."

But Elise and James were the only ones who had changed into gods.

Marion sat back, drinking her wine and trying to think of what the world must have been like before Genesis. Seth and Rylie fighting against an ancient God, with the help of a half-sister whom Marion's father had created.

Even if Marion's memories had been intact, she doubted she would have remembered the days when Seth had fought alongside this Elise person. During the time of Genesis, Marion had been barely more than a toddler. It was unlikely she'd been directly involved in the battles.

Marion did almost remember a garden, though. And a boy in the garden who looked much like Seth.

No matter how Seth denied it, there was

something to those memories.

"I'm not the same as I was before Genesis." Seth took a sip of the wine and grimaced. "They changed me when they brought me to life again. I need to know how more than why. The symptoms..." He trailed off, staring hard at his hands. "I'm getting worse. I need you to ask Elise and James what they did to me."

So that was what Seth valued more than his anonymity, more than getting away from the mage who'd been dropped into his emergency room.

He wanted his identity.

She couldn't blame him. Marion was aching pretty hard for the same thing.

"I doubt I'll need my memory for that," Marion said. "If I've been able to contact Elise and James in the past, then I should be able to do it now, too." She twirled the glass between her forefinger and thumb. "You said you're different since Genesis. Different how?"

Seth finished his wine and set the glass on the coffee table beside the apple. The remaining drops of wine pooled in the bottom of the bulb. "Different."

"Is this another of those secrets you claim has nothing to do with me, even though it clearly does?"

"I don't know all the ways I've changed. But look at me, Marion. Just *look*." He pointed at his face. "Do I look like I'll be hitting forty years old soon?"

He didn't. If anything, he looked younger than

when Marion had met him a week earlier.

"And that's the only difference you've discovered since Genesis," she said.

"It's one of the big ones."

"Very well." She set her wine glass beside his. "I'll see if I have any way to contact my half-sister. Are you in a rush to leave?"

"Not at the moment," Seth said. "Charity was planning to hit up tea time at the Empress Hotel. She'll be entertained for a little while."

She scooped the apple off the table. "I'll pick through my journals, then. Make yourself at home." Marion dropped the apple into his hand. They both held it for a moment, touching through the apple without making any kind of contact skin-to-skin.

"Thanks," he said. The state of his agelessness wasn't the only thing that had changed since Marion had last seen him. His irises had gone from very dark brown to black.

She turned to leave. "You're welcome."

"Marion?"

"What?" she asked.

Seth twisted the stem off of the apple. "I am sorry. I didn't want to lie to you."

A smile twitched at the edges of her lips. "I was wrong." She swirled to leave, striding up the stairs.

"About what?" he called after her.

Marion shot a grin at him over her shoulder. "Your apology did make me feel better."

FIVE

The library in Marion's home was larger than her private pool, the kitchen, and the master bathroom put together. That was where she'd found all of her personal journals last Wednesday, which she'd systematically yanked off of the shelves and arrayed on tables for easy reading.

"I've been studying myself in my free moments, of which there are few." Marion moved stacks of journals off of one table so that she could reach the oldest ones at the bottom. "If I can't get my memories back, then I assumed that I'd be able to fake it in the meantime. I've been doing well, if I do say so myself. Few at the summit seemed to realize anything was awry."

Seth wandered into the room behind her. He was gazing around her shelves with some awe— the first time he seemed to have been impressed by her home. He'd had quite a few books in his old house too. A man after her own heart. "You still haven't told me how things at the summit unfolded."

"Terribly. The majority voted to keep the angels out of the Winter Court." She waited, but Seth was walking through her room, inspecting the spines of her books. "Aren't you going to ask me how I voted?"

"Nope. Whatever you voted, it was right. And wrong. There was no good answer to this. Either you piss off Elise by defying her will, or you piss off the angels by refusing to give them what they want."

"It's hideously unfair that I'd have been put in such a position. The gods must not think much of me, if they have me bearing such news to the summit."

"Or they think you can handle it," Seth said. "You have a chance to read the Bible?"

"You can see my entire reading list for the last week right here." Marion patted one of the journal stacks.

"The Bible's an old book that some religions follow. More so before Genesis. It's full of sayings, lessons for life, stuff about God. The old God. In Corinthians, there was one passage that said something like, 'God won't give you more trouble than you can bear.'"

"And then my half-sister killed that God and dumped all her crap on me to share with humanity," Marion said.

Seth laughed. She loved his laugh. The way it came to him so easily, the hint of embarrassment in his eyes. "You might not have your memories, but you've got a good grasp of what your sister's like."

"War, Seth," she said. "There's going to be war, and being placed in charge of the Winter Court means I'm at the crux of it, with no memories, virtually no army, and no clue how to protect myself."

"You're not getting in on all the defenses the Autumn Court's been setting up?"

"They're setting up defenses?" Another thought struck her. "How do *you* know about that?"

"Nori mentioned it," Seth said.

No, Marion hadn't been included. Her conversations with Konig had mostly been centered around what he would do if they took charge of Niflheimr, with occasional interjections about his mother's preferences about their decisions.

As for communications from the king and queen of the Autumn Court, there had been only dead silence.

It was feeling a lot like she was stuck at the far end of the table again, hanging out among the speakers for the least important factions when she should have been in charge.

"Mind if I look at your journals?" Seth asked.

Marion waved dismissively at the stacks. She was sick of looking at them. "Much of it is truncated netspeak, and some of that in French. You're welcome to read anything you can understand."

He flipped through one of the journals. "This is all printed off of the computer. I'd been expecting something handwritten."

"Yes, the printing thing is explained in a later journal. I used to do all of my journaling on the internet, but an enemy hacked my accounts and exploited the private information for several assassination attempts." Marion imagined that it should have been embarrassing to confess that, but she had no attachment to any of it. None of the journals had stirred a single memory.

She didn't feel attached to her own thoughts. Her home. *Anything.*

"How old were you when that happened?" Seth asked.

"This was five years ago."

"Your mom let you have unsupervised access to the internet when you were fourteen?"

"I was also behind the election for the office of Alpha at that age," Marion said. "I don't think anyone was concerned about what I was doing online, though clearly they should have been."

"That's ridiculous," Seth said.

She shrugged. "Even then, I was the Voice of God."

"Yeah, and a *kid*. You needed boundaries."

"You're all about boundaries, aren't you, Luke?" she shot back.

He set her journal down. "Okay," he said

slowly. "But you haven't found anything about how you contact the gods in your writing."

"I never elaborated on it. Why would I? If I'd been chatting with the gods since Genesis, it would be like elaborating on something as mundane my hair care rituals." Marion wished she'd gotten a bit more specific about her hair, actually. Humidity did unpleasant things to the curls.

"Maybe the answers aren't in your journals, then," Seth said.

"It's the only thing I have," Marion said.

"Not the *only* thing." He flipped the cover on her journal shut. "You woke up thinking that Seth Wilder could bring your memories back. So..." He offered a bare hand to her.

Marion edged away. "You didn't want me reading your mind."

"You already know what I was trying to keep to myself," Seth said. "No point in trying to protect my identity now. If the two of us are going to get what we want, this seems like the fastest way."

Fastest, but perhaps not the easiest.

Seth may not have had more secrets to protect, but Marion wasn't sure that she wanted him in her head now. She had been thinking about him over the last week a lot more than a girl with another boyfriend should. Sometimes those thoughts had been riddled with frustration. But they mostly had not. Really, really not.

He held his hand patiently outstretched, unwavering. The skin on his knuckles was a more ashen shade of brown than the rest of him, like he'd been punching things. His palms were callused.

Marion could get her memories back.

"I'm not sure it's safe," she said. "My magic flares up whenever we, um…" She pointed at his hand.

"You can't hurt me," Seth said.

"Another of your post-Genesis changes?" she asked. He nodded. And he kept waiting.

Well, there was no point in putting it off. It meant she wouldn't have to read another of her embarrassingly frank preteen journals, and hopefully her thoughts would remain firmly within her head.

Marion rested her fingertips in Seth's.

The physical contact was light, and the mental collision was equally peaceful.

For once, instead of feeling as though her skull were blasted open by lightning, her mind seemed to blossom. The library whited out with swirls of magic. Seth's face and hand and everything else vanished from view.

The ground shifted beneath her feet.

Marion.

She was standing in the garden again—a place of towering trees, a dense canopy, and mossy floor.

There was a door between two of those trees.

Marion drifted toward it, and she had no clue if she was moving physically or simply imagining it.

She didn't bother reaching for the handle. She simply rapped her knuckles against the frame, and the knocking resonated throughout the entire garden, making the trees sigh and the leaves rustle gently.

The door swung open.

For once, there wasn't another world on the other side—only a pedestal that held a jar.

The Canope. A voice supplied its name as she approached. *Find it. Take it. That's yours, and once you have it, you'll be whole.*

Marion reached out to grab the Canope. Her hands contacted smooth clay.

And the vision terminated.

The garden vanished, and Marion was back in her library. No time had passed. Nothing had changed. The only difference was that she must have started to fall, because Seth was holding her upright.

Though they were similar in height, he felt so much stronger than she was, sturdy and safe. He pushed her hair out of her face. Cupped her cheeks in his hands.

Seth looked at her closely, as though trying to see if she was still herself.

"Marion?"

Her knees wobbled. She rested her forehead on his shoulder and wrapped her arms around him.

Marion's mind from the time two weeks prior was still a giant blank.

"I don't remember anything new," she said.

He sighed, and she wasn't sure if it was relief or regret. "Damn. You didn't get *anything* out of that?"

Well, Marion was currently getting a hug from sexy doctor Seth Wilder, so that wasn't exactly nothing.

Konig certainly wouldn't have thought it was nothing.

"I saw something," she said, peeling away from him guiltily. "The Canope."

"The what?"

"I'm not sure." Marion found a blank piece of paper and pen on her desk. She sat down to sketch what she had seen. Her motions were confident—she was good at illustrating.

It only took a few minutes to sketch out a large jar. It was plain, made of clay, without handles. It had two stripes of strange runes, which Marion had to be vague about, as she couldn't remember those in detail.

"I'd say it's approximately fifty centimeters high, perhaps twenty in radius. Quite heavy." She sat back to study her own picture, nibbling on the tip of her pen. "I heard a voice tell me that it would make me 'whole.' What do you think it is?"

"Let's find out." Seth snapped a picture of her drawing with his phone. "I'm sending it to Brianna. If anyone's heard of this Canope thing, it'll be her."

Marion sighed, dropping her pen. "I can't believe that's all I got out of you. This feels like some kind of cruel joke."

Seth stroked his fingers along the back of her hand. Bare skin against bare skin.

Nothing at all happened now.

"Seems like that's the only information you

were supposed to get," he said.

"*Merde*." She shoved the chair back and stood. Disappointment choked her, and she needed to move, needed to distract herself—needed another glass of wine, perhaps.

Seth's phone rang. He answered it. "You do?" he asked after a moment. "Wait, I'm with Marion right now. I'm going to put you on speaker." He pushed a button.

"Hey Marion," said Brianna Dimaria, her voice crackling from the cell phone. "Where'd you see the Canope?"

"I remembered it," Marion said. "It's the *only* thing I remember. Do you know what it is?"

"Yeah, that's what's weird. Dana McIntyre had it about a month ago. She was hired as courier to transport it into Sheol, since she's the only badass bitch who doesn't mind taking stuff into the Nether Worlds."

Marion's eyes widened. The Nether Worlds were similar to the Middle Worlds, in that they were a separate plane of existence than the one that Earth resided in. However, instead of housing the sidhe, the Nether Worlds were home to demons.

"Sheol?" Seth asked sharply. "Who was she taking it to in Sheol?"

"You'll have to ask her. She's in Las Vegas right now, working a case with the vampires. She told me she'd be meeting at the Trump Tower this evening."

"You're friends with this Dana McIntyre?"

Marion asked.

Brianna paused for a long time. When she spoke again, her words were slow. "Yeah, I am. I bet she'll be at the Trump for the next hour, at least. You need to know anything about the Canope, you should hit her up."

"Thanks, Brianna. We will." Seth hung up.

"Wait," Marion said. "What does it matter where Dana McIntyre is right now? Isn't Las Vegas further than an hour from here?"

"Depends on how you travel."

"I don't think there's any mode of travel that would put the southwest within an hour of Vancouver Island."

"That's not entirely true," Seth said, "I can show you."

Marion folded her arms. "Okay. Tell me where we're going."

He spread his hands wide, as though inviting her for another hug.

She laughed hesitantly. "What are you doing?"

"I said that I changed in a few different ways during Genesis. This is one of them," he said.

She finally stepped into the circle of his arms.

Seth embraced her gently. She was enfolded in his warm, leathery scent, and every hesitation vanished. She let her cheek rest against his shoulder.

"You might want to hold your breath," he said.

Marion had momentarily forgotten that they weren't simply hugging again. "Why?"

"Just trust me."

She held her breath.

And Seth snapped his fingers.

The shift between Vancouver Island and Las Vegas was nearly instantaneous, but somewhere between her last heartbeat at home and her first in Nevada, Marion felt as though her entire body had been plunged into fire.

She materialized and instantly vomited on the pavement.

"Holy crap," Seth said, stepping back.

Marion collapsed onto all fours. She barely managed to keep her right hand out of the bile puddle, which was tinted red from the wine she'd been drinking. "Gods," she rasped, clutching her throat.

Seth dropped beside her. "Are you okay?"

"I should have held my breath longer." It felt like she'd inhaled lava. She wanted to touch her tongue to see if it was blistered, but the idea of touching her mouth when it hurt so much was appalling.

"You shouldn't have gotten hurt. I've never gotten hurt doing that."

She swiped at her mouth with the back of her hand and gazed blearily around the street. Marion had managed to shift one of her contact lenses out of alignment when they'd teleported, too. She had to blink a few times to get it to slide back into place.

Yes, they were in Las Vegas. They were outside the shopping mall across from a hotel that she assumed to be the Trump Tower, given the large, gaudy letter T emblazoned on the sidewalk.

"You're a planeswalker like Nori," she said, gulping back another surge of nausea. "I don't get sick when I go with Nori."

"I don't think it's the same thing. I'm not confined by the ley lines." Seth lifted Marion from the ground. She swayed into his grip, unable to stand alone. Her legs felt like they might melt underneath her.

"Stop it," she said, pushing at him.

He peered closely at her face. "Stop what?"

"Stop being so close to me. I threw up. I must smell awful."

"I was a doctor for over ten years," he said. "I dealt with a lot worse than vomit from my patients."

Marion locked her knees, trying to stand upright. "I'm not your patient anymore."

He didn't let go of her. One of his hands was curved around her neck, his palm rough against the soft skin, thumb resting against the underside of her jaw. He was staring very intently at her neck.

"Checking for a pulse?" she asked faintly, trying to smile.

Seth's hands dropped to his sides. "Sorry."

"Next time you decide to teleport me, I'd appreciate warning," Marion said. It was a little easier to breathe now. She wiped her hands off on her jeans. "At least we got here quickly. Now let's see about finding this Dana McIntyre person, shall we?"

"I think we already have," he said, gaze fixed across the street.

Even Marion recognized the sound of flesh slapping against flesh and the crunch of bone.

A window shattered outward. A body flew out of the Trump's lobby, smashing into the divider and crumpling on the pavement.

A second body followed, landing atop the first.

Seth pushed Marion behind him. "Stay back."

Magic fizzled over the street, swelling so hard and so sudden that Marion nearly gagged on it. It was gaean magic, a human creation, but it fed on such rage that it nauseated her.

The remaining glass shivered, then pulverized. It rained to the sidewalk outside of the Trump's lobby in a wave of shimmering glitter. Then the person who had cleared it out of the frame stepped over the remnants of the frame.

She could only be described as fat, and she wore it with authority. Leather and black cotton stretched across her rock-solid body. The woman was busty, with virtually no waist because her core muscles were built as solidly as the pillars of the Coliseum. Stone gauntlets gripped her fists, her forearms. The spells originated from the gemstones set into those gauntlets. Electric magic lanced up her armored shoulders and crawled over the skin of her round cheeks.

Her hair was cut short, very short, and the

spikes were dyed bright blue. Her eyes were hard. Her nose was button-like, almost cute, although Marion suspected that describing her in such words would have been a great way to get one of those gauntlets shoved down her throat.

She stalked toward the people she'd thrown across the street, crushing glass under the heels of her studded combat boots. Leather straps swung from her belt like a Roman gladiator's skirt, punched with metal spikes that sparked with more magic.

"Oh my gods," Marion said, eyes widening. "Is that—"

"That would be Dana McIntyre, yes," Seth said.

One of the vampires was scrambling to his feet, trying to escape before Dana reached him.

She punched his head into the ground.

The other vampire rose, and she mule-kicked one of those chunky heels into his jaw, sending his skull spinning almost a full ninety degrees.

A half-dozen vampires flooded from the lobby she'd evacuated.

"Ooh," Marion said. Eight against one. The odds weren't good. "Shouldn't we help?"

"No, I don't think so," Seth said.

He was right. Dana thrust a gauntleted fist toward the newcomers. Pure white fire flooded from her palm, chewing over their desiccated flesh, melting it away.

Only one of the vampires was left.

Dana marched over to him and kneeled on his chest. He thrashed, but she must have been a good two hundred and fifty pounds, most of it muscle; an animated cadaver didn't stand a chance of escaping her. "Do we have an understanding now?" she asked.

He struggled to suck air through his dried throat. "But—I don't—you killed them!"

"They might recover with blood. They won't if I decapitate all of you." The threat in her tone seemed sort of redundant, considering she was digging her studded combat boots into his sternum.

"Okay, okay! We have an understanding! You'll have your tithes!"

Dana released him and stood. "Good."

She finally noticed that she had an audience. Her eyes narrowed at the sight of Seth—and then she spotted Marion behind him.

The glow vanished from her enchanted gemstones instantly.

"Shit," Dana said. "What the hell are *you* doing here?"

SIX

Dana McIntyre lived in a condo in the Allure Tower, up near the top floor. Its windows offered an excellent view of the rest of the Strip: circling tourist helicopters and signs advertising residencies by the likes of Serafina the Siren, succubus strip clubs, and witch burlesque shows.

One entire wall of the condo was used to display weapons and armor. Some were guns. She had a few axes, too. But mostly she had more enchanted stone pieces, like a helmet, and some knee guards, and even a breastplate.

Dana stripped the gauntlets off as she strode into her condo, tossing them onto a leather couch. "Yeah, I took the Canope to Sheol. What's it to you?"

Marion gaped at the enchanted armor. The magic was complex and unlike anything that

Marion had seen before. The gaean spellwork she'd sensed when Dana had been tossing people out of the Trump Tower was only a fragment of it, woven into threads of magic that seemed ethereal and—Marion had to guess—infernal too.

Dana didn't emanate even the faintest hint of witchy power herself, so Marion had to assume her collection had been gifted or purchased. She clearly knew how to use them, though.

"The hell are you staring at?" Dana asked. Marion's jaw snapped shut.

Seth slipped into the room. "Who gave you the Canope courier job?"

"I don't know. It came to me through the darknet. Picked it up from an anonymous drop point and did my job, like I always do."

"Where was the drop point?"

"Outside Vegas," Dana said.

Seth and Marion exchanged looks. As far as they knew, Marion hadn't been anywhere near Vegas recently. "We need to know where you took the Canope so we can get it back," Seth said.

"I don't share my clients' secrets," Dana said.

Seth surveyed Dana with surprisingly fond eyes. "You don't remember me, do you? I was acquainted with your dad, Lucas McIntyre."

Marion felt a jolt of shock. *Lucas?* When she'd met Seth, he had been going by Lucas as a pseudonym—now an obvious homage to the father of this woman.

"Dad had a lot of acquaintances," Dana said.

The bedroom door creaked open. A woman

peered through. "Dana?"

"Stay in there," Dana said. "I'm doing business."

The other woman's eyes flicked between the people in the living room. Her skin was green, her eyes flat brown, her underbite accented by tusks. She was something gaean that Marion hadn't seen before.

When the green woman realized that Marion was looking at her, she popped back into the bedroom and shut the door.

"I don't do favors for anyone, even Dad's acquaintances." Dana plopped onto the couch, unlaced her boots, and kicked them off. She was wearing striped ankle socks with holes in the left big toe and bumblebees on the heels. "If I did, I'd owe something to thousands of people. He was too popular. And a hell of a lot more personable than I am."

"That's Brianna's work." Seth pointed at the breastplate.

Dana dropped her boots with a *thud*. "You know Brianna?"

"They dated for a week," Marion said before she could stop herself.

"I had no idea Brianna was a cougar," Dana said. "Nice."

"Brianna sent us to you," Seth said. "She said you'd be able to help us track down the Canope. I'm Seth Wilder, by the way. This is Marion Garin. We have reason to believe that the Canope is holding memories stolen from Marion."

"*You're* Seth Wilder?" Dana gave Seth another once-over and grunted. "Huh. Sorry."

"For what?"

"I should have been expecting you, I guess." Her jaw clenched. "Both of you."

"I'm sorry, do we know each other?" Marion asked. "You look very...angry."

"Do you remember me?" Dana asked.

The specific phrasing of the question made Marion inclined to think the answer was yes. They did know each other. The relationship didn't seem to be friendly, though. "I might remember you if we could get the Canope from Sheol."

Dana rolled her eyes. "I guess that's the point, isn't it?"

"I'm not following you," Seth said. "The point of what?"

She grumbled as she pulled herself off of the couch. Without the gauntlets and with her bumblebee socks exposed, Dana looked less like a warrior from the days of yore and more like a disgruntled cashier from Hot Topic. "Hey! Penny!"

The bedroom door opened again. The green woman emerged hesitantly. She was taller than Marion had first realized, tall enough that her coarse brown curls brushed the top of the doorway. She was also broad-shouldered and as muscular as Dana, though she had less body fat, and also seemed to prefer flannel and pajama pants to leather.

"What's up?" Penny asked. She spoke surprisingly clearly around those tusks.

"Go find my maps of the Nether Worlds," Dana said.

Penny shot a shy smile at Marion, slipping into a second bedroom.

Dana waved Seth and Marion over to her kitchen island. "The buyer's a guy named Arawn. He's one of the Lords of Sheol. The other big one is Nyx, who rules from a palace called Duat. Are you following?"

"I'm following." Seth sat on one of the bar stools.

Penny returned with a thick piece of folded paper. She weighed its corners down with a barbecue spatula on one side and an empty snifter on the other. "There you go, sweetums." She kissed Dana before shuffling back into the bedroom.

"Here's Sheol," Dana said. "This here's the hive." She pointed to a mess of streets on the left side of the map. "Arawn's got a place there, but he also shares space in Duat, over on the other side of the Dead Forest. It's easier to get into the hive. You can start out looking there. Stay out of the forest. The Hounds roam there, and you don't wanna deal with the Hounds."

"What makes the hive a hive?" Seth asked.

"Buggy-type demons chewed tunnels into the rock, and it's big enough that it's basically become a city of its own. Believe it or not, the hive's the safest place to start off. Most of those demons only eat smaller demons of the same persuasion."

The idea of going anywhere near so-called "buggy-type demons" made Marion feel queasy.

"And you think that Arawn will have the Canope in his home in the hive?"

"Hopefully," Dana said. "He'd be keeping the Canope somewhere safe. He has to be careful with it. Really, really careful. It's designed to hold souls. If it breaks, the soul's gone."

"It holds souls?" Marion asked, eyes widening. "Or memories?"

"The essence of a person. Whatever you want to call it. If it breaks, whoever's being kept in there will be pretty much dead."

Marion's essence—her memories—had been sold to a demon in Hell.

No wonder she didn't remember anything at all once she touched Seth. She'd already remembered everything that remained within her mind. Everything else was locked away in the Canope.

Seth took her hand and squeezed it. "We'll get it back. Don't worry."

Was her fear so transparent?

"Yes, thanks," she murmured.

She edged away from the island while Seth and Dana continued to discuss the map.

Dana wasn't as much a fan of books as Marion, or even Seth, but she had a few shelves. Most of her collection was trashy science fiction. Old stuff that had been read so much that the spines were illegible from being creased so much.

There was a piece of paper sticking out from between two books. Marion glanced at Dana, who was still distracted, before tugging it free.

It was a photograph of three women at a sunny

beach: an adult and two teenagers.

The moon-faced teen on the left with the spiky pink hair was clearly Dana, though she wasn't quite as fat as she'd grown to become. Less like a tank, more like an armored car. She wore a halter bikini top with board shorts that showed off her powerful thighs and the pleasant rolls of her belly.

The adult woman was someone that Marion had seen in photos of her own: Ariane Kavanagh, who looked like an older, whiter-skinned version of Marion. Ariane was dainty and mischievous around the eyes, as though she were hiding secrets.

The third woman was Marion herself.

She was younger, skinnier, cute rather than beautiful. Her hair was concealed by a headscarf, emphasizing her luminous blue eyes. And the teenage Dana was easily hefting Marion's lanky figure above her head, like Marion was a barbell, while Ariane watched the two of them. Ariane looked like she was either laughing or horrified.

Marion wore a string bikini, which showed off her abdomen. She had no silvery scar on her ribcage. The photo must have been taken before she started dating Konig.

Together, the three women looked happy.

Like family.

Marion stared at Dana in the flesh, where she stood under the pool of light shining on her kitchen island. The huntress didn't look like she'd been happy in a long time. Like she might have never once smiled since becoming an adult.

Were they sisters? Marion and this stocky, armored, angry lesbian?

"Gods," Marion breathed.

"Take the map," Dana was saying, oblivious to Marion's exploration. She folded the parchment and handed it to Seth. "Once you get in Sheol, there'll be a dot that shows your location. Bring it back to me once you're finished down there."

Seth picked up the paper, studying it closely. "Loaning your enchanted map to me? That's showing a lot of trust for one of your dad's worthless acquaintances."

"Not that much. It'll spring back to me if you die."

"Interesting magic. Very strong, very privileged, unseelie magic." He directed that toward Marion.

She came up behind him to look over his shoulder. Seth was right. The map was riddled with complex unseelie magic similar to the kind that had connected Oliver Machado to the unseelie. "You're a triadist," Marion said. "Aren't you, Dana?"

"Triadist?" Seth asked.

"They're a church that thinks the gods aren't dead and have dedicated their lives to worshipping them." At Seth's confused look, Marion explained, "Konig told me about them. He said that the triadists are connected to the previous rulers of the Winter Court."

Dana folded her arms. "What about it? Who cares if I am?"

"I believe that triadists recently tried to kill

me," Marion said.

"Konig thinks your assassins were triadists? Huh." Seth took folded pages out of the inside of his jacket. Showed them to Dana. They were drawings of men: Oliver Machado and two that Marion didn't recognize. "Do you know any of these people?"

She studied the pages from a distance without taking them. "No."

"Not even this one?" Seth lifted the picture of Oliver Machado.

Dana shook her head. "I doubt all triadists want anyone dead. That'd be like saying bald people want you dead. Triadists aren't a unified community—just a bunch of people who agree on a few philosophies. Like the fact that there are three gods kicking around."

Marion frowned. "Three?" The triadists couldn't know too much, then. The only gods were Elise and James.

"Yeah. Three. And yeah, we've got access to unseelie magic," Dana said. "This one triadist, Brother Marshall, had friends among the old Winter Court. He shares with anyone who can find his church."

"So you didn't have anything to do with the recent attempts on Marion's life?" Seth asked.

"I've got better shit to do than that. A city to run. Vampire asses to kick." Dana finally took the drawings. "I can pass these around to some triadist friends of mine. See if anyone knows who they are." She spotted the photo that Marion was holding. She ripped it out of Marion's hand. "Don't touch my shit."

"We're cousins or something, aren't we?" Marion asked. "That's why you're a triadist. You believe in the gods because you're related to me."

"Your mom raised me after my parents died," Dana said. "We don't have one gods-damned drop of blood in common."

"But we did grow up together."

Dana scowled, shoving the photo into her pocket. "Yeah."

And here Marion had been thinking she only had one sister, who was a god. She really had two. This one seemed to hate her even though they'd looked so happy in the photograph.

Now that Marion realized they had a relationship, she knew why some of Dana's enchanted armor resonated with her so strongly. There *was* ethereal magic woven in with the gaean, unseelie, and infernal stuff. "I made that helmet," Marion said. "Didn't I?"

"Penny made the helmet, you enchanted it. It's not like I even wear it most of the time."

But when Marion stretched out her senses, she felt her magic coming from the gauntlets too. Those fireballs that Dana had been throwing— those were Marion's design. "Why don't you like me?"

"That's cute, that's really cute," Dana said. "Don't tell me I've hurt poor Marion's *feelings*."

"Hey," Seth said sharply.

Dana jabbed her finger at the map he was

holding. "That's everything you need to find Arawn and the Canope, if you're smart about it. You'll have to find your own way into Sheol. I'm not giving you my contacts to get into the Nether Worlds."

"I think we've gotten enough from you," Seth said. "Come on, Marion."

She didn't follow him to the door. She gazed in hopeless confusion at Dana.

That look of anger, annoyance, hatred—it wasn't unlike the looks that Marion got from various members of the Autumn Court, the angels, and almost everyone else who had known her before she'd lost her memory. "I can't make things right between us if you don't give me the opportunity."

"Tell you what," Dana said. "You get the Canope, you get your memories back, and you remember it all on your own. If you're still feeling all butt-hurt about this, we'll talk. But I think you'll get it, and you'll feel like shit for having the nerve to show up in my city once that happens. Now go away."

Seth's hand slipped into Marion's, holding her firmly as he guided her out of the condo.

Everyone who knew Marion hated her. Even someone who had been raised as her sister.

Maybe she was better off without the Canope.

"You look like you could use a drink," Seth said once they hit the street. The Las Vegas night was warm and busy, illuminated by so many brilliant witchlights that it nearly seemed like daytime.

"I'm only nineteen and you called me a kid earlier," Marion said.

"Yeah, well, I didn't know how bad a day you were having earlier. Come on, I know a place you'll love. It's fancy. Big crystal chandeliers, classy wait staff, very clean."

Marion's smile was still a little too hesitant. "That sounds wonderful."

They walked all the way down the Strip and through a labyrinthine casino in silence. Seth had a hard time remembering where to go. Lots had changed since he'd lived in Las Vegas after Genesis. Magic and technology had fused. There were as many witches at the blackjack tables as mundane dealers, and the air was thick with spells, flying decks of cards, and even sparkling chips.

Many things hadn't changed, though. That included the cocktail waitresses, most of whom wore skirts so skimpy that they verged on illegal. They were happy to give Seth directions in exchange for tips. Marion didn't look surprised by the way that the cocktail waitresses dressed. They must not have impressed her after all the debauchery she'd seen in the Middle Worlds. Sidhe were far worse than Las Vegas.

"Here we go," Seth said, getting off at the top of an escalator. "It's right down here—wait."

The bar he'd expected to find around the corner was a Cheesecake Factory now. A chain restaurant. Clean, yes, but not the bar he remembered. Not the one he'd gone to with Brianna Dimaria so many times, along with the other preternatural investigators in their company.

"Can I help you?" asked the hostess with a too-bright smile.

"How long has this been here?" Seth asked. "What happened to the bar?"

Her cheer cracked. "I've only been working here for two years, but...I think this restaurant has been in this spot since like '22?" Eight years earlier, during the time when Seth had been firmly entrenched at Mercy Hospital.

"It's fine," Marion said, glancing uneasily at the crowd surrounding them. "I should get back to the Winter Court and address a few things before we go to Sheol."

Seth backed out of the restaurant, trying to shake the malaise that had settled over him. "No. No way. We're getting drinks."

"My pick this time," Marion said. "I promise to choose nothing called the Salty Anything."

They didn't have to go too far to find something more palatable than a Cheesecake Factory. The next casino over was brand new, something called Valhalla, and it was nothing but dark décor and sparkling chandeliers that glimmered with pixie light.

Marion was as good as her word. She selected a bar that was called the Endless Battle. It was packed that time of night by beautiful young people—all very fashionable, happy, and drunk. None of them held a candle to Marion. Even in jeans and a blouse, she managed to look like she was walking the runway on the way to the bartender.

Seth slipped in between a couple and took the stools they'd vacated. He wiped off the one to his left with his sleeve. "There you go."

"Such a gentleman," Marion said.

"It had overpriced cocktail on it. Knowing you, those jeans are worth a few hundred dollars. Can't get them wet."

He was rewarded with one of those dimpled smiles. "You're still teasing me. Have you forgotten what a dreadful day I'm having?"

"You don't get out of anything that easily," Seth said.

"A demon has my memories in a jar. If that's not an excuse for you to take it easy on me, then nothing is." She perched on the stool, tucking her boots behind the footrest.

"What can I get you guys?" the bartender asked. She was a busty vampire with a tiny waist and lips red as blood.

Seth barely glanced at her. "Long Island Iced Tea for my friend. For me, whiskey straight up."

The bartender left to get their drinks.

"Whiskey?" A smile flitted across Marion's lips. "You're having that kind of week too?"

"That kind of lifetime," Seth said.

It only took a moment for the vampire to serve

them. Seth paid and tipped her.

Marion was giving him a funny smile when the bartender finally left.

"What?" he asked.

"Most women who see you are immensely attracted to you. She was no exception."

Seth hadn't noticed. "So what?"

"You aren't attracted to her."

"You're reading my mind?"

"I often don't need to. Some emotions are strong enough that I have no choice but to read them," Marion said. "I'm getting a lot of strong feelings from the men in the bar about the vampire. Some of the women are having strong feelings, too. Not you."

"Hate to repeat myself, but...so what?"

She stared at his forehead as though trying to get into his brain. Her skin was tinted blue-green in the pixie light, making her eyes glow even more brightly. Her hair seemed black where it curled against her cheek. "I thought that you were going to leave for good. Why did you come back for me?"

"I told you," Seth said. "I need your help."

"The help you need resembles helping me rather strongly."

"Would it be a problem if that was the reason?" he asked.

Marion bit the inside of her cheek. She sipped her Long Island Tea, but he thought she was hiding a smile. "Rylie said that you and I don't have a history. We've never met."

"Nope. That's what I told you before, wasn't it?"

"It destroyed my theory as to why we have a connection," Marion said. "I've formulated a new one about you. Would you like to hear it?"

"I'm not sure I do," Seth said.

"You're a hero, and I need help, and you're incapable of going about your business until you've saved me." She'd stopped smiling by the time she finished speaking.

Seth took a long drink of whiskey. It was much more tolerable than the wine from her house.

"I voted to give the Winter Court to the angels," Marion said suddenly.

He swirled the whiskey in his glass. The ice glittered like gemstones. "That's not what the gods told you to do."

"Where are they?" she asked softly, quietly enough that nobody else in the bar would be able to hear. "How much can they care if they've left me like...this? They deserve no better than my defiance."

"You're probably the only person who could get away with trying to piss them off like that. Elise never let anyone else get away with anything, aside from her husband, whom she let get away with everything."

"You didn't like them."

"It's complicated," Seth said.

"That seems to be your favorite word for the gods."

It was the only word he could use.

"It's not about thumbing my nose at them," Marion said. "There are people suffering in the aftermath of the civil war between sidhe. Survivors. If we can appease the angels, thereby preventing further fighting, I'll be able to keep the refugees safe. Yet almost everyone voted against me in the United Nations."

"You're steward of the Winter Court now," Seth said. "You don't need UN permission to give Niflheimr to the angels."

"But then I don't have backing from the other preternatural factions. Where do I put the refugees if nobody will help me? They're all afraid of defying the gods."

"Konig won't take them?" Seth asked.

"He hasn't offered. I assume he would if he could. Regardless, this is all academic. I can't make a deal with the angels if Leliel won't meet with me." She propped her forehead on the heel of her hand, glaring into the dregs of her Long Island Iced Tea. "There are so many nuances to pleasing all of the factions, protecting the refugees, and preventing war."

"You can handle it."

"That's what people keep telling me." She tipped her head to gaze up at him. A curl tumbled over the bridge of her nose. "What would you do?"

He rubbed a hand over his upper lip. "I'd take it sideways. Figure out what Leliel wants. Find her weaknesses. What do you know about her and her allies?"

"She had Oliver Machado," Marion said.

"I'm not sure he was *directly* involved with the angels." Not that they could ask, since Charity had ripped his head off. "That doesn't mean they aren't linked. Like you said—nuances. What connected Ollie to the angels?" Seth snagged a dry napkin. "Got a pen?"

Marion gave one to him. Like everything else she owned, it was an expensive brand, made of silver and platinum, with a nib that made it look like a quill.

Seth wrote Ollie's name in one corner and "the angels" in the other. The Autumn Court went in between them.

He drew a line between the angels and the court. "We know these two have an alliance. Right? Oliver was a triadist, and the church has friends among the Winter Court." He added those to his diagram. "What else?"

"The only connection there is between the Autumn and Winter Courts. They're both unseelie. But Konig said that they went to the grave hating each other."

"What could motivate collusion then? Money? Everyone likes money," Seth said, drumming the end of the pen on the bar. "Or it could be something like revenge."

"Or love." Marion was watching Seth even as she continued stirring her remaining ice in ongoing loops. "Nothing motivates people to commit more evil than love."

"That's funny coming from you. You're the one who said love and loss are integral to the human experience. I'd think you were more sentimental about it."

"I'm having quite the week," she said softly.

The conversation clearly wasn't improving anything. He hadn't taken her out for drinks to make her more miserable.

Seth stuffed the napkin in his pocket. "Hopefully Dana McIntyre finds something. Help us draw a few more lines."

"I don't see how it will help me with the angels."

"Nuances," he said again. "The angels, they're shameless. They won't care what we find about them. They won't care if we know what they're doing or why. If they've got friends supporting them, though... They might care more about their reputations. If we remove the angels' support, we mitigate the amount of trouble they make. Rather than appeasing or fighting the angels, you can cripple them."

"Take it sideways," Marion mused. "That sounds like the subtle tactics I used, back when I was still myself."

"You are yourself," Seth said. "Everything you are right now, this is you."

"Is it?"

Her hand was resting on the table between them. Seth thought about taking it. Offering comfort.

Her pulse was fluttering in her wrist.

Seth finished his whiskey and set the glass down hard. "Wherever this goes, whatever rabbit holes we end up diving down in the investigation... Don't give the Winter Court to the angels.

Appeasement never stops the greedy. They just take and take and keep on taking."

"I appreciate the advice. However, speaking of Niflheimr—duty calls. I have to go back for at least a few minutes to sort things out." Marion pushed the rest of her drink away.

Seth stood when she did. "I can take you."

"That won't be necessary." She took a small white statuette from her pocket. It looked like a key made of marble. "This gets me in touch with Nori. She'll pick me up." Marion gave a small smile. "It doesn't make me sick when she pulls me between planes."

Seth understood. He had things to do anyway —things with Charity that he needed to address before they could journey to Sheol. "I'll go to Sheol soon. I'll get your memories back from Arawn. I promise."

Her eyes widened with alarm. She reached for his hand. "*You're* going to get my memories? But Seth—"

He vanished from the bar before she could finish.

SEVEN

Marion returned to a Niflheimr that had been changed. Someone had activated the wards on the exterior of the castle, making the interior temperature a balmy five degrees Celsius. She was still chilly in the clothes she'd been wearing in Las Vegas, but not so chilly that she ran for the furs.

Better still, Konig's knights had rearranged the inner courtyard to serve as a refugee camp. There were more than enough bedrooms in Niflheimr to give one to each family, but they were in various states of disrepair; each room would need to be inspected before moving anyone in.

For now, everyone had beds and tents in the cavernous courtyard, and it was so populous that it was starting to look like a village.

"How wonderful!" Marion said, unable to keep from beaming at the sight of it. "This is *much* better."

"Thanks," Nori said. "Uh, not that I had much to do with it. It was the knights, mostly."

Marion leaped back when a gaggle of sidhe children ran past, nearly knocking her over. Ymir tagged along at the back of the crowd, along with Cyprian and his daughters. It was funny to see the boy—the supposed frost giant—playing with two little unseelie girls. Marion almost believed he would one day grow into a giant by the clumsy way he chased after them. His hands and feet were so big for his body that he kept tumbling all over himself.

He wasn't laughing, but there was a little bit of a smile lingering around his haunted eyes.

"We'll need to get everyone into private rooms as quickly as possible," Marion said. "On that note, have you prepared my bedroom?"

"Yes, of course. I've moved the clothes from your second walk-in closet in your Earth home, as well as your bow and quiver, as you asked," Nori said.

The bow and quiver were the entire reason that Marion had decided to return to Niflheimr. "Excellent. Thank you again."

Marion headed for the hallway that led toward the rooms.

"*There* you are, princess." Konig swept out of the door before she could reach it, followed closely by a pair of his knights. Konig's violet eyes were usually warm with a mixture of love and lust when he looked at Marion. But right now he was all business. "Where have you been?"

"I've gotten a lead on restoring my memories. I had to follow through." Marion kissed him in greeting, as the sidhe usually did, and clutched both of his hands.

"What did you find?" Konig asked.

She shrugged. "Not the memories—yet. But I've a better idea of where to look for them. Have you ever heard of an infernal artifact called the Canope?"

"Never. I can ask my parents to look into it."

"No need. We've already found that it's been bought by a Lord of Sheol. How or why it happened, we really don't know, but—"

His tone went sharp. "We?"

Cyprian's daughters and Ymir chose that moment to laugh. The sound made the frosty halls seem a little less remote and alien.

Oops. Marion had meant to ease into the subject of Seth more gradually than that. "Why don't we talk in my room?"

"What did you do?"

"Nothing," she said. "But Seth's the one helping me find my memories. Seth Wilder."

"Lucas Flynn."

"The one and only," Marion said.

Konig's features darkened. Sidhe were transparent about their moods: when they became angry, the entire world surrounding them crackled. "We were never certain that he wasn't trying to take advantage of you leading up to the summit."

"*You* were never certain."

"It must be nice to have the privilege of being so naïve," he said, cupping her cheek. "This, Marion—*this* is why I'll be the one to talk to the angels when they arrive. Aren't you lucky to have me?"

"So lucky," Marion said without irony. "I trust your judgment where the angels are concerned, and I wish you'd trust that I know Seth well enough."

"I can't believe I'm hearing this." Konig sounded like he was working up to a much bigger rant, but he cut off when one of his knights hurried over.

"Heather Cobweb is here, my lord," the knight said. "She has messages from your parents."

Konig looked torn. Marion gently urged him, "Go ahead. I'll keep supervising work on the refugee camp."

"I'm not worried about the refugees. This conversation isn't over," Konig said.

"Agreed," Marion said. He kissed her, and it was much briefer than she would have liked. As cold as Konig was, he was still several degrees warmer than the Winter Court.

As if sensing her reluctance, Konig only stepped away for a moment. And then he kissed her again. Slower. Deeper.

Marion clutched at his shirt in both of her hands, enjoying the heat of his chest.

"Don't go far," Konig said.

And then he was gone to meet Heather.

Marion traced her fingers over her lips.

A cold wind whirled through the courtyard, waking her up enough to remember what she'd come to Niflheimr to do. She hurried into the hall.

Nori showed Marion to a bedroom beside the king's. It was smaller, but significantly warmer, as Konig had promised. Lush green trees grew within the sitting room. Vines crawled up the icy walls. It was so muggy that a layer of dew clung to the furniture.

With Marion's belongings in boxes around the bed, it felt as homey as her house on Vancouver Island—or anywhere, really.

She popped open boxes to search for her bow.

"You found your memories?" Nori asked.

"I've found who has them," Marion said. Her bow was in a protective wooden box of its own. She pocketed the oily package of strings, slung the bow across her shoulders, looped her belt through the quiver.

"You're arming yourself. Does the person with your memories live in a war zone?"

"Something like that."

"Marion..." Nori sat on the edge of her bed, clutching her clipboard in both hands. She'd been getting personal information on all of the refugee families to make sure that they were accounted for. "Jibril's going to be here soon to talk to you."

"I know," Marion said. "And Konig has made it clear that he's got everything under control. He'll also have your help. You'll assist with negotiations, won't you? After you return me to Earth, of course."

Nori's eyes turned to big circles. "You have a lot to do here."

"That's why I'm so grateful for your help. You're ethereal Gray too. You know as much about the angels as I do—more, since you've worked with them directly in Dilmun. And I know that you'll represent our interests to the best of your ability." Marion switched out her boots for sturdier boots that laced up to her knees.

Nori floundered. "I guess, but—Konig won't be happy, and I doubt Jibril will be thrilled, either."

"I'm the Voice of God," Marion said. "But I'm useless until I've restored myself. I won't do much good against the angels without my memories and magic."

"*Against* the angels?"

"Do you really think that talks with Jibril will lead to peace between us?"

"We won't get a chance to find out if you skip out on it," Nori said.

"I'm not skipping out. I'm delegating responsibility. And I take great comfort in knowing you'll be in charge while I'm busy," Marion said. "Now, let's get to the Empress Hotel. I have memories to restore."

Seth took a shower as soon as he got back to the Empress Hotel in Victoria. He turned the heat to its maximum setting and stood under the flow with his eyes shut for at least an hour. He told himself that it was because he didn't know when he would get to shower again—who knew how long he would be in Sheol?—but mostly it was because he didn't want to deal with reality.

Teleporting Marion to Las Vegas had made her sick, and Seth had been able to feel it the same way that he had felt Agent Hanes having a heart attack.

He'd been as fixated on her sickness as he had been on the heart attack, too.

It had been easy to focus on Marion herself when they'd been together. Her personal pain after meeting Dana McIntyre was adequately distracting, as was the attempt to connect Oliver Machado to the angels.

Once she'd been gone physically, she hadn't been gone from Seth mentally.

He kept thinking about when she'd collapsed in Las Vegas. He thought about Marion getting sick, and how weakly her heart had beat for a few moments.

Worse, Seth thought about Agent Hanes's death and the taste of cooling blood on his fingers.

What's wrong with you?

He let the water wash over his body, but it couldn't clean the parts of him that were in most desperate need of purification.

Charity was waiting in the room. She wore a fluffy bathrobe and was watching trashy TV in bed. The happiest, most comfortable revenant that

Seth had ever seen.

Of course, she was also the only revenant Seth had ever seen.

She groaned when he came out. "Does this mean it's time for us to go to Sheol?" She'd been insistent that she wanted to help him track the Canope down in Sheol, but she hadn't needed to work hard to convince him. Going into the Nether Worlds was less intimidating when he knew he'd have something of her power at his back.

"I was hoping we could talk first," Seth said. "I can't stop thinking about it." What he meant was, *I can't stop thinking about her.*

Charity understood what he meant. She pushed her glasses up the bridge of her nose, squinting at him through lenses strong enough that they made her eyes look big. "What have you tried to help you control your instincts so far? Meditation? Emptying your head out?"

"You mean whiskey?"

"Until you know what's happened to you, it's probably better to go easy on your liver, doc." She sat up and turned the TV off.

"Honestly, I haven't tried anything to get myself under control. It wasn't much of a problem until recently. How did you resist drinking blood for so many years?" Seth asked.

"Meditation," Charity said. "I can show you how I do it." She scooted off the edge of the bed and gestured for him to join her on the floor. "Get comfortable."

"I'm comfortable."

"You're going to wear your shoulder...thing?" She pointed at his underarm holster.

"I'm more comfortable with my gun than without." He'd been carrying a Beretta for literally as long as he could remember.

"Take it off anyway," Charity said. "We're emptying our heads of violent thoughts. Guns are violent."

"Guns save lives."

"And kill people, as we saw a little too often in the emergency department. Hunting accidents, misfires..."

"I'm not exactly the average gun owner," Seth said.

"Isn't that what they all think?" Charity asked. "Anyway, you're the one who asked me for help, so let me help you. Do it my way. Take your shoes and gun off."

Getting barefoot made him feel almost as displaced as he did once the shoulder rig was resting in a puddle of straps by his right knee. He rolled his shoulders out, exhaled slowly.

"So is this where I go all full lotus, say some prayers?" Seth asked.

Charity tipped her head back, eyes closed. A gap in the curtains let light spill over her cheeks. She'd been eating well lately, so her hair and skin looked strong, healthy. "This is where you relax, doc. Can you relax?"

"I'm always relaxed." But he took a few deep breaths as she instructed.

The problem was that once he closed his eyes,

he didn't have as many distractions from his thoughts.

Like how it had sounded when Charity shredded those agents.

Or how the blood had tasted, cooling on his fingers.

It wasn't even the flavor that had appealed to him. It had been the way that he could taste them rushing toward death.

The same way that Marion had rushed toward death in the instant they'd teleported.

"This isn't helping," Seth said.

Charity sighed. "It's been five seconds."

"I can't stop thinking about everything. How's sitting around taking deep breaths supposed to make me stop thinking? Does it make you stop craving blood?"

"Not really," Charity said.

Seth's eyes popped open. "Then what are we doing?"

She hugged her knees to her chest. "You're not going to stop craving blood. I think about it every waking moment. *Every moment*. The hunger is my life. Meditation doesn't make those thoughts go away. In fact, it makes me overwhelmed by them. But in the eye of the hurricane, there's calm. Get used to living in the storm."

He was supposed to get used to the idea of wanting to tear Marion's throat open?

Seth let his eyes fall shut, but this time, instead of focusing on breathing, he thought about how he was going to leave. Get away. Find Marion's memories, and then never see her again.

People moved elsewhere in the Empress Hotel, their voices murmuring on the other side of the walls. Distantly, teacups clinked against saucers. Wind sighed past the windows.

And Seth thought of blood.

He kept thinking about it. He was trapped in a loop—thinking about the blood he'd already tasted, the deaths he'd seen, and the deaths he wanted to see, and then how he would escape.

Even if he never saw Marion again, the hunger wasn't going to go away completely.

She'd collapsed at his feet. Her heart had stopped beating, and for one sweet second, he'd thought it might never start again. When he'd helped her off of the ground, he had realized that he could inflict that death upon her personally.

Those were thoughts he hadn't lingered on before. Not even briefly. Now he lingered on them, reveled in them.

Get used to living in the storm.

Seth didn't want to.

"Whiskey's better," he said, grabbing his holster off of the floor and standing.

"You need total honesty," Charity said, watching him move from her spot on the floor. "Maybe for you, it's not enough to be honest with yourself. You've got to be honest with Marion, too. She's the problem, isn't she?"

Charity was much too perceptive. "How'd you know?"

"You went on a field trip with her and came

back for a cold shower. I mean, it's not very subtle."

"The shower was hot, actually. And it's not like that with Marion."

"Why isn't it?"

"Let me count the ways. She's got a boyfriend. And she's nineteen. And I don't date anymore, period."

"I didn't think you were dating," Charity said. "Whatever is going on with you, it's a little bit more, um, *intense* than that."

"Yeah, like I keep thinking about killing her," Seth said.

Charity blinked. "Oh. Well, you should probably talk about that, then. Before Marion gets the wrong idea."

"No. *No*. I'm not going to tell a woman that I'm thinking about killing her. That's creepy as hell. I'm going to figure out how to deal with this on my own—and with your help. That's all the honesty I need."

Her eyes went unfocused, as though she were listening to very quiet music. "Here's your opportunity to be honest right now."

Someone knocked at their hotel room door an instant later.

Seth didn't have to check to know who it was.

He'd seen Marion's face when he'd said that he planned to go to Sheol without her.

Maybe that was the subconscious reason why he'd chosen to take a long shower—not to calm himself, but to wait for her arrival.

He opened the door. Marion stood on the other

side with her fist uplifted, as though preparing to knock again. She was dressed for travel into Sheol: long-sleeved blouse, jeans, boots, a headscarf. She even had her unseelie bow slung over her shoulders and a quiver at her waist. Marion looked far too conspicuous to wander around the Empress Hotel, so Nori must have dropped her off in that hallway.

All that effort he'd put into controlling himself —clearing his mind of thoughts and hunger and *need*—vanished in a heartbeat. The sight of her pulse pushing blood underneath the veil of her skin tossed him back to the detention center, licking the blood off of his fingers.

The deaths of angels, immortal as they were, would be sweeter than the deaths of human OPA agents.

Seth was horrified by the thoughts, as foreign to him as though he had some parasitic brain-slug narrating the violent fantasies.

Hell, maybe it *was* a parasitic brain-slug. Weirder things had happened during Genesis.

"Hi," she said, giving him a dimpled smile. "What are you guys doing?"

Charity gave Seth an expectant look, encouraging him to respond. He cleared his throat. Stuffed his feet into his shoes. "Guess you could say we're enjoying our luxury amenities for a few last minutes. Nowhere in Sheol has high tea."

Charity made a scoffing sound.

Marion wasn't oblivious to the mood. Amusement darkened to suspicion, and hurt. "Is that it, then?" Damn, she must have thought they'd been talking about her. It would have been so much worse if she'd known what Seth was really thinking.

"That's it," Seth said.

The mage girl looked between Charity in her bathrobe and Seth, who wasn't wearing his holster and was putting on his shoes, in the hotel room that they were sharing.

He finally made the connection Marion did.

She wasn't feeling self-conscious. She thought Seth and Charity were getting dressed together. Never mind that Seth had sworn to spend the rest of his life alone—or that Charity was, despite her frightening vampiric charms, the emotional equivalent of a little sister to Seth.

He squared his shoulders. "Charity's coming with me to Sheol."

"The more the merrier," Marion said brightly. "I'll be happy for the assistance."

"You're not coming," Seth said. "Did you forget about what happened when I pulled you down to Las Vegas?"

"I'm fine. I'll be better prepared for it this time." She smiled at him toothily, and it was more of a challenge for him to defy her than her normal charming grin. "I don't have anything better to do."

"Really?" Marion had made no secret about the work to be done in the Winter Court.

She lifted her chin in defiance and crossed her arms over her chest. "Really. Nothing is more important than getting my memories back.

Perhaps you don't need me, but I won't let you go without my company, so here we are."

"That's very *honest* of you," Charity said, shooting a pointed look at Seth. She dropped the bathrobe. She was fully dressed underneath, wearing a tank top and shorts that would be suitable for Sheol's warmth. "I think it'll be good to have Marion help us."

Because that meant Charity could keep bullying Seth into telling Marion the truth.

Two against one. It wasn't fair.

"Then let's go," he said, holding his hands out.

Charity took the right hand. Marion the left. Even through the gloves that he wore, Seth could feel her pulse, strong and sure. He could hear her heart. See the flush of blood on her throat.

She was watching him so closely, he wondered if she was catching glimpses of his murderous thoughts.

Seth yanked all of them into Sheol before Marion could hear the worst of it.

EIGHT

Seth leaped into Sheol. It was always unsettling to teleport somewhere that he hadn't visited by normal means first. He hated stepping out of the world without being certain where he'd step back in.

Stepping off of the Earth to a place where he knew there would be nothing waiting for him but demons—that was something he dreaded even more.

He appeared in a cramped tunnel. Thankfully, he was still clutching both Marion and Charity.

"Is everyone all right?" Seth asked.

"I think so," Charity said, patting herself down. Marion nodded silently. She was very pale.

He stepped up to the edge of the tunnel, lifting Dana's map to compare it to what little he could see of the hive.

Seth's first impression of Sheol was that it was claustrophobic. The tunnel that they'd appeared in was too short for Marion to walk through without stooping over. She'd have to duck under the doorways.

The fact that there were open windows along the side of the tunnel wasn't much improvement; all they could see was a honeycomb of other cramped tunnels, along with heavy iron doors, pipework vanishing into the walls, and ooze.

He spotted a row of shops at the end of the tunnel because he could see the end of a sign marking a butcher's shop. Seth located it on the map. They had appeared exactly where he'd intended, and, just as Dana had promised, a tiny red dot appeared to mark their position.

"Let's find Arawn," Seth said.

Marion only took two steps down the tunnel before her knees buckled. She struck the ground on all fours.

She coughed. Seth smelled her blood before he saw it, and the coppery scent was stronger than the metallic tang suspended in Sheol's air.

The hunger roared through him.

The *need*.

His human instincts were, for the moment, stronger than the inhuman ones. Coughing blood might not have been worrying if the amounts were small. But when he kneeled to help Marion, he saw splatters the size of a fist. It looked like she'd regurgitated coffee grounds.

Internal bleeding.

She turned pained eyes on him. "Seth?" And then those eyes unfocused, rolling into the back of her head.

Marion stiffened. Fell over. The bow bent strangely under her, but she didn't respond to being jabbed in the side by the stave.

She began to shake.

Seth moved on instinct—making sure the space around her was clear as she seized, ensuring her airway was clear—but there was another instinct that was far too interested in the wavering jitter of her heart. An instinct that told him she was dying. He didn't even need to hear the raspy, labored intake of her breath to know that.

It was Agent Hanes all over again. He was frozen, knowing that he needed to resuscitate her, but without a clue as to how that should happen.

"I'm going to look for a doctor," Charity said, grabbing the map. He hadn't realized he'd dropped it.

She ran off before Seth could tell her to stop. They weren't going to find a doctor in Sheol other than Seth.

He clutched Marion's shoulders and focused on teleporting back to Earth, where they had come from. Back to Marion's home. Back to mage-friendly atmosphere and medical care.

Nothing happened.

He'd never been stuck before. It was like the ability simply wasn't there anymore.

Charity raced back toward him. "There's an apothecary down by the butcher. I don't see anything like a hospital."

An apothecary. Leave it to demons to have some archaic Dark Ages shit in their new version of Hell when Marion was going toxic. She needed real medical care. Not an *apothecary*.

Seth gathered her into his arms. She was his height in bare feet and continuing to tremble, so it was awkward hefting her. He held her tight. Refused to let go.

Her heart was speeding, but erratic.

I never should have let her come.

Charity raced down the tunnel, glancing over her shoulder to make sure that Seth was keeping up. "It's around the corner," she said.

Marion went limp. The sticky black blood was caking her chin, her chest. Her skin was colorless.

They rounded the corner to see a milling trio of insect-like demons. One clung to the wall. They all looked at Seth with bulging stares that were too human to match their segmented carapaces, as though someone had yanked eyeballs out of a human body and hot-glued them to giant beetles.

The two on the floor skittered forward. They must have smelled the death on Marion, just as Seth did.

"Get out of my way!" he roared.

They clicked to each other. The sounds that came from their mouthparts didn't resemble human language, but Seth understood it.

It's them.

Go get the guard.

He was so shocked to understand that he

missed a step. "*What*?" He stumbled, clutching Marion tighter to keep from dropping her body.

The demons dispersed, vanishing into burrows in the lava rock. If they'd been hoping to get to the Canope without being spotted, they were out of luck.

A bell tolled over the apothecary's door when Charity shoved it open. The sound was heavy with power.

The shop was clean but cramped. Shelves had been built out of scrap metal, displaying books, glass jars, a few body parts that might have come from creatures similar to the ones outside.

"We need help!" Charity cried, running toward the back of the shop. It seemed to have been fit into one of those burrows, so it curved toward the back, preventing Seth from seeing through to the end.

He shoved a few boxes off of the counter next to the register, laying Marion's body where the space had been cleared.

There was no longer a pulse of energy under the semi-translucent skin of her throat. There was blood flowing underneath, but it was too slow to resemble life.

Charity returned moments later. "I found the shopkeeper."

A woman drifted toward them from behind Charity. At least, Seth thought that it was a woman. Her face was a skinless skull with exposed teeth, hollows where her eyes should have been, and wisps that resembled hair. Her waist was tiny, her legs misty. She dragged a cloak of shadows behind her.

The instant that she spotted Marion, she stopped.

"Mage." The word slithered through yellowed teeth. The hollows of her eyes turned on Seth. "And...*you*."

She swept through the shop, shadows billowing around her, and reached for them. She stopped an inch in front of him, shoving her face into Seth's. Her eye sockets weren't empty after all. Smoke stirred within their depths, tickling along the upper rims of bone.

"So this is when it began," she said. "I've been waiting for you."

Seth's shoulders were so tense that the muscles could have ripped his spine apart. "Me?"

The door slammed open again. There was no chime of a bell this time.

A demon appeared in the archway. He was tall and tusked, much like Dana's girlfriend Penny, and he had a long-legged dog on a chain. It snarled, lunging and snapping at Seth's legs.

"They're here!" the demon shouted.

And then there were more of them—five, six, a dozen—and they were all jamming into the shop. They looked like a biker gang on Halloween. The leather they wore wasn't all in shades of black. Some of it was pink, olive, brown. Nothing that looked like it could have come from animals.

They were carrying chains and blades.

Seth jerked his Beretta out of the holster, but

he didn't even know where to begin shooting with that many demons coming toward him.

They encircled him. They reached for Marion.

"Get back!"

He fired one shot directly into the face of the nearest demon. Its head snapped back. It stumbled, smashing into the demon behind it. They fell like dominoes into a shelf. Glass sprayed across the floor.

Seth looked to see if the apothecary would attack him for it—but she had vanished.

In his instant of distraction, two demons grabbed his arms.

"Arawn's going to be excited to see you," one of them wheezed down his neck, its breath hot.

Arawn?

Charity grabbed her glasses as though she were about to remove them.

"Wait!" Seth said. "We'll go peacefully!"

She stared at him. "We will?"

"Yes," he said, "we will."

The demons laughed as they dragged them out of the apothecary. They didn't seem to think that Seth had any choice but to be taken peacefully—not surrounded by so many enemies.

He could have figured out how to take them. It wasn't like they could kill him. Given infinite time, Seth could have handled infinite demons.

But he wasn't alone.

One of the demons had scooped Marion off of the table. She hung over its shoulder limply, smelling of blood and death.

Seth would go anywhere they took her. Literally anywhere.

Luckily, the demons were taking them exactly where he wanted to go.

He was carried on a tide of the gang's bodies, shoved down the halls of the hive, helpless to fight back. That long-legged white dog nipped at Seth's boots, snarling and drooling. "Give me the word," Charity said, bumping against his side. "Just tell me when." The guards weren't watching her as closely as they should have. They had no clue she was anything strange.

"Do you still have the map?" he asked.

"Yeah, why?"

Because they would need to find somewhere to hide soon. The demons were taking a revenant straight to their leader, Arawn—the guy who had bought Marion's memories.

Seth didn't doubt he could steal the Canope. But he didn't know how to get back to Earth if he couldn't teleport.

The demons carried their party through so many twisting corners of the hive that Seth lost track of direction. They passed pools of bubbling magma, open fire pits surrounded by shadowy forms, rooms that were webbed over with sticky gray fiber.

Then they arrived at a tunnel that turned vertical at a ninety-degree angle. Seth gaped up at it. Insect demons scrambled up the rock surface as far as he could see—at least a few hundred feet before foggy darkness concealed the upper levels.

"Welcome to Arawn's tower," said Seth's captor.

That was when he noticed there was a door by the tunnel's juncture. It was surrounded by demons lounging on crates wrapped with barbed wire, forming makeshift barriers.

They kicked the door open and shoved him through.

He found himself in a tattoo parlor.

There was a demon lying in a chair that looked like it belonged in an old-fashioned dentist's office. The chair was upholstered with red leather and lifted on gears of shiny gold to make the demon's arm accessible to the man who sat beside it.

That man was holding a tattoo gun, its spiraling cables vanishing into the darkness behind the table. He was etching occult symbols onto the demon's fragile, papery flesh. The lines tore cuts into its arm and ichor dribbled onto the table.

The demon had the ugly, stretched features of a nightmare. All nightmares looked like they had been sculpted from putty by someone who'd only ever heard humans described in loose terms. It must have been powerful to have substantial human-like form, even if the tattoo gun did shred its skin.

But the nightmare wasn't the guy in charge.

There was no power resonating from the tattoo artist. None at all. He looked like an ordinary mortal man wearing a tight-fitting laced leather jacket and boots that would make him too tall for the hive. His skin was human brown. His hair was twisted into black dreads.

The fact that Seth felt no power from him at all meant everything.

He was the leader because he was strong enough to hide it.

"Arawn, sir," said the demon gripping Seth's shoulder painfully tight. "We've got prisoners for you."

Unsurprisingly, it was the tattoo artist who responded. "I don't want them." He wiped ichor off of the nightmare's arm, exposing an illustration of looping, interlocking circles that radiated dashed lines.

"Then what should we do?"

"Kill them," he said without looking up.

Marion was limp in the arms of the demon beside Seth. She didn't react to the threat.

"Okay," Seth said.

That was the only word Charity needed.

She ripped the glasses off of her face, disabling the glamour spell that made her look human.

The revenant emerged.

For all the horrors of Sheol, there were none quite like Charity. She seized the nearest demon by the throat and smashed his face into the wall. Her serpentine tongue wrapped around another demon's head, and the texture was so coarse that it stripped the flesh right off of its skull. Her claws gutted a third before the second had time to scream.

The guards exploded into chaos.

"Seth!" Even though he knew Charity well, the

sound of his name coming out of a revenant's maw made his heart skip a beat. She thudded toward him, smashing through the guards effortlessly.

Arawn finally lifted his gaze from the tattoo. He flipped his magnifying lenses onto his forehead to expose eyes that were nothing but pupil—endless, inky black.

First he focused on Charity. Admiration curled his lips into a big smile, and his short-trimmed mustache bent along with his lips. Arawn had jackal features, stretched and mean.

Then he looked at Seth and Marion, and the smile turned into surprise.

"Wait!" he yelled to his guards. "Don't kill them! And you—get off of my table."

The nightmare sat up, twisting his arm to look at it. "You're not done."

"Get off of my table!" Arawn surged to his feet so quickly that his stool fell over. His jacket flared behind him. The tattoo gun clattered to the floor.

Charity had cleared a path to Seth, breaking at least a half-dozen necks on the way. She plucked Marion away from a demon and shoved the mage into Seth's arms. "Get out! I'm right behind you!"

Seth gripped Marion to his chest and bolted.

He didn't even make it to the door. More of Arawn's gang swarmed in.

Charity cried out. Not a battle shriek, but a shriek of pain.

Arawn had seized her. In her exposed revenant form, he only came up to her chest, but he'd caught the bony spurs of her elbows in both hands. He locked her in place. Grinned up at her with that cruel jackal face.

"Stop breaking my toys," he said.

He slammed her into the dentist's chair, holding her down with one arm though she thrashed. And a thrashing revenant was nothing that Seth would have ever screwed with.

Guards swarmed Seth and he dropped Marion. "No!"

He had both handguns drawn instantly, bringing them to bear. But his wrists were caught. Twisted behind his back. He was disarmed and hurled against the moldy, peeling linoleum an inch from Marion's blood-crusted face.

"Take them upstairs," Arawn said.

"Which ones?" asked the demon with a boot planted squarely in the middle of Seth's back.

"All of them. And be nice." He howled with delight. "These are our guests!"

Marion dreamed of war. It wasn't the first time she'd had that dream. It wasn't even the first time she'd had it that week.

She walked the streets of Victoria and found it as ravaged as Leiptr in the Winter Court. She stepped among the broken bodies of innocents and children, all of who had faces like Ymir's, a little frost spirit waiting to become a giant.

He would never grow up, and it was because of

the war.

The sky wept crimson rain. Magic burned over it all.

Marion's magic.

But it was only a dream, just as it had always been. It faded away and her senses returned.

Reality was not much more pleasant than what she'd been dreaming.

A man sat inches away, his face shoved into hers. He had a black goatee, dreadlocks, and goggles that had been pushed onto his forehead. Red rings encircled his black eyes. "I wasn't sure that would work," the man said.

Marion tried to jerk away from him, but she had nowhere to go. She was in a bed crammed into a tiny metal room. Ichor dripped from a cracked pipe thrusting out of the ceiling. It dribbled by the wall at her elbow, and she cringed away from that, too. "Who are you? Where am I?"

"I'm Arawn, Lord of Sheol, and you're in my tower." He sat back with the creaking of leather. The man wore so much of it that he must have killed an entire herd of cows to dress himself for the day.

Gods, Marion hoped that reddish leather had been made from cows.

Her eyes burned, as though her contacts had dried out and adhered to her irises. Marion felt like she needed to firehose eye drops onto her face. For now, she settled for blinking repeatedly as she struggled to focus beyond Arawn.

She was so confused by the strange setting—

the skulls mounted on the walls, the patchy rug, the dripping ichor—that for a horrible instant, she thought that she'd lost her memories again. Then she saw Seth in the corner, arms folded tightly across his chest, holsters empty.

Marion hadn't forgotten Seth. She'd never forget Seth.

"Sheol," she said. The man had said his name was Arawn. She sat up straight. "You have the Canope. My memories. You bought them."

"Looks like you're not brain dead. Hurrah." Arawn rose from the chair beside her bed. "She'll be fine for a few hours, but humans have a hard time acclimating to the Nether Worlds. She'll likely need another dose of this by the time the clock strikes twelve." He shook a vial of red jelly at Seth.

Marion instantly knew the red jelly was the reason her mouth tasted so disgusting. He'd fed that to her. And it had revived her.

Seth reached out to take it, but Arawn pulled back.

"I don't think so," Arawn said. "I don't want the two of you trying to run off."

Two of you. "Where's Charity?" Marion asked.

"Elsewhere. Think of her as additional leverage."

"For what? What do you want from us?" Seth asked.

Arawn ignored the questions. "I expect you're here for the Canope. You can't have it. I paid for it, fair and square, and it's mine. You're now my guests and absolutely will not leave this room until I say that you can." He rattled it off rapidly, as though reciting a short monologue that he'd practiced.

He headed for the door. Seth barred his path.

"Why do you want it? Her memories are worthless to you," Seth said.

"The memories of a mage?" Arawn cackled. "If you think those are worthless to a demon, then you've got no imagination. Anyway, they're *mine*. You can't have them. And now you're my guests."

"If I'm a guest, then have someone attend to me," Marion said, gathering her strength to sit up straight. "I need to wash. I need replacement clothes as well. And this room will not do—not at all. Do you realize how filthy it is?"

"You don't get to make demands here," Arawn said. "You're in my world now. Both of you are."

He brushed Seth aside and left.

A heartbeat after the door shut, Seth tried the handle. "Locked." He pounded his fist into the wall.

"We're so close to the Canope. *So close.*" She patted the bed around her. "My bow and quiver—"

"Taken," Seth said. "They're probably with my guns. We're totally disarmed."

She tried to get out of bed, but when she moved, everything hurt—her lungs, her knees, her back, her skin. She gasped for breath. Sat back on the mattress. "Gods, I wish I had water."

Seth sat on the bed next to her. "Are you still feeling sick?"

"Very. How lucky that there's a doctor in the house." It hurt when she tried to laugh. Marion settled back against the wall with a groan, clutching her chest. It felt like she'd been breathing pure acid. "What happened to me?"

"I don't know. You collapsed as soon as we entered the Nether Worlds."

"It feels like when you teleported me to Las Vegas multiplied a thousand-fold. When you teleport, you must be passing through the Nether Worlds. Has that occurred to you?"

"I can't be a demon. The tests we run at the hospital to figure out what breed people are—the infernal sensors don't react to me."

"But every time you teleport, it smells as sulfurous as the air here."

"I'm not a demon," he said sharply.

Marion dropped her gaze. "I'm just trying to understand what happened to me."

Seth sighed. "Yeah, I know. Sorry."

They sat in silence for a few moments, gazing in opposite directions. Marion couldn't stop edging away from whatever substance was oozing down the wall. She'd have preferred to cough up an entire lung than have whatever that was touch her skin.

She curled up into a ball, trying not to touch anything that she didn't have to. But there was no escaping from herself. She was bloody, sticky, as foul as the rest of the Nether Worlds. None of that was quite as bad as the sandpaper burning of her eyes, though.

"I'm going to take my contacts out," she said. "This is ridiculous." She tipped her head back and peeled the silicone off of her irises. It ached to remove them, and it felt like she was trying to rip the eyeballs out of her skull.

"It's weird that you haven't gotten surgery to fix your eyes," Seth said.

"I did, once. I talked about it in my journals. It simply didn't work. The laser technology we have right now doesn't work on angel eyes, for whatever reason." She cringed as she dropped the contacts onto the floor. She wouldn't be using those again.

Once they were gone, and after she blinked her watering eyes a few times, she could see better. Everything was blurry, but it was a normal amount of blurriness.

"This shirt needs to go too," Marion said. She unbuttoned her bloody blouse to look at her body. Even shifting a little bit hurt, as though her clothes had been turned to sandpaper by Sheol. It wasn't a change in her outfit. It was that her skin was shredded, fragile.

Seth stood up suddenly. "Don't."

Her hands froze on the buttons. "I'm wearing a camisole under the blouse. It's not like I'll be naked."

"Just *don't*." He was glaring at her hands—at the bloody patch on her shirt. Seth sounded so *angry*. "I'm going to look for Charity. Stay here."

He tried the handle again. Still locked.

"Please, Seth," she said. "I can't sit here alone."

The look in his eyes was chilling. It was a look

very much like hate.

He snapped his fingers. With a swirl of brimstone, he vanished.

NINE

Nori had to take several deep breaths before she could bring herself to enter the throne room of Niflheimr.

On the other side of that door, Konig was meeting with Jibril, and Marion should have been with them. Nori had agreed to stand in when Marion asked, but it wasn't until the meeting actually arrived that the gravity of her agreement sank in.

She had seen Marion perform negotiations before. The woman was as determined as she was charming, capable of convincing anyone to give her anything she wanted. Her powers of persuasion were incredible.

Nori was not Marion.

They were cousins, and both had angel blood, but that was where similarities began and ended.

Nori cried over everything. Literally everything. Including sentimental car commercials. And while she believed herself to be as intelligent as any angel, she was too terrified to speak up and make use of that intelligence.

She could perform acts of subterfuge well enough. Spying on the Autumn Court and reporting to Marion had been fine.

Pretending to be Marion was not fine.

Unfortunately, it was too late for Nori to back out.

She closed her eyes, counted to ten, and walked into the throne room.

Jibril snorted when he saw Nori enter, as though her mere presence insulted him. He'd never warmed up to her presence in Dilmun. Encountering her in the wild didn't evoke a more positive response, either.

At the sound of the doors closing, Konig turned. The prince's eyes fell on her, and his gaze sharpened. "Nori. There you are."

Pleasure rippled down her spine. He remembered her name. Of all the times they'd interacted in the Autumn Court, the gorgeous, stately prince had never addressed her by name before.

"Yes, my lord?" she asked, her pitch a little too high.

"Where's Marion?"

Right. She was nervous for a reason. "She's attending to business elsewhere, so I'm standing in for her while she's gone."

"What an attentive steward," Jibril said dryly.

"She's fully capable of multitasking," Nori said. "That's why I'm here to help in her stead. I have her authorization to facilitate whatever deal we decide is mutually beneficial." It came out more acid than she'd intended, but perhaps that was good. The angels needed someone to call them on their crap once in a while.

She squirmed under the combined gazes of the two men, though for very different reasons.

Jibril, because he looked annoyed by her existence, as he always did.

Konig, because he was staring at her as though she were the only thing in the universe—a puzzle he needed to solve.

Jibril folded his arms. "Let's ignore for a moment how insulting it is to talk to the assistant of a steward—not even the steward herself—and say that I'm willing to commit an act of treason against Leliel to save the angels from extinction. Why should I put my neck on the line when Marion won't even show up to discuss it? I should go back and tell Leliel that the court's undefended, without a leader—"

"You'd be lying," Konig interrupted.

"With all due respect, you're no more in charge of Niflheimr than I am."

The prince drew himself up to his full height. It was easy to see his relation to the King of the Autumn Court whenever he became angry, though he had too much of his mother's lovely features to look as intimidating. "Do you question my ability to take care of the Winter Court?"

"I don't feel like there are many questions surrounding the situation."

"We can give you space in the Wilds to nest if you can usurp Leliel's leadership," Konig said. "Surely you have questions about *that*."

The angel was obviously tempted, but he shook his head. "I won't speak with anyone but Marion. My offer to negotiate was to her alone. I won't accept flimsy promises from her boyfriend, her cousin, or any other bit player she thinks to throw at me."

Jibril drifted toward the window, his wings unfolding behind him. They appeared as ribbons of shimmering light that slowly took form into true appendages, feathered and each twice as long as he was tall.

"Where do you think you're going?" Konig asked.

"I sneaked out of the EL to talk to Marion today, so I should get back before I'm noticed. Leliel's been planning to take action. She'll have an announcement soon. I'd hate to miss it. I want to know what she's organizing."

Panic surged within Nori, strong enough that her eyes pricked with tears.

All the work they were doing to protect the refugees, all the work to rebuild Niflheimr...

But Marion had gone tilting at windmills, leaving them exposed to war. Unable to make a deal because the angels wouldn't talk to them without her.

Speak up, Nori. Marion trusted you to take care of this. It's your job, stupid, so speak up!

"Marion wants to find a way for you to have the Winter Court," Nori protested. "If you leave now, you're burning your bridges. Talk with us. Please! We can work something out." She sounded more whiny than commanding. Even a tiny fraction of Marion's confidence would have tripled her authoritativeness.

"Words are hollow." Jibril stepped over the edge of the window, flared wings catching the icy breeze.

He swept away into the eternal night.

Nori's heart was pounding in her temples. It only pounded harder when Konig turned slowly to face her with anger in his eyes. The annoyance he must have felt at being dismissed by Jibril had no outlet other than Nori.

Perhaps it wasn't such a good thing that Konig knew who she was after all.

"Where is Marion?" he asked. "I told her that she needed to be here for this."

Nori hadn't planned to tell Konig the truth about Marion's whereabouts. She'd felt guilty enough delivering the mage to the Empress Hotel to see Seth, like she was helping her cousin cheat on Konig.

Even though Nori was relatively certain nothing was happening with Seth, Konig wouldn't care. Marion had once made the mistake of talking to a male member of the Autumn Court over dinner and Konig had almost murdered him over it. Once he found out Marion was spending time with Seth again... Nori didn't want to imagine it.

But he was advancing on her, backing Nori toward the melted lump that used to be the throne, and her fear was too much to lie. Tears swirled at the bottom of her vision. "Marion went to find her memories."

"She went with that doctor. Didn't she?"

Nori cringed. "Well..."

Konig's upper lip twitched. His nose wrinkled. It was like the effort to control his emotion was a living thing skittering under his skin. "I'll kill him. I should have killed him when he first set foot in the Autumn Court."

"You'll never get Marion to work with us if you do that."

He glared at her. "Us?"

The failing scraps of her courage wriggled in her stomach. She pressed a hand to her belly to quiet it. "The way I see it, the steward has delegated her authority. We're the ones running the court while she's gone. This isn't a problem, but an opportunity to utilize tools she's too distracted for."

"But Jibril's right. Marion's words are just words, and we can't do anything binding without her here."

"I'm not sure we can do anything *with* her here, either," Nori said. "The Wilds will only respond favorably to allies of a true ruler, and she's a steward—not a queen. Not even sidhe."

Konig clenched his hands into fists. "I know.

We're incapable of cutting any kind of deal with the angels."

"Under these conditions, yes, but there are ways around that," Nori said. "I talked with Marion a lot before—you know, *before*, when she was still herself. We often talked about the magic surrounding the Middle Worlds, and the structures that were put in place during Genesis, and the hierarchies..."

He closed in on Nori. "And?" There was still anger in his eyes, but it was tempered by interest.

She took a step backwards. She couldn't seem to organize her thoughts when he was looking at her like that. "The magic inherent in the Middle Worlds will respond best to a true ruler—sidhe royalty. Marion's officially in charge, but she can't control Niflheimr, can't regrow the Wilds, can't activate a lot of the wards."

"You said that."

"Niflheimr still recognizes her as a leader to a small degree. We can tell because we haven't been ejected by the wards. If the steward somehow became sidhe royalty..."

Konig seemed to be catching onto Nori's line of thinking. His lips curved into a bow that might have been a smile or a frown. "Or what would happen if Marion became *wedded* to sidhe royalty?"

Yep. He was on the same line of thinking.

"The Winter Court wants to be ruled properly. The magic here would recognize you instantly," Nori said. "And once you've got the reins, you can do pretty much whatever you want—including forging alliances that the magic of the world will recognize."

"Gods, Nori," Konig said. "You're a genius."

Her cheeks went hot, which was near miraculous, given the temperature of Niflheimr. "Thank you."

Konig gazed at her intently, as though he were seeing her for the first time all over again. He seemed to like what he was seeing. "It's a shame I never spoke to you—really spoke to you—during all those months you served my parents in the Autumn Court. We're going to have to talk a lot more in the coming days."

Gods, it felt like she was going to catch fire with pleasure and embarrassment. "I'd like that. I would really like to have the ear of the King and Queen of the Winter Court, in fact."

A shiver rolled over Konig. "King of the Winter Court. But that can't happen if Marion is running around with that doctor."

"She told me that they would be going to Sheol to confront a demon named Arawn." When he rubbed the bridge of his nose, considering this information, Nori added, "I'm happy to arrange another meeting with Jibril in a couple of days. I'll also watch the refugees in the meantime if you want to take a trip anywhere else. Anywhere at all."

"Yes," Konig said. "Yes, I think that might be a very good idea."

Charity was alone in Arawn's tower for so long that she thought she had been forgotten. Enough time passed that fear subsided to be replaced by boredom, and she began to explore the confines of her new prison.

It didn't look much like a prison. She'd been ditched in an airy room with overstuffed leather furniture, much of which was decorated by bone. There were rugs and tapestries too. It might have been pleasant if not for the kennels along the walls filled with snarling white dogs.

She edged nearer the kennels, contemplating whether releasing the dogs might make enough chaos for her to escape. There was no consciousness in their hollow eyes. They also weren't locked in. Arawn wasn't afraid of her opening their cage doors, which meant that it wouldn't be in her favor to do it.

Not that Charity thought she couldn't kill the dogs. She just didn't want to.

The dogs weren't locked in, but she was. The towering double doors wouldn't open under her hand. She could hear Arawn's gang laughing outside.

And then she heard footsteps.

Charity stepped back as the doors swung open.

Arawn had returned.

She struggled against the urge to hide. They were in his tower, his home, his whole stupid plane of the Nether Worlds. Where would she hide that he couldn't find her?

"It's you," Arawn said with surprise. "You look totally different. What happened?"

Charity reflexively touched the frames of her glasses. She'd reengaged her glamour out of habit. Even in Sheol, surrounded by monstrosities, she was more comfortable looking human. She didn't exactly want to blend in with the locals.

"Where are my friends?" Charity asked.

He pretended not to hear her. "Take the glamour off. Stop hiding."

Charity was so offended that Arawn might as well have suggested that he tattoo a giant penis on her forehead. "No way."

"Gods, but *look* at you. So cool. So amazing." He tossed his hat onto his table and bounced over, like he was a fan getting to meet a celebrity for the first time. "What *are* you? You don't feel like anything I've ever met before!"

Charity backed up until she bumped into the window. It looked out of the tower, all the way down to the tunnel that had led to the entrance. "That's because you probably haven't met anything like me before."

"You're not a demon. I can't read your mind." Arawn only stopped walking once he was a few inches away, gazing at her human face intently. "Yet you're not mortal, either. I can't feel your death."

"My death?"

"I'm not merely a Lord of Sheol. I'm Death

himself, heir to the Pit of Souls. One day, when I've grown into my power as psychopomp, I'll walk all mortals to the other side." Arawn made it sound like she should have been honored to be in his presence.

She wasn't honored, but she was a little bit afraid. "You better back off. I'm a revenant. A kind of vampire. I don't want to hurt you."

"You don't, do you? All that power, and you don't want to use it." He lifted his hand, as though contemplating removing her glasses. He didn't touch her. But the look in his eyes was reverent. The words that came out next were not. "You're ugly like this."

Charity slapped him hard enough that his head snapped to the side.

Arawn worked his jaw around and rubbed his cheek gently. She'd hurt him. Good.

"That one's free," he said. "Next time you hit me, I'll rip your arm off. I'd rather leave every perfect inch of your body intact."

"My ugly body," Charity said. Not that she was insulted that some Lord of Sheol thought she wasn't pretty.

"*This* body is ugly. Your true form is...amazing. What you've got underneath this wretched spell is better than any of the artwork I've got in my entire tower."

He bent like he was going to kiss her.

Charity ducked away from him.

Arawn was so relaxed about the rejection that she thought she must have misinterpreted his body language. He sauntered toward the door, pulling out a pocket watch. It was the size of his fist, a complicated mess of cogs and ticking pieces.

"I need to know *everything* about you," he said. "We'll have dinner tonight so that we can talk, you and me."

"I'm not doing anything without my friends," she said.

"The 'friends' who make you hide your truth." They didn't make her do anything. It was Charity's choice—her way of keeping them from fearing her, a way to blend in. But what did Arawn know about that? He didn't know her. He didn't know Seth. "You should dress in proper attire."

She didn't have anything else to wear, but Charity was pretty sure he meant her revenant form.

"Not a chance in Hell," she said.

Seth had discovered that he could teleport by accident thirteen years earlier, and he'd resisted using the talent for a long time. He didn't know where the ability came from. He didn't know if it had a cost. Would it hurt him? The world around him? He wasn't sure.

His greatest fear had been getting spotted by a witness and losing his job as a doctor. That was no longer a threat.

Seth had no reason to avoid teleporting now.

He still couldn't leap back to Earth. But when he concentrated, he managed to jump from Marion's cold, dingy cell in Arawn's tower to the hallway six inches away. He stood immobile for a few moments, shocked that the teleportation had worked.

It wasn't that the ability had left him. Only the ability to leave Sheol.

That idea was equal parts disturbing and relieving. He couldn't go home, but he'd be able to jump back into Marion's cell once he was ready.

To save her, Seth told himself.

That wasn't where his thoughts were focused.

He could jump right back in and join Marion on the bed, where her blood was smeared like chocolate sauce drizzled over ice cream. Even now that she wasn't dying, it still smelled like the promise of death. Her weak heart was calling to him from the other side of the wall.

"Damn," he muttered, pressing his forehead to the door.

What kind of monster was Seth becoming? He was a doctor who refused to stay with a woman in need. A doctor who couldn't stop obsessing about her death.

Do no harm.

Seth punched the wall, hard enough that his knuckles cracked. It didn't hurt. Very few things hurt anymore—physically, at least.

The way that Marion had looked at him before he left had hurt.

He needed to find Charity.

None of Arawn's gang were guarding the hallway outside of the cell. They must not have thought there was a chance that Seth and Marion would be able to get out. And if Seth had been properly human, then that would have been correct. Between a mage who was allergic to her very surroundings and a mortal man, there was no way that they should have escaped.

Seth checked the other cells on that level, but they all stood empty. Wherever Arawn had put Charity, it wasn't in his dungeon.

A narrow paternoster waited at the end of the hall. It was an open-sided elevator that never stopped moving, requiring light feet to jump on and off on the desired floor. Rattling chains groaned as it chugged in an endless loop.

Seth stepped onto it. He descended to the next level and stepped off just as quickly.

He found himself in what passed for a home in Sheol. The hallway was cozier than the one above, if skeletons standing on pedestals like suits of armor could be considered cozy. The iron chandeliers were arguably similar to Halloween decorations. There were mirrors framed with black thorns.

None of the elaborate dressing could conceal the stark, industrial structure lying underneath. Rusty pipes embedded in the ceiling dripped steadily, leaving black puddles on the cement.

At least the ceilings were eight feet tall. Seth didn't feel like he was going to be buried alive while walking around.

Arawn's voice echoed down the hall. Seth followed the murmur to a pair of open doors, which led into sitting room.

At that point, Seth was unsurprised to see that Arawn's furniture was made of bones and leather and iron. Dramatic stuff. Didn't matter the era, before or after Genesis—demons loved the macabre. Arawn was no exception. It must have been boring to be such a stereotype.

The Lord of Sheol himself stood in front of a sphere the size of a bowling ball, which was lifted on a pedestal. Colors swirled over the surface. The steam billowing from its edges reminded Seth of dry ice.

The faint outline of a woman hovered over the sphere, her face level with Arawn's. "I know," she was saying. "I saw them first."

"They're going to want the Canope. Bring it to me," Arawn said.

"I'm not doing anything that will send the Hounds into populated areas."

"Did it sound like I was asking?" He gripped the sphere with one hand, fingers splayed across her face, like he longed to choke the woman. "I'm *telling* you to bring the Canope to me, and you better make it fast if you don't want to piss me off."

"Would you use that tone if you weren't speaking through the distant safety of a palantír?"

Arawn snarled. He sounded like the long-legged white dog that his gang had dragged around on a chain. "All right, try this on for size. Bring the Canope to me right now, *bitch*, or I'll—"

"Urinate yourself and curl into a shivering ball?"

"Bitch," he said again. "I know you took the Canope into Duat. I could come get it myself."

Duat? Seth eased back behind the shelter of the door and pulled Dana's map out of his pocket. Duat was a large city within walls called the Bronze Gates. There was no ruler for scale, but Seth estimated that it wouldn't have been a long walk—less than a day, if it had been on Earth.

That distance would be neither easy nor short in Sheol. There was no civilization between the hive and the Bronze Gates, and Dana had recommended avoiding the Dead Forest.

He could probably teleport into Duat, but not until he found Charity. And he wasn't going to teleport Marion again at all if he could avoid it.

Arawn continued bickering with the woman in the palantír. Seth slipped back from the doorway, darting along the relative safety of the shadowy hall edges to return to the paternoster. The echoing voices chased him all the way back until they were overwhelmed by rattling chains.

Duat. I have to get to Duat. Seth's mind was clearer once he had a goal more tangible than "don't think about killing Marion."

He returned to the cells on the higher floor without encountering another guard.

Every door was closed. He got no sense of life from any other cell he passed.

The only person on the floor with him was Marion.

Marion, and her beating heart, struggling in the harsh climate of the Nether Worlds.

Before Genesis, angels hadn't been allowed into Hell, in much the same way that demons hadn't been allowed into Heaven. Seth had been told that the restrictions had been in place to prevent invasion. Now he believed that they might have been in order to protect the angels and demons, too.

He never should have brought Marion there.

Seth jolted when he heard the murmur of voices coming from Marion's cell. All those years he'd spent fighting the urge to teleport were forgotten instantly. He leaped inside of Marion's room.

A tall form loomed over Marion's bed, bending over her supine body.

Seth didn't have his guns—didn't have any weapons at all. They'd been stripped away by Arawn's guards.

He gripped the shoulder of the man standing over Marion's bed. "Get away from her!"

"Seth," Marion said, "wait!"

The man spun at Seth's touch. He had violet eyes, copper skin, black hair. And his features were etched with rage.

Prince ErlKonig of the Autumn Court.

"What the hell are you doing here?" Seth asked.

"That's exactly what I was about to ask you," Konig said. "*Both* of you."

TEN

With Konig's arm around her shoulders, Marion suspected she was meant to feel secure.

In reality, she felt like a child being punished. Forced to sit in time out.

Konig stared at Marion like he never planned to let her out of his sight ever again, even as he answered the question that Seth had asked. "Ley lines extend into all of the planes. They're most common in the Middle Worlds, but they've got tendrils all the way into the Nether Worlds too. That's how I got here. I only needed to jump."

Marion kept her gaze fixed to her hands in her lap. She was holding a spare pair of glasses that Konig had brought from the Winter Court. She appreciated the thoughtfulness, even though she was reluctant to put them on. She sort of preferred being unable to see the dripping cell she was locked in.

"Nori told you where I went," she said.

"Yeah, you left her in a ton of shit," Konig said. "The angels won't even talk to us unless you're involved."

"But you said you wanted to handle it yourself. You planned to play hardball because I was too close to the angels after the summit," she said.

"Oh, so you think you can turn this around on me? You're blaming me for *your* failure to lead?"

Marion knitted her fingers together. "You said —"

"You're supposed to be steward," Konig said. "I came to help you. You should be thanking me, not leaving me to babysit your cousin Nori."

Her throat burned.

It wouldn't have been so painful to be lectured if his harsh words hadn't rung with truth.

"We don't need to negotiate a deal with the angels if I find my memories. I'll be able to protect the Winter Court once I've got my full power back."

"The Winter Court doesn't need your memories," Konig said. "It needs *you*." He gripped her shoulders, forcing her to look at him. His lips quivered with anger as he breathed hard through his nose. "*I* need you, princess. What would I do without you?"

Seth had remained on the edge of the room until that moment. When Konig became rough, Seth materialized. "You should take your hands off of her." It was amazing how he could manage to sound mild and threatening at the same time.

Konig's hands only tightened on Marion. "You should stay out of something that has nothing to do with you."

"We're close to my memories, Konig," she said, drawing his attention back to her. She hated the way that the men glared at each other. She didn't want to be in the middle if they decided to go for one another's throats. "Arawn's the one who bought the Canope, and that's where we are—his home."

"His dungeon," Konig said scornfully.

"The Canope's not here. While I was doing reconnaissance, I heard him say that it's in Duat," Seth said.

"Great." Marion slid out from under Konig's arm, trying not to wince at the motion. She put her wire-rimmed glasses on. The arms wrapped around the backs of her ears. "You can teleport us there."

For the first time, Konig seemed to notice the state of her clothes. "Good gods! What happened to you?"

"Nothing," Marion said. Being treated like a child seemed to have rendered her petulant. She couldn't help it.

Konig slammed his fist into the opposite palm. "You're a half-angel in the Nether Worlds. I should have realized—no, *you* should have realized! I'm taking you back to the Winter Court right now."

She wrenched herself away from the bed. "I'm not going anywhere until I have my memories back!" The spike in adrenaline made her start coughing again. Each time, it felt like having a car slammed into her chest.

Through watering eyes, she noticed that Seth recoiled.

Konig's face melted into patient annoyance. "I'll heal you, princess." He'd done it before when Marion had gotten stabbed by the leader of the ethereal faction. She'd felt cold for hours to come. But at least he would touch her, help her, take care of her. He wasn't recoiling.

"Thank you, Konig," she said pointedly, glaring at Seth.

Konig pressed one hand against her chest, the other against her back. Ice flowed through Marion.

She coughed twice. The first time, she expelled more of that foul-tasting gunk. The second time, her lungs breathed clear.

The sweet, flowery perfume of orchids wafted around her. It was even more of a relief than feeling the weight in her chest lift—a touch of the Autumn Court's beauty in the relentless brimstone darkness of Sheol.

"How do you feel?" Konig asked, pushing her hair behind her ear.

"Good enough to hunt down the Canope," she said. "I'm not leaving without it. The sooner you come to terms with that, the sooner we can get something done."

He snorted. "You're so damn *difficult*."

"That's what you like about me, isn't it?" Marion felt good enough to smile at him—that teeth-flashing, dimpled-cheek smile that often turned resistance into instant obedience.

Konig knew her well enough not to fall for it, but he did laugh. "My princess wants this...thing, this Canope?" He shrugged. "Then let's get your Canope." He plucked at her shirt. "Take this off."

Marion hastened to obey. The camisole underneath wasn't entirely clean, but it was an improvement over the blouse. "We can't just 'get' the Canope. We need a plan."

"Oh, please. I know what I'm doing," Konig said.

He walked over to the door and tried to open it. Confusion flashed through his eyes when he found it locked.

That was how he'd entered the room. He had waltzed in and let it shut behind him without seeming to consider that the door might open to let him in, but not to let him out.

"Let me try," Marion said, edging toward the door. "I'm sure that I can get us out of here." Her slowness to approach was only partially due to the weakness of her body. Konig was a wall of anger on her left, and Seth was eerie calm to her right. It felt like willingly wedging herself between the rock and the hard place.

The only way out was to pass through the door.

Marion's specialty was doors.

She knocked. The sound resonated through that plane and others.

The door swung open to expose another of those cramped, dirty hallways.

"I didn't think your magic would work in Sheol," Konig said.

That was the thing—Marion's magic likely wouldn't work in Sheol, even if she remembered it. But opening doors wasn't magic. It was because she had the attention of entities who could open doors for her, anywhere she was, in any world, at any time.

The gods truly could see her *anywhere*.

That shouldn't have been such an unsettling thought.

Konig strode into the hallway.

"Wait," Marion said, hurrying to follow him.

Arawn was on the rising paternoster as though he'd felt them opening the door to his cell. Konig strode toward him. He must not have realized that the unassuming man with a goatee and apron was a Lord of Sheol.

"Get back here," Marion hissed.

Konig marched on Arawn. The sidhe prince looked strangely small in the hallway, even though he was a very tall man, and it took Marion a moment to realize that it was because he had none of his usual unseelie aura. He wasn't cloaked in magic. He didn't warp reality or even glitter.

Outside of the Middle Worlds, Konig was little more than a man.

Conversely, Arawn was in his element. The air darkened around him when he realized there was an intruder, and Marion felt light-headed, as though the oxygen were being removed from her veins molecule by molecule. "Who are you?"

Arawn asked.

"I'm Prince ErlKonig of the Autumn Court. You're risking war with me by holding my princess captive, Lord of Sheol." Evidently he did recognize Arawn's power.

"War? Yeah, right. I'm shivering in my boots. Where did you come from?" With a flick of his wrist, Arawn was suddenly holding a switchblade —nothing compared to the swords Konig normally wielded, but the prince hadn't come armed. Arawn looked to have used the blade recently. It was rusted and dripping.

"No," Marion whispered.

But Konig didn't try to attack. "I challenge you to duel in the manner of the gentry."

Arawn barked a laugh. "A *duel*?"

Marion would have laughed too, except that it wasn't funny. They were in Sheol—a place where demons dwelled in giant hives and the walls dripped blood.

Duels were gentlemanly. Totally suitable for the sidhe. Totally unsuitable for Hell.

"Yes, a duel," Konig said. "When I win, you'll release my princess to my custody."

"And everyone else," Marion said. "Charity and Seth, specifically."

Konig shot a look at her. "Yes, you'll release all your prisoners. If you win—which you won't—I'll arrange for my parents to pay you a hefty bounty. They're the King and Queen of the Autumn Court. They can give you virtually any prize."

"This...dueling thing." Arawn gestured with

the knife when he spoke, not threateningly. "This is a tradition you people have up in the Middle Worlds?"

"The sidhe gentry, yes," Konig said.

Arawn smirked. "*Gentry*. How *pretty*." He touched the tip of the knife to Konig's breastbone, and the prince squared off, glaring at him regally. "I like the idea of it. I'll duel you for the freedom of your pretty little princess. When you lose..." Arawn flicked the knife. It flashed in the darkness. "I'll take a pound of flesh from whichever one of you I want. And I'll keep taking it every day until there's no flesh left to take."

He was looking at Marion with those shark-like eyes. It was clear whom he had in mind for his pounds of flesh.

She wanted to turn and run. To refuse. To find another way out.

But Konig said, "Agreed."

It turned out that Arawn hadn't been coming to Marion's cell because he'd felt Konig's intrusion. He had been retrieving them for a formal dinner. To commemorate the occasion, the Lord of Sheol had changed into a high-necked suit—black jacket on black shirt, leather on leather. Seth imagined that the brass-edged goggles nesting in his hair were his formal goggles.

Arawn's dining room was as cramped as the

rest of the hive, though it had less to do with inadequate floor space and more to do with the meat hooks lining one wall. The slabs hanging from those hooks had no visible legs or arms— only stumps where they had been severed—so Seth could imagine that those were sides of beef. He'd slaughtered a few cows while working at a ranch. Killed them with bolts to the brain, hung them up, skinned them, let them drain.

It had been fast and humane. Something that the ranch had done to earn income.

One of Arawn's gang leaned against a slab of meat, casually carving another slab as she spoke. The demons laughed, they slapped the bloody flesh, they stripped away tendon to chew upon. They tossed some of the scraps to the snarling white dog chained against the wall.

Seth doubted that the way that meat had been killed was humane.

He also doubted that the meat was bovine in origin.

Seth was more grateful than ever that Marion had been unable to walk to the paternoster for dinner, and even that Konig had stayed behind to care for her. She didn't need to see what Arawn considered to be fancy décor. And she didn't need to see how fixated Seth was on all that death.

Arawn shoved Seth toward the table. "Take a seat." There were three chairs, three place settings. A dozen demons from his gang were already lounging around the room, so the place settings clearly were only for the supposed guests of honor.

Charity appeared in the far doorway, entering from another part of the tower. She looked even more shrunken and nervous than usual, which was saying a lot. In her human form, she was so much smaller than all of the burly demons, and she looked especially innocuous among the leather-clad gang in her baggy sweater.

"Charity. Are you okay?" Seth asked.

"Yes, I'm—yes, fine," she said, eyes flicking toward Arawn. The Lord of Sheol had walked to the hooks to chat with his gang. He tossed a bottle of vodka to a demon, and they laughed raucously, shattering an empty bottle on the floor.

"Did Arawn do anything to you?" Seth asked in a lowered voice.

"That's what's weird. He's being really..." Charity shrugged uncomfortably. "Nice."

Of all the words Seth might have used to describe a demon of Arawn's stature, "nice" wouldn't have been among them, especially since Arawn had been threatening to take a "pound of flesh" from someone in their party. After seeing his dining room, Seth expected that threat to be literal.

It was much too easy to imagine Marion hanging from one of those hooks. He'd probably mount her on the one at the head of the room. Demons would love to have a half-angel. The only woman who could perform magecraft was an exquisitely rare prize.

The very idea of it made Seth's blood boil, just as much as it made him salivate.

"I told you to sit," Arawn called over to them. Seth and Charity took two of the positions at the table. The dishes were fancy china, the napkins black linen, the chairs hand-carved wood. "And now you could consider thanking me for my hospitality, if you were going to be properly grateful."

Charity didn't seem to hear him. She was gazing at the wall, pale-lipped and trembling.

Seth followed her gaze.

In the dim corner, barely touched by the light of the candelabra, skins had been stretched out on ropes. Someone was practicing tattoos on the skins. It looked to be common practice in Arawn's tower, because most of the skins had old drawings etched into them.

Those *definitely* weren't cow skins.

Arawn flopped into the third chair. "I appreciate that you chose to join me for dinner," he said, kissing Charity's knuckles.

She jerked her hand out of his grip. "Well, I was hungry."

"I sure hope you are."

"I'm not," Seth said. "I only came to talk business with you, Arawn. What will it take to buy the Canope off of you? I have money."

"So do I," Arawn said.

"Then what do you want?" Seth asked. "Tell me. I can get you almost anything."

"What if I told you that I want a mage girl's essence trapped in a jar? What if that's the whole point?"

"It's not."

Arawn leaned back in his chair, stroking his thumb along his mustache. "You can't give me what I want."

"Who can?" Seth asked. "Who'd you buy the Canope off of in the first place?"

"Look at you, starting to ask the right questions," Arawn said. "Not real surprising, coming from Seth Wilder. *Seth Wilder*. Son of Lucian Wilder, brother of Abel and Cain, descendant of the first man, Adam."

Seth kept his posture relaxed, back straight but not stiff. He still wasn't used to running across people who knew who he was. But it wasn't hard to learn Seth's history, especially not since Rylie had written that autobiography. There were extensive academic papers analyzing every aspect of her life. That included her exes. Seth was, unfortunately, an open book.

"It's funny, isn't it? Descendant of Adam. One of the few still kicking around with His blood. You belong in Sheol as much as the Voice of God does, but you're not suffering." Arawn twisted the edge of his mustache, curling it around his finger. "Wonder why that is?"

"Who sold you the Canope?" Seth asked.

Arawn picked at his teeth with his long pinky fingernail. "Dunno. Bought it off the black market. Didn't think about it all that much."

He was lying. That much was obvious.

Staff wearing black butcher's aprons emerged carrying lidded trays. They set one in front of each chair.

Arawn brightened at the sight of food. He leaned toward Charity again, putting his flirtatious look on as easily as though it were a mask. "I prepared a feast for you, my beautiful revenant. I think you'll like it. *Bon app?tit*." Marion would have cringed at his drawling, Southern American butchering of the French words.

The waiters whipped the lids off of the trays.

Charity had been served chunky crimson soup with lumps floating on the surface. The edge of her shallow bowl was garnished with a few teeth jutting from a curved jawbone.

She gave a tiny whimper.

Seth had to clench his fists on his chair to avoid making an equally miserable sound at the sight of his food. He'd been served something that might have been a fish once—or a rodent, it was hard to tell. Something small. Something that now writhed with maggots, chewing tunnels into its blackened, oily flesh.

Arawn grinned at their reactions. "Looks delicious, doesn't it?" Mocking laughter rolled through the gang in the room. Arawn forked the raw meat on his plate and took a bite with gusto.

Charity pushed her bowl away. "I don't eat that."

"A beautiful vampire such as yourself doesn't drink blood?"

"Generally, no," she said curtly.

His fingers played over the back of her hand, stroking along the bones in her wrist. "You smell like blood. You've tasted it recently. And you tried to eat my guys when they captured you."

Seth took the knife from his place setting and slipped it under the table when Arawn was fixated on Charity.

He studied the demon's features, searching for a weakness.

Wouldn't most things die if stabbed in the throat?

"If it makes you feel better, the asshole who donated blood to your dinner deserves to be eaten," Arawn said. "She tried to poison a shipment of lethe intended for Earth. She'd have killed everyone who shot up with those drugs— harmless, innocent junkies addicted to my brand."

Seth's fist tightened on the hilt of the steak knife. "You make lethe?"

He'd seen too many addicts pass through his hospital. Lethe was a horrible drug. Made it so that people didn't want to eat. They'd starve themselves and come in with organ failure, so deluded that they'd fight against anyone who tried to treat them.

"This is where lethe comes from. Sheol. We've got a river here that we drain, filter, inject into cubes, ship off to Earth." Arawn's gaze went dreamy. "Someday, I'm going to see where my product goes. Bet it's beautiful."

He was on the opposite side of the table from Seth. One quick motion away from getting a steak knife in his jugular.

If anyone deserved to be killed, it would have been Arawn.

Smooth fingers touched Seth's hand under the table. When he looked up, Charity shook her head fractionally.

They were surrounded by Arawn's gang in his tower. If Seth attacked, their chances of escape would have been poor.

But he couldn't stop thinking about violence.

No. Not the violence, but the death that would result from it.

What had Charity told him to do when he was fixated on ugly ideas? Accept it? Get used to it?

How was he supposed to get used to wanting to kill people?

Seth dropped his knife on the table. "Can we finish this mockery of a dinner and get to the part where you duel Konig?"

"As a matter of fact, we can't. There's etiquette surrounding sidhe duels. Prince ErlKonig was happy to enlighten me." Arawn took another bite of the raw meat. "Duels are done at times of day appropriate to the challengers' court, and since ErlKonig comes from the Autumn Court, that means we roll at sundown."

"There's no sun in Sheol," Charity said.

"We all live under the same sun. We duel at sundown, just like y'all would on Earth." He set his fork down, wiped his mouth off with the napkin. Blood clung to his goatee. "Funny thing, these sidhe. The unseelie can go anywhere they want, but they stick to the darkest corners of the Middle Worlds. Wonder why that is." He waved his hand. "Wine!"

An aproned waiter arrived with a metal carafe. Whatever he poured into Arawn's glass was sludgy and red. Seth didn't think that was a zinfandel.

The waiter was accompanied by another of Arawn's gang—a woman with gnarled dreads as thick as her wrist and an extra set of bony arms hanging from her spine. "Nyx is calling on the palantír."

Arawn's pleasant demeanor vanished. "Will you excuse me, darling Charity?" He didn't wait for a response before following the four-armed demon out of the room.

"What's going on?" Charity whispered, leaning toward Seth. "Is Marion okay? Where is she?"

"She's fine," Seth said. "For now."

"Is Arawn planning to do something to her?"

"Probably. I'm not sure that he's the real threat to her safety, though." He dropped his forehead into his hands. "When she collapsed—the way that her sickness smelled... Jesus, Charity, I didn't think I'd be able to control myself."

Sympathy crimped Charity's brow. "Did you tell her?"

And let Marion think that Seth was like the demons? The monsters defacing the skins of the dead with tattoo guns?

"Do you think Marion would speak to the gods on my behalf if she knew I wanted to kill her?" Seth asked.

"But you don't, really," Charity said. "Thinking about it doesn't mean you *want* to. Don't underestimate her compassion. She likes you. A lot."

Sure, Marion liked Seth right now. She might even forgive him for the monster he was becoming. But then the Canope would restore her memories, and she wouldn't be his Marion anymore.

Charity hadn't spoken to people like Dana McIntyre, who characterized Marion as relentlessly selfish.

"Be honest with her," Charity said. "You'll never be able to get control of your abilities if you're in constant denial of them. Just talk about it."

"I'll talk about it with you," Seth said.

"Right. Because I'm a revenant, so I'm even worse than you are."

"That's not what I said. It's not your fault Genesis did this...thing...to you."

"But it's who I am," Charity said, staring at the bowl of bloody soup. "I can't change it. I don't know why I hide it as much as I do." Her hand trembled as she lifted the spoon, lifting a chunk out of the soup.

Charity sipped it. Her shoulders relaxed.

Seth sat back, leaning away from her. Charity didn't look at him as she continued to eat.

"There," Konig said. "Try standing up again."

Marion pushed to her feet while her boyfriend hovered a few inches away. It was easier to get out of bed than it had been the last time. When she took a few experimental steps toward the door to her cell, she didn't get winded at all.

Konig's healing magic was working.

"Excellent," she said. She was going to be able to join Seth at Arawn's dinner after all.

But then her knees buckled. Only Konig's swift arms kept her from falling completely.

Marion dropped onto the edge of the bed again. She swore loudly in English and in French, using every single expletive she could summon to mind. Konig watched with amusement. He only spoke one of the languages, but he clearly understood the intent.

She flung her hands into the air. "How am I supposed to retrieve the Canope if I can't walk without becoming fatigued? I'll have to remain here, reliant on Arawn's potions that acclimate me to the environment—"

"Or go home and wait for others to retrieve your memories." Konig sat beside her. "If you're worried, I'll stay here to attend to it myself."

"That won't make me less worried." She could think of few ideas worse than leaving Konig and Seth alone together. "Regardless, I'm not some swooning princess waiting to be saved. I will get my own memories!" And she wasn't going back to the Winter Court until she could rule it properly, with the full might of her magic.

"I hate to break it to you, but at the moment, you're literally the definition of a swooning princess."

"I'm a swooning steward. Give me some credit." Marion flopped back on the bed, draped an arm over her eyes, and groaned. Inhaling that deeply made her lungs burn. "I'm going to get my memories. I *will*." The more vehemently she said it, the truer it would become.

"This is all your fault," Konig said.

"You're so sweet," Marion said.

"I'm not going to be sweet. There's no point in sugarcoating the truth. You've screwed up, princess. You didn't think twice about plunging into Sheol, and everything you're suffering now is your fault."

She peeled her hand away to glare at him. "It's not my fault that someone sold my memories into Sheol."

"It's your fault you're chasing them. Once you found out that they were in the Canope, you could have worked with me to get them," Konig said. "Yet, instead of speaking to me, you snuck off with Seth. *Again*."

This conversation.

It was the conversation that Marion least wanted to have.

"What are you suggesting?" she asked.

Konig's fists clenched, knuckles whitening. "I'm not *suggesting* anything. I don't need to suggest anything I'm not willing to say outright."

"Then speak plainly."

"Okay. There's something between you and Seth. Is that plain enough for you?"

Her cheeks went hot. Marion could hardly

deny Konig's claims when she'd said the exact same thing to Seth at his house in New York. "That's ridiculous."

"You haven't had sex with me in weeks. I can't help but wonder if you're getting it from somewhere else."

Her jaw dropped. "You know I don't want to have sex until my memories come back. That's the only reason."

"Waiting is painful to the sidhe," Konig said. "Every day I wait to have sex, I suffer, but I do it for you. Are you waiting for me? Are you respecting my sacrifice, or are you running off to screw the doctor every time my back is turned?"

"Seth and I have a working relationship," Marion said. "He doesn't even like me."

"I notice you don't say that you don't like him. It doesn't matter. You don't need words when your actions speak volumes. The way you flaunt yourself in front of him, flouting responsibility so that you can bat your eyelashes at the doctor—"

"Stop it!" Marion clawed to her feet. She stood over Konig with her chin lifted and shoulders thrown back, exuding every ounce of defiance that she could muster. "I'm not hitting on Seth and I'm not running from responsibility."

"You didn't attend the meeting with Jibril that *you* arranged."

She swallowed around the lump in her throat. "Jibril doesn't have the authority to cut deals. Only Leliel does, and she will never, not in a million years, agree to work with me. She wants war. She's going to get what she wants."

Konig surged to his feet. He slammed his fist into the wall by her head.

She flinched.

"Leliel doesn't have to be willing to work with us," Konig said in an acid whisper. "Her peace treaty with my parents has very specific terms. We can force the angels to leave the Winter Court alone."

Marion leaned hard back against the wall. The door itched inches from her left hand. "How?"

"Marry me," Konig said. "Unite your stewardship of the Winter Court with the angels' peace treaty with the Autumn Court. If Leliel attacks, the other angels will have grounds to remove her. Then I'll be able to activate all of Niflheimr's magic. I'll be capable of best protecting my people. *Our* people." His free hand raked down her body, pulling her hips flush against his.

"But—"

"We've talked about this before. We talked about it a lot. Nothing has changed except for Seth, and you claim that there's nothing going on with him," he said. "*Marry me.* It's the right thing to do."

She couldn't breathe.

Konig's face had become less foreign to Marion in the last weeks, working together at the summit and Winter Court. She'd never had trouble finding him attractive. They hadn't had sex since Marion's memory had been lost, though.

Until that moment, she'd believed Konig was fine with her reluctance.

It wasn't about Seth. It was about the fact that Marion always felt scared and vulnerable on some level, and she didn't feel safe with Konig. Not yet.

Did she love him? Yes, she thought so.

Would they eventually marry? She suspected they would, if things continued as they had been lately.

But now? Like this? For *these* reasons?

The door opened to the left. One of Arawn's gang members entered. "It's nightfall," the demon said in a deep, growling voice. "You're due in the ballroom, Prince ErlKonig."

For a moment, he didn't move, staring expectantly at Marion.

It wasn't just anger in him. There was vulnerability there, too—the need to be reassured that Marion loved him, that she would be with him.

When her silence stretched too long, Konig's expression shuttered. He gathered his arrogance around him like a suit of armor. "Then lead us to the ballroom."

ELEVEN

Arawn's ballroom was better than his dining room, but it would have been difficult for it not to be. The only thing Seth could imagine that might be worse than the meat locker was an actual grave pit filled with rotting bodies.

Seth didn't doubt that Arawn had one of those somewhere within his tower.

Stepping into the ballroom felt like stepping into an oversized iron maiden. Spikes thrust from the walls and ceiling. Only the concrete floor was polished smooth, glistening in the light from the jagged iron chandeliers.

On the left-hand wall, the spikes had been bent to act as hangers for weapons and armor. Arawn had everything that Seth could imagine. Guns, knives, swords, flails, whips, chains. They all resembled their Earthly equivalents, but the lines on them were skewed, as if hacked together by clumsy hands. They might as well have been stamped with "Made in Sheol" labels.

Dana McIntyre would have been jealous of the variety.

Arawn led Charity to an engraved wooden chair on a dais at the far end of the hall. It was positioned underneath a tattooed skin that had been framed and mounted like a painting. "Why don't you take a seat?"

Charity sat uneasily, and Seth stuck close beside her. There was no chair for him. Standing on the floor beside the stairs to her seat meant that his head barely reached the level of her knees. Unfortunately, that meant he got a great view of the carvings on the seat's base—all the naked human bodies folded in on one another, contorted into positions of agony.

Arawn's mismatched gang was filtering in through the narrow portal to the room, talking and laughing and shoving each other, as though they were going to a sporting match. Arawn watched his people enter with a smug smile. "I've been doing some reading on these sidhe rituals. We each get to choose a weapon, and then there's this whole ten paces thing. Isn't that adorably archaic? You wouldn't believe that the sidhe didn't exist prior to fifteen years ago."

"They've always existed," Charity said. "Just not in such numbers."

The lord waved her off. "What do you think would be the best way to beat Konig? I can't kill him—that would be ungentlemanly—but there are no rules against a little maiming." The switchblade flashed in Arawn's hand again, appearing from seemingly nowhere. "Cut a few pieces off his pretty copper face."

Seth could have told Arawn that a switchblade would be a terrible choice. There was a two-handed bastard sword hanging among all those weapons on the wall, so he knew what Konig would pick.

But he kept his mouth shut.

Seth's feelings about Konig aside, the prince was their way to get to Duat. In this matter, they were on the same team. He wasn't going to give Arawn any advantage against him.

Then Konig strode in with an arm around Marion, practically dragging her while she looked exhausted at his side. The sidhe healing hadn't benefited her for very long. Seth already knew that —she hadn't been able to get to the paternoster, after all—but the sight of bright, mischievous Marion barely shuffling into the ballroom still gave him pause.

Her skin had lost all its luster. Her curls were limp. And she reeked of death.

If Seth hadn't known better, he'd have thought she were a woman of eighty years, rather than someone who couldn't legally drink in the United States.

It took every ounce of self-control Seth possessed not to seize Marion the instant she entered the ballroom. Forget what damage she might experience if she teleported within the Nether Worlds again—he needed to get her out of that place of rusted spikes and meat hooks.

He needed to find a way to drag her back to Earth before she died.

Because that was where she was heading, no doubt about it. She was teetering on the precipice of death. Merely existing in Sheol was enough to suck the life out of her.

Konig set her on the top step of the throne beside Charity's legs.

"Watch, princess," Konig said, kissing her passionately. Much too passionately for someone who looked so weak. His fingers dug into her shoulders hard enough that it seemed like he'd break her in half. "Watch what your prince is willing to do for you."

"Clear the space," Arawn boomed to his people. "We're going to have a little show today." He stepped onto the floor with Konig.

The instant that the prince's attention was diverted, Seth dropped to his knees beside Marion. "Are you okay?"

Her gaze remained fixed to Konig's back. She didn't look injured—no more injured than she'd been when he'd left her, in any case. Yet some shadow had fallen over her entire demeanor.

The same seemed to have struck Konig. He was agitated. His motions were jerky and halting. He was no more injured than Marion, but something had happened between them—and neither was very happy.

Seth touched her shoulder. "Marion?"

She jerked away without looking at him.

"These are the rules as I understand them," Arawn said, addressing his gang like they were an eager audience. "Prince ErlKonig of the Autumn Court challenged me, so I get first pick of any weapon in this room. Because we're not the same species, we can't use any of our powers. We fight to defeat, not death." That sent cruel chuckles through his people. "Does that sound right, pretty little prince?"

"Don't call me that," Konig said.

"I could kill you where you stand, so I'll call you by whatever names I think suit your prissy ass."

"It'd be against the rules to kill me. You said it yourself."

"I don't have to follow the rules of the Middle Worlds if I don't want to. You're in Hell, pretty-boy. You'd best remember that." Arawn lifted his switchblade. "This is the weapon I choose. I won't need anything bigger to take a scrawny thing like you down."

Konig shivered with rage. The sidhe power that was suppressed by the Nether Worlds sparked to life and rippled down his skin.

He marched to the spikes on the wall, reaching into them to extract a sword as long as he was tall. It was huge to a theatrical degree, designed by demons more interested in instilling fear than producing a functioning weapon. There was no doubt in Seth's mind that it would be sharp, though. The twin edges gleamed with murderous promise.

"I pick this one." Konig's arm muscles didn't even strain to lift it.

For the first time, doubt shifted through Arawn's eyes. "Big toy for such a little boy."

"I'll make you regret saying that to me," Konig said. "I'm going to make you cry in front of your gang."

Arawn gave a booming laugh. "That would be a sight!"

He shared chuckles with his gang. One of them had brought that long-legged white dog, and it howled at the sound. The chain around its neck rattled when it threw its head back.

Arawn lunged for Konig before they'd even stopped laughing.

So much for ten paces.

He danced into Konig's guard, slashing his switchblade with the swiftness of a cobra. The point sliced from the prince's belted jeans to the v-neck of his shirt. The cloth parted as easily as paper. Arawn didn't cut his undershirt because his touch was so light.

It was a move meant to show Arawn's speed, not hurt Konig.

The prince didn't have a chance to retaliate. Arawn leaped back as quickly as he'd leaped in, cackling wildly.

He whirled around Konig. Another couple of slashes destroyed Konig's belt, and then one more sent a lock of glossy black hair floating to the ground.

Each time, Konig tried to hack with the bastard sword, but he was so much slower than the demon.

"You must have thought you'd be able to win when you challenged me to a duel, little prince." Arawn was addressing the gang more than his opponent, sauntering along the ballroom to high-five demons. "As if the sidhe could ever stand up to the might of the infernal forces!"

Something in Konig snapped.

Seth could see it. He could *feel* it.

Konig roared, swinging the sword in both hands. He swept up, hooked high, slashed it across Arawn's back.

He wasn't trying to humiliate Arawn. He was trying to cut deep.

And he did.

The blade opened Arawn's jacket and dug deep. The blood that spurted forth was as black as Arawn's eyes. The muscle within looked rotten. His spine glistened when exposed.

He fell against the spiked wall, grabbing one of the iron points to hold himself up.

Arawn wasn't laughing now.

"Fight me!" Konig shouted.

He thrust the blade forward, aiming for Arawn's gut.

The demon leaped away. The bastard sword smashed into the spikes with a sound like a blacksmith's hammer striking an anvil.

Marion tensed all over and Seth reached over to take her hand. She turned to him, startled.

Confusion filled the paleness of her eyes. "Seth," she said, squeezing his fingers for a moment.

She pulled her hand out of his, shrinking away.

The tone of the fight had gone from jovial to grim. The gang was silent except for the white dog. It howled, thrashed, rattled its chains.

Arawn circled Konig with a little more caution. He seemed to be rethinking his switchblade.

"You got me good once, I'll give you that," Arawn said. "But you can't keep it up. You're not man enough to follow through, pretty-boy."

Konig's lips spasmed.

He missed with his next swing, but not the one that immediately followed. The bastard sword bit into Arawn's wrist. The demon dropped the switchblade.

Disarming him should have been enough to end the fight.

They'd won. They were free.

But Konig didn't stop.

He swung again, and again, driving Arawn backward. "You think I can't follow through?" Konig snarled. "I'll show you follow-through!" Magic rippled over him, building and frothing and pulsing in time with his anger. The music of the Middle Worlds shouldn't have been able to reach them there, but Konig was strong in his fury. He dragged the full might of the Autumn Court into Sheol as he pursued Arawn.

"Wait," Marion said, surging to her feet.

She stumbled. Seth grabbed her.

"Careful," he said.

"But Konig's not giving up," she whispered. "He's—he's so angry, and—"

"Cheater! *Cheater!*" Arawn shrieked.

It was chaos in the room.

The gang was screaming.

Arawn was running for another weapon.

The white dog bayed.

Konig swung, and Arawn had to drop to the floor or risk getting impaled on one of his own spikes.

Once he was down, Konig didn't relent. The prince crouched atop Arawn, slamming the pommel of the sword into his face again and again.

"I concede!" Arawn finally said.

"Konig, *stop!*" Marion shouted.

It was against the rules to continue fighting after someone conceded. Until that moment, Arawn had been following those rules perfectly, even though he didn't need to. Most likely it was out of some perverse sense of amusement rather than honor.

But now that Konig was breaking his own rules, there was nothing to keep Arawn from breaking them, too.

Arawn disappeared from underneath Konig. He reappeared a few inches away. Seth thought he'd intended to go further, but failed to put adequate distance between himself and Konig; he had to be caught by one of his gang to avoid collapsing into a bloody mess.

For the moment, nobody was moving in to attack Konig. Spattered in the blood of a Lord of

Sheol, towering taller than any demon, holding a mighty sword, he was even more frightening than Arawn.

"I am the Prince of the Autumn Court, and *you will respect me!*" Konig roared to the room at large.

But he was looking at Marion.

The gang surged forward, collapsing around Konig.

A dozen demons. Two-dozen. Seth hadn't bothered to count the gang when he'd entered, but he knew that the prince was vastly outnumbered.

Seth was tempted to let him get murdered. It would be a death of his own making, and the promise of oblivion hung heavily in the ballroom, as though vultures were perched in the chandelier, waiting to descend upon the carrion in the aftermath.

But Marion was clinging to Seth's arm, and he knew she was aching to help, unable to intervene.

"Damn it," Seth said.

He gently pushed her into Charity's waiting arms and leaped into the fray.

Seth yanked one of the guns off of the wall.

He picked something that looked like a hunting rifle—the kind of weapon he'd trained with as a boy. It was heavier than he expected and the trigger was too far forward. He was clumsy bracing it against his shoulder, aiming into the mass of demons.

Seth squeezed. The gun exploded in his hands, discharging something that sparked with brimstone.

A white fireball punched into the back of a female demon. She didn't have bones or muscles like Arawn did. She was yellow on the inside, rather like a blister brimming with pus.

She burst.

Fluid spattered over the other demons. Several swung around at the sensation, and a dozen black eyes focused on him.

He only had time to shoot twice more before they were on him.

Seth's feet went out from under him. There was no making sense of the attacks—who was grabbing what, or which blows connected which parts of his body. He was punched and bitten.

He kept shooting until the rifle didn't work anymore.

Claws slashed across his chest, and the scent of his blood filled the air. A demon with feline features tried to dig her hand into the wounds.

Seth shoved her back. Rolled both of them. Ended up on top, dripping blood into her face.

"Seth! The dog!" Marion's voice carried over the cacophony.

He sat back to search for what she was talking about, and he found that the white dog was straining against its chain. Its nostrils flared. Its eyes were huge.

It wanted Seth's blood.

The chain snapped.

It bolted through the mess of demon bodies, skirting Konig's wide-sweeping sword, and leaped.

Seth flung himself off of the demon before the

dog could strike. It didn't bother chasing him. It wanted Seth's blood, and there was plenty of it on the demon who had cut his chest.

Its mouth opened wide—and then wider, wider. Its toothy maw opened far larger than should have been possible with a skull so narrow. And then its mouth snapped shut on the demon's face, ripping her skull off with an easy toss of its head.

"Holy crap," Seth said.

The dog looked at him, mouth closed and throat distended with the mass of the demon that it had devoured. Its long tongue licked its chops.

Konig hacked through the last of the surviving demons, slicing a man from nether to shoulder. His upper half slid sideways off of his body. There was nothing inside but a sludgy black mass that might have been organs.

The only survivor was Arawn, and he didn't look good. He was sitting in a puddle of his own fluids. He was struggling to move.

The dog bowed its head to the demon to keep eating.

Konig glanced at the dog, and then at Seth. He seemed to be trying to decide if he wanted to save Seth or go after Arawn.

After an instant of hesitation, Konig attacked the dog.

It was sluggish from its oversized meal and didn't stand a chance of escaping. The dog barely dragged itself three steps before Konig cut it open. The demon it had eaten spilled out of its belly.

Distracted by the dog, Konig didn't see Arawn phasing across the ballroom. He reappeared on the throne with a swirl of black smoke.

"No!" Seth teleported too. He crossed the distance in a heartbeat, and he dragged Marion out of the demon's reach.

Arawn wasn't looking for his pound of flesh, though.

He wrapped an arm around Charity's throat.

"You miserable child," Arawn hissed at Konig, blood spraying from his shattered nose. "You stupid little *asshole*."

Charity turned wide, terrified eyes on Seth. "Doctor?"

"I'll see you sacks of shit in Duat." Arawn swept his arm under Charity's legs, holding her against his chest.

He vanished, taking the revenant with him.

TWELVE

Arawn and Charity appeared in a room of crumbling stone in the space of a blink.

She hurled herself away from him, out of his arms.

"Seth!"

Charity stumbled on a piece of uneven floor. The landing shocked through her body.

"Relax," Arawn rasped. "They're gone."

She got onto her knees, eyes wide as she looked around for her friends. But he was right. They weren't in Arawn's tower anymore. They were in a room with no furniture, arched ceilings, and walls of obsidian. Murals depicted eerily long-legged jackals, like an entire pack of those white dogs from his home.

"Where are we?" she asked. "What did you do?"

He laughed. "What did *I* do? I'm not the asshole sidhe prince who broke his own rules!" Arawn spat onto the floor. It was more ichor than sputum. "That shithead is going to pay for what he did to me!" He flung his arms wide to show his body to her.

Arawn's clothes were torn open to expose lengths of desiccated skin, which Konig had carved into with that massive blade. Nothing looked to be healing. Demon he may have been, but preternatural regeneration didn't seem to be among his skills.

The slashes in his jacket revealed extensive tattoos. Until that moment, he had been covered from throat to ankles and wrists in clothes. Charity hadn't realized he would be marked. Now she could glimpse detailed illustrations over the remainder of his wrecked body.

Arawn was tattooed in suns, moons, and whirling planets, shaded with elaborate stippling. The imagery was strangely beautiful for a demon.

And Konig had cut through much of it.

Yet even though glistening ribs were exposed on one side and dried muscle dangled off his opposite shoulder, Arawn didn't seem to be in pain. He limped over to Charity and helped her stand.

"Where am I?" Charity asked again,

"I've brought you to Duat," Arawn said. "What are the chances they'll come for you here?"

If it had been Konig and Marion alone, Charity doubted that they'd put the effort into saving her.

But Seth was with them. The man once known as Dr. Lucas Flynn.

Even if he hadn't needed Charity's help to control his growing inner monster, and even if they hadn't been coworkers for years, he would have saved her. He was just that kind of guy.

"Let me go," Charity said.

Arawn physically released her, but he remained close. "I asked you a question."

"They'll come," she said with no small amount of despair. "I know they'll come." Seth would never leave her trapped with Arawn. He was going to hunt her down to fight this hideous demon with the ripped muscles and exposed bones.

"Perfect." He clapped his hands. "I'm here!" A pair of beetle-like demons scuttled around the corner, carapaces clicking. "Tell Nyx I'm within the walls. I want to see her." They left, but not before Charity had to swallow down a bellyful of burning bile.

Giant beetles. Sheol was so screwed up.

Arawn offered his arm to her. "In the meantime, would you like a tour of Duat, beautiful one?"

Getting out of the tower to rescue Charity was only second priority. Seth's first priority was to locate the potions in Arawn's storeroom.

He had to walk through more bodies hanging

from meat hooks, ankle-deep sludge, and crates cluttered with bones to find the potions. Arawn kept them on a shelf in the back. There were a dozen different types in a dozen shades of crimson. All were nearly indistinguishable to Seth.

"Can you tell which one's meant to heal you?" Seth asked, handing one to Marion.

She was sitting in the dentist's chair where Arawn had been tattooing a nightmare earlier. Konig had carried her downstairs before leaving to search for their missing weapons.

Marion held one of the vials to the light to study the consistency. "This is the one, I think." She drank it down, and then a second identical to the first.

While her head was tipped back, Seth could see the lacy pattern of veins under her semi-translucent skin. They brightened and faded with each heartbeat.

For several long seconds after drinking the second potion, her heart didn't beat at all. The cloying veil of death clung to her.

Then her weak heart thumped.

Seth didn't breathe until it resumed a regular beat. He forced himself to look at her face instead of her neck, her chest, the vessels visible on the insides of her wrists. "Are you okay?"

Marion nodded, eyes screwed shut and nose wrinkled. "I should be grateful I was unconscious last time I drank these. They taste dreadful." She tossed back a third vial before finally standing.

Seth hovered nearby, watching to see if she was

going to fall.

For the first time since entering Sheol, Marion looked fine.

She wasn't fine, though. She'd pushed death back by a few hours and no more.

"Perfect." She picked through the remaining potions that he'd brought, discarding a handful of them and stashing the rest in a plastic bag. "These should last long enough for us to reach Duat." She sounded much more optimistic than Seth felt.

She could take more potions when the first three began to wear off. Arawn had stored enough that Marion might be able to last a few days by taking those every time she started to feel ill again.

It didn't change the fact that being in Sheol was killing her, slowly but surely, and Seth had a hard time thinking about anything else.

"I hope we didn't make Arawn so angry that he shatters the Canope," Marion said. "Dana said that breaking the vessel would allow my memories to escape, and…" Her shoulders sagged at the idea. "It would be quite the act of revenge, wouldn't it?"

Seth was a lot more worried about poor Charity in the hands of a creepy Lord of Sheol. "I don't think there's a chance that Arawn will screw with the Canope. I spoke to him about it at dinner. I don't think he bought it for fun—I think he was hired to hold on to it for some reason. Maybe even bribed."

"That doesn't make sense," Marion said.

"It does if someone wants to lure us to Duat."

As she considered this information, she pulled

her curls back from her face, tying them into a loose ponytail. She missed a few strands near her face. They dangled in her eyes. "What's in Duat? Aside from the Canope, that is."

"We're going to find out," Seth said grimly. "It's not like leaving your memories there is an option."

"Not for me," Marion said. "You have alternatives."

"No, I don't. I really don't. I'm not leaving you, Marion." Even if leaving her might have been the best thing for her safety. Her movements had gotten Seth transfixed by her throat again, and the lingering aroma of death that wafted toward him every time she shifted.

"Oh, Seth," Marion sighed. "You're kinder than I deserve."

He folded his arms tight enough that his shoulder blades ached. "Trust me, I'm not."

Konig reentered the tattoo parlor. "I found your bow, princess." He'd washed himself of Arawn's blood since Seth had last seen him. He had also stolen a black t-shirt from the Lord of Sheol and wore the infernal bastard sword across his back. Konig did a great impression of a demon. "And your guns, Doctor."

"Thanks," Seth said. He returned his Beretta to its position in the holster under his arm. He stashed the other handgun at the small of his back.

"You're welcome." Konig said it so graciously, like he was doing a huge favor for them. Like Seth wouldn't have been fully capable of locating his own damn weapons without help from a

SM Reine

temperamental unseelie prince.

Marion threaded her belt through the quiver and slung the bow over her shoulders. "Okay. What's our plan from here? How do we get to Duat?"

"According to Dana McIntyre's map, the only route is directly through the Bronze Gates," Seth said.

"Let me see," Konig said. Seth handed the map over. The prince studied it, rubbing a hand over his upper lip. It was strange to see five o'clock shadow appearing on a sidhe's jaw. Seth hadn't thought they could even grow facial hair. "Unfortunately, no ley lines cross through Duat, but I can jump us across the Dead Forest. There's a ley line here." Konig pointed to a spot between the Bronze Gates and the river Mnemosyne.

"Seth could teleport us into Duat," Marion said.

Konig's brow lowered over his eyes. "You can teleport? You're a planeswalker?"

"Yes, but no," Seth said. "I tried to teleport out of Sheol earlier, and I can't for some reason. I also won't teleport Marion anywhere now. It makes her sick."

"Then how will we get through the gates?" Marion asked, folding her arms. It looked like she was gearing up to argue with Seth.

Konig spared him from the fight. "I'll have to do reconnaissance," he said. "I can figure out a way in, rest assured. Even if it requires killing every demon on the wall."

It was a stupid plan. No, worse than that—it was no plan at all. But Seth didn't have any better suggestions, and he wouldn't be able to come up with anything until he could study the gates in person.

Seth wasn't confident he'd be able to come up with anything once they got there, either. Marion was a few feet away, her heart steadily fluttering along.

She was watching him. Distracting him.

Konig's stupid non-plan was still a thousand times more useful than Seth at the moment.

"Where do we go to catch the nearest ley line?" Seth asked.

"A juncture crosses through the tower. We don't have to go anywhere. That's how I reached Marion without being disturbed." Konig wrapped his arm around her shoulders, pulling her tight to his side.

"That's poor planning for security purposes," Marion said. "That means the sidhe could have invaded Arawn's tower at any time."

"His stupidity is lucky for us." Konig extended a hand toward Seth. "Are you ready?"

Not even remotely.

Seth grabbed the prince.

Being pulled through the ley lines felt nothing like teleporting. It was one thing to willfully propel himself across the planes, and quite another to be dragged by an outside entity.

Passing through the ley lines made Seth feel like toothpaste forcibly extruded from a tube.

All of Sheol stretched underneath him. The Nether World was completely contained within a cave with walls pocked like a stony sponge. The hive was burrowed into those holes. The Dead Forest, on the other hand, grew from the loamy quagmire collected along the bottommost curve of the cave, dampened by a network of rivers that flowed in spirals around Duat at the center.

Only one ley line crossed the entirety of Sheol, slicing a path from the hive to the Dead Forest. Seth extended from one position to the next, out of body, out of mind, beyond sensation.

His heart plummeted into his stomach and he reappeared on the banks of Mnemosyne. He stumbled as though he'd been dropped twenty feet, trying not to collapse onto his knees. The river's crystalline waters sloshed inches from his toes.

"What just happened?" he asked, looking up for his companions.

Marion and Konig weren't beside him.

He turned to orient himself. Seth had fallen out of the ley lines on the wrong side of the river. Instead of being on the banks nearest the Bronze Gates, he was at the edge of the Dead Forest. The skeletal shapes of the trees were eerie silhouettes in a thick, hot fog that smelled of animal waste and rotting flesh.

Konig must have ditched him a few hundred

feet too early. They were probably safely on the other side, where Seth couldn't see them.

"Goddammit," Seth muttered.

In all fairness, it was his mistake for thinking he could trust the prince.

He took Dana's map out and found his dot on the edge of the Dead Forest. There was no bridge crossing Mnemosyne nearby. He traced its looping path around Duat and realized that there were no bridges marked anywhere at all.

Dana had warned him that the Dead Forest was patrolled by Hounds. If they were anything like Arawn's white dog, Seth didn't want to encounter them.

He shut his eyes and focused on teleporting across to the other side.

"I wouldn't do that if I were you," said a soft voice.

Seth looked around. The dark form of a small boat had appeared on the calm waters, and it now drifted toward him.

A cloaked creature stood on the aft of the gondola, pushing it toward him with a long pole. It wasn't until the gondola struck the shore nearby that he realized that it was the apothecary again. That feminine spirit with the exposed skull for a face and pits for eyes. "Hello again." Her voice slithered through his ears, penetrating the fog effortlessly. "Looking for a way across?"

Seth took a step back, resting a hand on his gun. "I can get around on my own."

"You might, if you can teleport without

touching the wards," she said. "Do you know where the warlocks have placed their spells?"

He didn't. And he couldn't sense them without help of a witch like Marion, which meant that they may or may not have been there at all. The source of the information didn't exactly seem trustworthy.

Her gondola was matte black. It didn't seem to become damp where the water touched it. He wasn't entirely sure that the water *could* touch it.

Seth surveyed the demon without releasing his gun. "You're not an apothecary, are you?"

"Not usually." Her semi-transparent cloak billowed around her in a wind he couldn't feel. "I pulled you from your friends so we could talk."

So it wasn't Konig's fault they'd been separated. "All right. Talk."

A skeletal hand swept toward the prow of her gondola. "The Dead Forest isn't safe for you in this form. We'll talk in privacy as I take you across. It will be a short passage, I promise."

It couldn't be that short. He couldn't see the other side.

Short or not, it wasn't like Seth had a lot of options. He could hear howling in the Dead Forest.

He clenched his jaw and climbed in. The demon towered over him, a gangly specter with arms longer than her legs and a spindly neck of exposed bone. She pushed them away from the shore.

"Do you remember the Pit of Souls?" the demon asked.

He checked Dana's map. Yes, there was a Pit of

Souls inside of Duat, apparently located underneath the temple. "I've never been there."

"Arawn is heir to the Pit of Souls and the title of Death." She remained poised above Seth as they glided serenely across Mnemosyne.

"Yeah, he told me that."

"Did he tell you that he'll only inherit if Death concedes his throne?"

"I think that's kind of implied with the whole 'heir' thing," Seth said. "Who's Death right now?"

"Death is Death," she said simply.

"All right." That was about as unhelpful as Seth could imagine.

"Arawn doesn't want to inherit," the demon said. "He hungers for the Middle Worlds. He's been pushing against his boundaries for weeks, sending spirits to Earth to possess humans and quietly forming an army."

"Why? To conquer?"

Her tone became thoughtful. "Isn't that what you would expect of a demon? Driven by need to conquer?" She pushed the pole again, and they glided a few more feet. "Arawn longs for the sunlight of the Middle Worlds. Don't give it to him. Don't go after the Canope."

Seth stared up at her emotionless face. "How did you—"

"The Canope is the only reason that you'd have come here again," she said. "It's also the only reason that Arawn would have assigned his Hounds to guard it. The instant you touch the Canope, they will come for you. They will devour you. You'll be trapped."

"I can handle them," Seth said. If Konig could kill one of those dogs, then Seth could surely take them, too.

"The domesticated Hound in Arawn's tower was a crossbreed, an impure bastard. Even you can't survive a mauling from the true Hounds. That's the whole point."

"The point of what? Did Arawn take the Canope so he could kill me?" It didn't make any sense. Seth hadn't known Arawn existed until he'd spoken to Dana, and Seth wasn't important enough to have Lords of Sheol going after him.

"I don't blame Arawn for doing whatever it takes to escape," Nyx said. "You became tired of Sheol's darkness within a span of centuries, too."

The gondola stopped abruptly. The river that had seemed endlessly wide when he stood on the opposite shore had taken barely moments to cross.

She didn't have to tell Seth to get out. He'd never wanted to set foot on land more urgently.

"I'm not staying in Sheol for centuries," Seth said the instant his feet touched colorless grass.

By the time he turned back to look at her, gondola and gondolier had vanished. There wasn't even a ripple to show that a boat had disturbed the water.

The only thing that remained was a sense of unease weighing heavily within Seth.

"Seth!" Footsteps whispered through the grass. Marion appeared, eyes glowing white-blue in the darkness. She stopped a few feet away, even though it looked like she wanted to tackle him. It wouldn't have been the first time. "I thought we'd lost you. Damn it, Konig—"

"It wasn't him." Seth's gaze was fixed to the inside of Marion's wrist. She clutched her bow in one hand and arrow in the other, and he could see the blood flowing under the surface of her skin with every thump of her straining heart.

She swept her eyes over the river as if looking for something to shoot. "Then how'd we lose you?"

His conversation with the apothecary—or gondolier, whatever—had left him itchy all over. *Don't go after the Canope.*

"I fell out," Seth said.

Marion crossed her arms. "You...fell?" Her jaw tightened, and the tension rippled through her entire body. Her heart was beating sluggishly again. The three potions she had drunk in Arawn's tower were already wearing off. "What aren't you telling me?"

You became tired of Sheol's darkness within a span of centuries, too.

He wasn't telling her a lot of things.

Honestly, he wasn't sure what he'd tell her at that point even if he tried.

Seth trudged up the hill toward her without answering. "Where's Konig?"

"He's trying to find a way into the Bronze Gates," she said. "He's performing what you might call reconnaissance."

He could imagine how terribly that must have been going. Konig wasn't a subtle man. "All right.

We better get up there and help."

Marion hesitated. "I'm afraid." She didn't give Seth an opportunity to ask why before plowing on. "I'm afraid of going into Duat. The Bronze Gates are making me uncomfortable."

Seth rubbed a hand over his jaw. "Uncomfortable how?"

"It feels like something is calling to me from the other side."

"It's probably your memories," Seth said.

"It feels bigger than that. Less like I'm being pulled and more like I'm being...pushed. I know it doesn't make sense. It must sound insane. Here we are, so close to my memories, and I fear crossing over."

"You don't sound crazy." He sighed. "Look, I know you're having second thoughts. After the way everyone's been treating you, especially Dana McIntyre... I can see how you might be reluctant to go back to your old self." Seth had thought more than once that he didn't want Marion to change. The fact that he liked that horribly selfish idea so much made his words come out harsh. "You have to get your memories back, though. It's the right thing to do."

Marion blinked rapidly, as if slapped. His hostility shocked her. "I don't think that's the reason I'm afraid."

"Then why?"

"I think it has something to do with the gods," she said.

That statement left chills rippling down Seth's

spine. He glanced around the gray banks of the river, half-expecting to see Elise and James walking toward them out of nothingness.

She went on. "I knocked on a door in Arawn's tower, and they opened it for me. They're watching. I think they're pushing now, too."

"That would be a good thing, wouldn't it?" he asked. "They're helping you."

"Yes..." She ducked her head, removed her glasses, and polished the lenses with the hem of her shirt. "I suppose it *would* be a good thing. So why am I filled with dread?"

Something soft brushed along Seth's hand. He looked down to see Marion's fingers.

She was seeking comfort from him, which he had often given in the past.

But he hadn't given it when she'd radiated such weakness.

Seth didn't want to risk getting any nearer to Marion, not when she was so weak and he could feel himself hungering. He didn't even have words of comfort for her. There was nothing comforting about the horrors of the Nether Worlds.

At the contact, the taste of her sickness rolled through him. Sheol was sucking Marion's life away, her light flickering on the brink of extinguishment. Every fiber of Marion's body was suffering in Sheol. Getting away from the harsh, dry air of the hive didn't help. The fields outside Duat were no more hospitable.

He knew he should have stepped away, but the allure of the illness fixed him where he stood. She was gravity, and he was a helpless star circling the event horizon, only inches from falling over the edge.

Marion's tongue darted out to wet her lips. The motion drew his gaze to her face. She was staring at him through the glimmering ovals of her glasses.

What was she going to think when she found the Canope, restored her memories, and read the hunger in his mind?

He needed Charity. Not only to get her away from Arawn—who would seriously regret it if he'd so much as cracked one of Charity's fingernails—but because Seth wasn't sure how much longer he'd last without talking to her.

"We're almost out of Sheol. This is going to be over soon." He pulled his hand away and took a step back. "Drink another potion and let's go help your boyfriend."

She did as ordered. Color returned to her cheeks.

"There," he said. "Better already."

Marion didn't smile.

Seth hurried up the field toward the Bronze Gates. She was silent behind him.

The wall emerged from the fog. The Bronze Gates were only a couple of stories high, but they would have been impossible to climb. As far as Seth could see, there was only smooth metal, without a single crack, bump, or foothold.

Seth could make out the lights of a city beyond its top, as though Duat were hovering in the sky beyond. Konig lurked near the base of the wall, having a conversation with an armored demon. The top of its head didn't quite reach Konig's shoulders, but the curled horns thrusting from its cracked scalp made it two feet taller.

Konig and the demon exchanged something that Seth couldn't see. And then Konig was stepping down the hill to wrap his arm around Marion's shoulders like he always did when Seth was around. "He'll take us through," Konig said. "We can go in the back of his truck when they open the gates to change the guards. They're expecting him to deliver lethe from the hive."

"What did you give him?" Seth asked.

"I came prepared from the Winter Court." He took gems out of his pockets—glittering shards of permanent ice, which shone dully with magic suppressed by Sheol.

"And he agreed to trade our passage for something like that?" What the hell was a demon going to do with enchanted ice from the Middle Worlds?

"I'm convincing." Konig glared, as though waiting for Seth to challenge him.

He didn't bother.

The weaker Marion got, the hungrier Seth felt, and the worse the distraction became. Marion wasn't the only one getting screwed up by too much time in Sheol.

You got tired of Sheol's darkness within a span of centuries, too.

Dammit, Seth wasn't going to be in Sheol for

centuries.

And he wasn't a demon.

He *wasn't*.

"Okay," he said. "Let's get inside Duat and get out of here."

THIRTEEN

It was strange to be escorted around Duat by a demon Lord of Sheol acting like he was taking Charity on a date. Arawn was charming, gallant, and free with his compliments—offset only by the bleeding gashes all over his body, which didn't seem to bother him in the slightest.

Stranger still, Charity wasn't sure how much she was bothered by it, either.

"Duat is a temple transplanted from an undercity that was on Earth before Genesis," Arawn explained. He held Charity's hand in the crook of his elbow, forcing her to walk alongside him like some old-time lady.

"What's an undercity?"

"Demons have long been a chthonic race, dwelling beneath the world that humans enjoy. Every major city once had demon hives underneath them. Some bigger than others."

"Demons on Earth." Charity shivered.

She'd known that demons had been around before Genesis—it would have been hard to miss the wars that preceded the void—but it was frightening to think of how long they'd been boiling under the ground, waiting to emerge.

"The Nether Worlds aren't under the Earth's surface, are they?" she asked.

"We've tried to dig through the roof of our caverns and never reached anything but vacuum. It seems that the gods saw fit to give us our own world." Arawn scowled. "It's a compliment, I guess. The gods like demons better than angels so they freed us to this miserable, cramped wasteland. Hurrah."

What he called a miserable, cramped wasteland appeared to be ancient ruins perched atop a hill in the center of Sheol. The city was surrounded by a wall of shining metal that didn't remotely match the industrial iron and steel of the hive's hallways. It was beautiful in a strange way.

It did look like the gods had been trying to do a favor for demons, in their strange way.

"So you used to live on Earth," Charity said, following Arawn. There was little else she could do. Those scuttling bug-demons were following them again.

"I wasn't a Lord of Sheol before Genesis," Arawn said. "I lived in the City of Dis. I worked in the palace. I was an artist before the Breaking, and a guard afterward, all the way through the wars.

Do you remember the Breaking?"

It would have been impossible to forget. Charity had barely finished college when giant rifts had been torn into North America, allowing the forces of Hell to spill onto Earth. "Yes, I do. I evacuated to San Francisco. It was far enough from the fissure that things stayed relatively normal until the end. The smoke, though. It was always so bad."

"It was as bad in Dis. The fissure carved through our world. When the wind blew right, it cleared the air enough for us to see the sky on Earth." Arawn had stopped walking. He gazed up at the black roof hanging low over Duat. "Eventually, the Dis army was evacuated to Earth. It was raining. There were clouds. And then…"

Arawn drifted in memory. He looked only like an ordinary demon—not so different from a human man—dreaming of better times.

"I saw the sun once," he said. "Just once."

"You want to go back, don't you?"

His black eyes dropped to hers. "I'd do anything for that."

A greater demon pining for Earth. The twist of sympathy in Charity's heart was unexpected, but not unwelcome.

"How did you end up as a Lord of Sheol, then?" Charity asked.

He led her down to an open area that might have been considered a garden, if bushes and trees of sculpted iron counted. "I was friends with one of the generals in Dis's army. Terah taught me how to manage people, how to be a leader. She inspired me to rally a gang after Genesis. I carved out a place in the hive, and the other Lord of Sheol let me get away with it because Nyx is sick of the job."

"She's the one with the Canope."

Arawn shook his head. "The Canope's mine. I cut the deal for it. She's just been hanging on to it."

"Possession's nine tenths of the law."

"I feel the same. But as any demon who'll possess a human can tell you, that last tenth is a hell of a lot bigger than you'd think." Arawn smirked at her as he stroked his mustache thoughtfully. "What about you? What's your story of transformation? I assume you haven't always been as fantastic as you are now."

Charity had once been very much the way she looked when she wore the glamour: a small, unassuming woman much more concerned with her studies than looking good.

She missed it. A lot.

"There's not much of a story. The Genesis void took me when it took everyone else," she said. "I came back to a city that was totally fixed. No more ash from the Breaking, no sign of the riots, nothing. It took me a few hours to realize that I had come back almost a month after Genesis."

"One of the mysterious delayed returns," Arawn said.

Charity nodded. "It could have been worse. Some people took a whole year to come back for whatever reason."

"The gods work in mysterious ways." He

laughed as though he'd told the funniest joke of his life.

"Well, a month was long enough that my friends kind of assumed I was dead," Charity said. "And when I came back looking like...you know, the way I do now, I didn't bother hooking up with any of them. I only tried to track down my boyfriend from before Genesis. His name was Mike. I wanted him to know I was okay."

"Mike is a pathetic name," Arawn said.

Charity caught herself smiling. Mike *was* a pathetic name. "He came back mundane after Genesis."

"What did Mike think of you?"

She had never been deluded enough to think he'd want to be with her once he saw her revenant form, but she'd thought he would be relieved to know she was fine.

"He threw things at me," Charity said. "Said I shouldn't have come back. So I left, found a witch who could sell me a fancy glamour, and mortgaged my old townhouse to pay for it. I got a job at a hospital and didn't talk to anyone from my old life after that."

Arawn took her hand. "The glamour's a waste of money. Whatever you spent wasn't worth it."

"Don't call me ugly again," she said. "I'll scalp you."

"I'd love that," he said, as though she'd offered to go down on him. She couldn't tell if he was serious. "Mike didn't deserve you. Anyone who doesn't admire you—the *real* you—doesn't deserve to breathe the same air that you do."

It was perverse how much she liked hearing that. Just as it had been perverse how much she enjoyed sipping on that blood soup he'd given her.

After years of hiding herself away, someone wanted to see her for what she was. He *liked* it.

Maybe Arawn wasn't that bad, even if he did have a dining room filled with human meat. It was better than a lot of the online dating Charity had suffered through in the last decade.

Charity touched her glasses. "I'm going to take the glamour off."

He grinned. "Good."

She pressed her thumbs to the gems inside her glasses as she removed them.

Charity didn't need to look at herself to know what was transforming. Her gut was nothing under the hollowness of her ribs. She had claws. Her skin was brittle, deathly pale, dried out.

She looked like something that should have lived in the Nether Worlds.

Once the glamour was gone, she stood even taller than Arawn. He gazed up at her with open adoration.

"You are *perfect*," he said.

And she believed that he meant it.

Another demon entered the garden. Charity prepared to put on her glasses again, but then she realized that this demon was as inhuman as she was. Her cloak covered her face, but the hands that emerged from the robes were skinless. She also didn't seem to have legs.

Arawn groaned. "What do you want, Nyx?"

"I want you to leave Duat," she said. "I didn't invite you here."

"You've got my Canope. It means that I have an open invitation to your place until you give my property back."

"Yet you didn't seek me out to take ownership of it. You took a woman to view my gardens." Nyx surveyed Charity. It was impossible to see the face within, but Charity could feel the weight of her gaze. "You're only here for another distraction, Arawn. You leave the burden of ruling upon my frail shoulders."

"Of course I do," Arawn said. "It's not like I'm going to be in this shitty little pit much longer."

Charity was surprised. "What?"

"Yes, I'm planning to go to Earth," he said. "I thought I'd mentioned that to you when I was explaining my Genesis story, didn't I? As soon as your friends take the Canope, my path will be clear. I'll see the sun again. Myself, my gang, and a few thousand demons who are as sick of the Nether Worlds as I am."

"You'll be interested to know that her friends have arrived outside the Bronze Gates," Nyx said serenely. "They've come for the Canope."

Arawn beamed at Charity. "And this is how it begins."

Seth was surprised—and disappointed—to find that it was even darker in the demon merchant's truck than it had been in the rest of Sheol. The shadows were absolute underneath the protective canvas. Only Marion's faintly glowing eyes offered a dim light in the back of the truck, but it was no comfort; that made it impossible to ignore the way that she was still staring at Seth.

Maybe she could already read his mind.

"You okay?" he whispered.

She shook her head.

Marion only looked more miserable as the truck carried them closer to Duat. She was a strong woman—one of the strongest that Seth had ever met, irritatingly defiant yet charming in her willpower. Yet she looked like she was going to be sick all over the back of the pickup.

He wanted to tell her that it was okay to be afraid—that he'd been afraid every single time he'd fought the bad guys, every time he'd hunted a werewolf, every time he tried to save lives. Fear was part of life. Fear kept him safe, strong, and alive.

But there was no time for a pep talk.

The truck stopped outside the Bronze Gates. Seth watched through a hole in the canvas as the merchant talked to a creature wearing layers of black leather and carrying a butcher's knife. Its face was covered in tattoos, which were clearly Arawn's work.

"I can't hear what he's saying," Seth muttered. For all he knew, the merchant was selling them out.

"You don't need to hear them." Konig was relaxing against the back of the truck with Marion clamped tightly to his side. They were packed in among closed crates of lethe. "He'll do what I told him if he wants to get the rest of his payment."

Those stupid frost gems. Every ounce of Seth's common sense told him that demons would never risk their necks for something so petty. But those ounces of common sense were also telling him how delicious it would be to murder Marion, so perhaps it wasn't best to listen to himself.

The merchant returned to the driver's seat. The engine grumbled to life again with a crimson spark of warlock magic.

The truck jerked forward.

Within the outer wall of the Bronze Gates, the dry grass and loam had been stripped away to expose bare stone. Every inch of the ground was coated in warlock runes. They were more jagged than the kind of spells cast by gaean witches or mages. Seth didn't need to be able to read them to know they were deadly.

According to Dana's map, there was only a good quarter of a mile between the two layers of city walls, but the pickup trudged slowly across the warlock runes.

"What do we do once we get in?" Marion asked.

Seth started to respond. "We should get Charity and—"

"I'll find the Canope for you," Konig interrupted. "I'll grease a few palms to find out where it is and cut my way straight to the prize. You'll have your memories soon, princess." He stroked the bastard sword jutting over one shoulder, like one giant blade would be enough against the numerous demons of Duat.

"We can't stir up violence until we're sure Charity is safe," Seth said.

"If we find her first, we'll tip off our arrival to Arawn. He'll hide the Canope somewhere else," Konig said. "You think that finding some revenant is more important than the memories of the Voice of God?"

"I think we should be focused on saving lives," Seth said. "Marion?"

He expected her to agree with him. But she shrunk against Konig's side and said, "Charity can probably protect herself. She *is* a—" Howls resonated outside of the pickup. Marion sat upright and clung to Konig's arm. "What is that?"

The pickup jerked to a stop halfway between the walls. The engine died.

And the howling grew louder.

"I don't think the merchant cared for your bribe," Seth said.

Anger flashed over Konig's face. He dislodged Marion. "It's more of Arawn's dogs," he said dismissively. "I took care of the first in Arawn's tower, no problem. I'll get these, too."

He whipped the canvas aside and leaped out of the truck.

"Wait!" Seth said. "The warlock runes—"

Konig landed outside the pickup. The magic

flared around him, and he cried out, legs buckling underneath him.

"Help him!" Marion cried.

Seth rolled his eyes, but he leaped out of the pickup, too. He took care only to step on the marks that Konig had already activated. Like landmines, they could only blow once; nothing hurt Seth the way that it had hurt Konig, writhing on the ground while infernal flame leaped over his body.

Seth stood over Konig, drew his guns, and faced down the howling dogs.

For an instant, he thought that there were werewolves in Duat. They were big enough— bigger than the werewolves he'd known in his youth, in fact. But these animals weren't as shaggy as werewolves, nor did their fur have the multicolored hues of shapeshifters.

These canines were sleek and white. Their legs were long the way that the gondolier's neck had been long. Their perked ears were tipped with red that was the same color as blood. Their feet didn't contact the ground when they ran, so they were immune to activating the warlock runes, with full mobility that Seth didn't have.

They were at least triple the size of the dog in Arawn's tower, and ghostly. Not domestic beasts, but the wild hunt.

The Hounds that Dana had warned him about.

When Seth saw them, all he could think was, *These are Death.*

They weren't animals the way that coyotes were or even the way that werewolves were. They were the cold physical embodiment of inevitability.

And they were racing toward him.

The dogs were only a hundred feet away by the time Seth realized he'd frozen.

He fired.

There was no way to tell if his bullets hit. If they did, it didn't matter to the dogs.

Konig struggled to his feet, flames continuing to lick along his shoulders, his spine, his hair. It didn't seem to hurt him once he got over the shock of it. Seth had underestimated the sidhe prince's strength.

"Run, Marion!" Konig commanded. He thrust his hand away from the dogs, toward the gate that would lead into Duat. Sidhe magic foamed over the warlock runes. They ignited as his spells passed, and went dim.

He'd cleared a path for Marion.

Then he leaped in front of Seth. Not to defend him—*never* to defend Seth. But because he was the Prince of the Autumn Court, and he *would* be respected. He would kill the dogs. He would protect the princess. Not Seth.

Konig met them with the blade.

They parted around him like a river parting around stone. Their bodies slammed into Seth and knocked the breath out of his lungs.

He hit the ground on the edge of the safe path Konig had created. Inches from an incendiary warlock rune.

Seth kicked both boots into the face of a dog when it tried to bite him. It felt like kicking an iron statue. The pain of it resonated all the way into his spine.

The dog's head reared back. Its mouth opened, similar to the one in Arawn's tower, but even wider —so huge that Seth could see all the way down its crimson throat into the boiling acid of its belly. Its jaw had thousands of teeth. Millions. And the teeth had teeth, layers upon layers of jagged razors the color of bone, running in long lines down its gullet.

Forget the warlock runes.

Seth hurled himself away, rolling out of the dog's path. He felt the demon spells catch underneath him.

He was consumed by fire.

It burned over his jacket, melting his skin. Seth ripped the coat off with a cry.

The dog lunged again.

He whipped the burning cloth in front of him, smacking the flaming sleeve right into the dog's face. The fire spread over its fur too. It caught as quickly as though it had been drenched in accelerant. The warlock flame wasn't ordinary fire, and thank the gods for that, because it meant Seth had a weapon.

With a yelp, the dog receded. But another took its place.

Seth tried to strike it with the fire too, but missed. It was ready for him now. And it darted forward, chomping on his boot. Teeth penetrated the steel in the toe. Sharp fangs scraped the tops of his toes.

He wrapped the jacket around the dog's muzzle, wrenching its head to the ground. He stomped its skull.

The fire on Seth's jacket crawled up toward his fingers. He had to drop it. The remnants of the cloth vanished into cinder.

"Konig!" Seth shouted. "Help!"

The prince was surrounded, but his head snapped up at the sound of his name. A smile sparked in his eyes. He liked having Seth beg for assistance. "Just a second!"

Konig whirled with incredible speed to swipe the bastard sword through two of the dogs in a single gesture. Even without full access to sidhe magic in the Nether Worlds, he was still a consummate warrior, as anyone trained in the Autumn Court would have been.

The sword helped.

Seth wished he had a sword.

Another of the dogs changed direction, charging him with two others on its tail. Seth thought fast.

He'd fought hundreds of werewolves in his day for fun, and for survival. These were bigger, meaner, and distinctly more infernal. But that didn't mean some of the same tactics wouldn't work.

"Come on, you ugly mutts," he muttered, crouching low, hands extended to either side.

The dog at the front hit him.

Seth was ready.

He wrapped his arms around its neck, his chin

ducked to his chest to protect his soft parts. And he let the force of the contact carry them onto the warlock runes.

When they hit the ground, Seth made sure the dog was on the bottom.

Its fur went up in blue flame.

He was surrounded by a yelping, thrashing mass of burning demon dog. The warlock fire was crawling over its thorax.

Seth kicked it into the two other dogs, putting the flaming Hound between him and his attackers. The fire spread and kept on spreading. No matter how they rolled, the fire wouldn't go out.

"Konig!" he shouted again.

And the unseelie prince was suddenly there. He carved through the dogs, putting them out of their misery with a few swift gestures.

His violet eyes were bright with the satisfaction of violence.

When he was done, he stood on a safe spot on the ground, drenched in ichor and grinning. There were pieces of the Hounds everywhere, but nothing living within sight. Maybe Konig hadn't been speaking from pure arrogance when he'd said he would carve his way to the Canope.

Konig offered Seth a hand up. He took it.

"Thanks," Seth said.

"But of course," Konig said. A thought struck him. He spun on the spot. "Where's Marion?"

Seth leaped to the truck bed and ripped the canvas aside. The only things inside were crates of lethe.

Marion had run.

At least, he *hoped* she'd run.

FOURTEEN

Marion wanted to pretend that it was strategy that compelled her toward Duat. Strategy, or maybe even cowardice—two completely normal reactions to being attacked by Hounds in Sheol.

It was neither.

She was propelled away from Seth and König's fight against the Hounds by a force so strong that she didn't look back. Two men she would have been stricken to lose were struggling for their lives, and she was fixated on the door leading into Duat.

With each step she took toward it, she felt doors opening in her mind.

The clicking of locks disengaging rattled through her skull.

Marion stopped in front of the door, gripping the stave of her bow in one hand and an arrow in the other as she studied the Bronze Gates.

As her mind opened, she could see with more than her eyes. She saw the magic layered over the gates, under them, throughout them—not too dissimilar from the magic that had been woven into the throne room of the Autumn Court.

The door existed on multiple levels.

It wanted her to knock.

No, that wasn't a want from the door. It came from the same gods who were shoving her toward Duat.

Marion didn't need information from her old journals to identify the feeling that grew within. It was the gods filling empty holes as though she were nothing more than a vessel for their presence.

She took a few steps to the right and knocked on the wall instead of the gates themselves.

A door appeared.

It swung open, revealing Duat.

The black city towered over her, enormous in its scale and familiar in the shapes of its blocky towers. She'd been there before. It was a city of the gods as much as it was of demons, and Marion knew it the way that she sometimes knew magic.

At the sight of it, all of her trepidation vanished.

Marion was exactly where she was meant to be.

Everything she could remember from the moment she had woken up in Mercy Hospital had been leading to this arrival.

She also knew that there were guard towers concealed within the inner walls of the Bronze

Gates, and that demons would be coming for her.

It felt like she turned around in slow motion to look for the guard towers. As she expected, demons were clambering down from the concealed windows, easily finding traction on the smooth metal. The door that she'd used to pass through the wall had already vanished. Her opportunity for escape had disappeared with it.

She didn't want to escape. Not anymore.

The demons hit the ground and raced toward her.

Marion lifted her hand. "Stop," she said, and there was borrowed power in the word.

They stopped so fast that they tumbled into each other. They stared at her in befuddlement, torn between the urge to attack and the urge to obey.

"I want the Bronze Gates opened," she said.

They didn't move.

Marion summoned every scrap of arrogance she possessed. These were the same instincts that had made her want to steal Charity Ballard's glasses and use Seth's money to buy couture.

The entitlement. The nobility. The self-certainty.

All those things that made everyone from her past loathe her, she donned like the robes of a queen.

And she said it again.

"I want the Bronze Gates opened *now*."

The first of the guards to break was some kind of human-like creature with snakes rather than hair—a megaira, Marion thought. She wasn't sure how she remembered the name. Maybe she didn't remember it. Maybe it was something that she was borrowing from the gods, much like whatever happened when she knocked on the wall.

The megaira stumbled past her with glassy, confused eyes. Only the serpents that flowed from its scalp watched Marion, exposing their needle fangs with loud hisses. They weren't susceptible to her commands. They would have bitten if they'd been close enough.

"Where's the Canope?" she asked the others as the megaira climbed into the guard tower again.

All of them turned slowly, painfully to point up at the tallest tower within Duat: a temple that was protected by statue versions of the Hounds who'd attacked outside.

Marion's heart almost stopped beating.

Her memories were so close. *So close*.

Fear grew within her throat until she choked on it.

There were two forces battling within Marion. The first seemed to be from the gods, who were pushing her toward her memories. The second seemed to be herself—the shadow of the woman Marion used to be, which was urging her to run away.

The gods were stronger.

She faced the demons again. "Get out of my sight and tell nobody you found me."

After a moment, they all obeyed, drifting away throughout the city, propelled by commands that hadn't come from Marion.

She was the Voice of God, and she was being controlled as surely as the guards were.

Konig and Seth went from one side of the Bronze Gates to the other to search for Marion, but there was no sign of her. When they got back to the inner wall a second time, Seth tried a hundred times to teleport through the inner wall of the Bronze Gates to reach Duat. He shut his eyes and squeezed his hands into fists and tried to jump with all of his willpower.

It felt like smashing his face into a wall. He moved nowhere.

"Damn!" Seth slammed his fist into the gate. This time, he punched hard enough to make sure it hurt, if briefly.

"Incapable of teleporting?" Konig asked.

"That seems to be the case, yeah."

"They clearly have wards against it. You shouldn't waste your energy trying."

Seth gritted his teeth, trying to ignore Konig's know-it-all tone. They were on the same team. The sidhe prince had saved him. They needed to get along, damn it.

Marion's life depended on it.

He could feel her, even now that they were physically distant from one another. Specifically, he could feel the line of her life slicing through

Sheol, edging closer toward death the longer she lingered. He was as acutely aware of her existence as though she stood right behind him with a hand on his shoulder.

Whatever she was doing—wherever she had gone—she was dying, moment by moment.

"Back to the truck," Seth said. "It might have something to get us through the Bronze Gates—something that would let the merchant access Duat."

"Why bother? I'll cut through the door," Konig said, swinging the infernal bastard sword at his side, as though to warm up his shoulder.

Seth had never heard anything so stupid in his life. Well, he probably had—he'd dealt with his brother Abel for a long time, and Abel was the master of stupid ideas—but this particular stupid idea was delivered with more self-assurance than Konig deserved.

He rounded on the prince. "What the hell is with this attitude you've got? Can't you listen to one goddamn idea you didn't come up with on your own?"

"I am the Prince of the Autumn Court—"

"And you *will* be respected," Seth said. "Yeah, I heard you the first million times. That doesn't change the fact that there's no way a demon sword is going to cut through that door. Like you said, it's clearly buried under wards. If I can't teleport through, then you can't cut it open."

Konig was haloed by shivering anger. "You don't want me to get to Marion."

That was the new stupidest thing that Seth had ever heard. A world record broken within a span of seconds. "I'm not listening to this." He headed for the truck.

"I see the way you've been looking at her," Konig called to his back. "I know your game."

"It's not what you think."

"Then what is it? I'm all ears. I would *love* to hear why you keep running off with my woman."

Seth stopped walking.

My woman. He would have laughed, except it wasn't remotely funny. Juvenile, yes. Exhausting, definitely. But funny? Not at all.

Seth had sworn off relationships exactly to avoid this kind of bullshit. He'd have rather cut his own throat than deal with that brand of jealousy ever again.

But he needed Konig's help. He needed Konig to *understand*.

"I was changed in Genesis, and I don't know how," Seth said. "I'm starting to think there's something seriously wrong about me. I've got these...instincts." He wasn't going to force himself to share the painful details with a dried-up crouton like Konig. Seth kept the explanation simple. "I keep thinking about killing Marion."

Konig surprised him by laughing. "You want to *kill* her?"

"No, I don't want to. I'm not a killer. But I'm thinking about it, all right? It's been all I can think about since we arrived in Sheol. I think it's because she's got angel blood, and she's dying, and for whatever reason it makes me like a greyhound after a rabbit." Or like a werewolf with silver poisoning.

"Then why are you still dragging Marion around, if you don't want to kill her?" Konig asked.

"Once she's got her memories, she can talk to the gods on my behalf and figure out what happened to me in Genesis. It's the only way I can get fixed."

The prince was still laughing. "Oh, this is great. Marion's been pining over you for weeks, and you want her *dead*."

Seth entertained the thought of punching the sidhe prince in the throat. "I wouldn't have brought her if she hadn't insisted. She's persistent."

"You could say that a thousand times and it wouldn't be overstating," Konig said. His laughter faded. He gripped Seth's shoulder. "If you hurt Marion, I will kill you. Let's make that clear."

"Konig, if I hurt Marion, I'll kill myself," Seth said.

That didn't seem to comfort the prince in the slightest. His lips drew into a thin line. "You're not in love with her. You promise that?"

"Goddammit, how many times do I have to say this? I don't want her within a hundred miles of wherever I am." Seth shook off Konig's hand. "As soon as we find her, you have to take her back to the Winter Court. I'll get the Canope, save Charity, and return as soon as possible."

"Done," Konig said. "Whatever you want."

Seth didn't tell Konig the truth—that he didn't

truly want Marion to leave. He wanted her right beside him, her heart beating sluggishly and breaths slowing as she labored toward the precipice.

And that was the problem.

The men walked back the way they came one more time, searching for the pickup. The distance only seemed to stretch the further that they walked together.

Seth would have been happy to walk in silence, but Konig seemed to feel differently. He was happy now that he'd heard Seth's confession. Practically skipping.

"Tell me more about yourself, Doctor. Clearly you can teleport yourself and friends," Konig said. "And clearly you want to kill people, particularly those of the beautiful princess persuasion. What else changed about you in Genesis, eh? Any fun party tricks?"

Seth shook his head. "Not that you need to worry about."

"You're great at pretending to be human. There must have been something that tipped you off to the way you'd changed when you came back from the void."

There had been a great many things that tipped Seth off, and he didn't want to discuss them. "Did something change in you?"

"Sure," Konig said. "I came back as a five year old who could do *this*." He snapped his fingers. Nothing happened. "That was supposed to generate flame. I seem to be running dry after fighting with the Hounds."

Seth shrugged. "Nether Worlds." That was all the explanation either of them needed.

"Well, I returned magical. Quite the handful for my parents, but nothing they couldn't deal with. And you? Did you come back a baby demon? Horns sticking out?" Konig shot him a look, as though double-checking to make sure he hadn't missed any infernal features.

"I'm not a demon," Seth said.

"Could have had me fooled."

"Charity drinks blood, and she's gaean. Not a demon."

"So you drink blood," Konig said.

He wasn't going to let up.

Years of frustration and despair built within Seth. "I came back from Genesis and thought things were normal. I was working with some preternatural investigators. Things were fine for a few months."

"Wait," Konig said. "An elementary schooler doing investigations?"

"I'm older than I look."

"Another demon feature, I'm sure."

Seth stopped walking. "I told you, I'm not a demon. I *know* I'm not a demon."

Konig rolled his eyes. "All right. Go on. Things were fine for a few months, and..."

And then Seth had gone with Brianna and another friend, Anthony, to rescue a guy from a den of vampires lurking under the Las Vegas strip.

That had gone fine.

They'd saved the victim's life, but not before a lot of blood got spilled. About a dozen vampires had been staked. There had been some collateral damage in the form of mundane partiers who'd been donating blood to vampires.

So much blood.

Seth had been in medical school at the University of Nevada, Las Vegas at the time. After saving the victim on that case, he'd gone to his rounds at the hospital like everything was normal, trying to ignore the senses that told him everything *wasn't* normal. That something was painfully different about him.

He never should have gone to the hospital like that.

"I killed one of my first patients," Seth said. "It was an accident. He was dying anyway, in a lot of pain. I touched him and..." The patient had died instantly, leaving a cooling corpse under Seth's hands.

The shock of it had made Seth teleport the first time. He'd appeared in the Nevada desert, alone, afraid, regretful.

By the time he'd gotten back to the hospital, the patient had already been cremated, and Seth's mind had been decided. He couldn't work with his friends when he was like that. Not when he had no clue what had changed about him and what his boundaries were.

He'd transferred to a different college, changed identities. Only Brianna had any clue what had happened to him...until now.

"So all you have to do to kill Marion is touch her," Konig said.

"I don't think I can do that to anyone who's healthy, and Marion's not usually near death."

"*Usually.*" The prince laughed again. "Oh man. I can't wait to see her face when I tell her about this."

Anger swelled in Seth. He advanced on Konig. "You're not going to tell her anything I just told you."

"Why not?"

Seth just stared at him. He let the anger show —the pain that he usually cloaked under a thousand layers of carefully maintained calm.

He let himself show the hunger for death.

Something must have visibly changed in his face, because Konig took a step back, alarmed.

It took him a moment to recover, but not before he started sweating.

"I see the pickup," Konig said. He was right. It had finally appeared from the fog between the Bronze Gates, exactly where they had left it. The bodies of the Hounds had gone missing.

Seth let out a long, slow breath, reassuming his mask of calm. "Yeah. Let's get in and find Marion."

And then she could go somewhere better than Sheol—and far safer than being trapped with a man who couldn't stop thinking about killing her.

Marion waited in the open gate for Konig and Seth to return. It felt like she was alone in Duat, but she didn't drop her guard; she kept her bow and arrow at ready.

For the first time since landing on the banks of the river Mnemosyne, she felt calm. She was no longer afraid.

She was exactly where she was meant to be—just a few minutes away from finding the Canope, once Konig and Seth located her.

The fact that her fear had disappeared was its own kind of terrifying.

But she was numb to it.

The power of the gods weighed heavily on her mind, like a sedative holding her in place.

She wasn't certain how much time passed before the merchant's pickup appeared on the other side of the open gate. She only knew that time did pass, and that the pickup came, and she was no longer alone. Seth had arrived. He was meant to be there, just as she was.

The bumper stopped a few inches away from her shins. The men leaped out.

"Marion!" Konig reached her first, sweeping her into his arms with a grip so tight that it was painful. She didn't like when he grabbed her like that—especially not now, when she felt sickly all over. The power of the gods could only buoy her so much in that environment.

She pushed him away gently. "Are you guys okay?"

"Of course we are. What about you?" Konig asked. "How did you get the gate open?"

Marion arched an eyebrow. "I knocked."

Emotion skittered over Konig's mind. With all of the doors that had been opening in Marion's mind, she found herself easily reading his thoughts: his annoyance, his anger, even his insecurity. It bothered him that he hadn't needed to rescue Marion from Duat. He'd wanted to ride in on his white horse to impress her.

"The guards?" Konig asked, his expression immutable.

"I told them to leave me alone." She spread her hands before her like she had when she'd cast magic in the past. There was no light now. She didn't need spells with the power awakening inside of her. "Nothing can stand between me and what I've lost." She pointed to the temple. "My Canope is there."

Konig turned to Seth. "Did you hear that?"

"Yeah," Seth said. It seemed to take physical effort for him to look down at his feet. Whatever was going on in his head was much more subtle than Konig's, but Marion could feel around the edge of it.

He felt disgusted. And worried.

Marion's display of power didn't threaten him the way that it did Konig, but Seth didn't seem to be much of a fan.

"Let's go." Konig startled Marion by grabbing her elbow so hard that she couldn't pull free.

"What are you doing?" she asked when he began walking her toward the pickup—away from the temple, toward the exit to Duat.

"I'm taking you home," he said. "To the Winter Court."

"What? *No*. I'm so close!" He dragged her through the gates that she'd had opened by sheer force of will, and Marion reached for Seth. He was the one who was supposed to be there with her. Both of them were fated, dropped into Sheol by the gods, and Konig was trying to ruin destiny. "Don't let him take me!"

Seth didn't move to help her. He didn't even look up.

Magic appeared at Marion's fingertips, glowing with white lightning.

Konig's hand touched her skull before she could cast.

"Sleep," he said. "We'll be home soon."

Sidhe magic breathed through her skull.

The last thing she saw before passing out was Seth turning away from her to walk toward the temple alone.

FIFTEEN

Marion woke up because she plowed into six-foot-deep snow. She was instantly buried, instantly freezing, and instantly furious.

Konig had used his magic to knock her unconscious.

He had taken her from the Canope.

The fury that surged within her was stronger than the smell of brimstone in Sheol. She clawed her way to the top of the snow bank, and she emerged screaming, punching her fists in the air.

Konig was already melting the snow a few feet away. He'd fallen nearby, standing underneath the shimmering black disc that suggested a ley line juncture.

"What did you do?" Marion roared, staggering toward him. The snow weighed heavily on her clothes. She had dressed for the warmth of the

Nether Worlds, not for the Winter Court. The wind sucked her breath away.

Konig grabbed her. His hands felt warm for once. "I'm saving you, dummy. Stay close. I can jump us right to Niflheimr." The castle of ice was on the horizon, suspended in the middle of a frozen ocean with no path to reach it aside from a narrow bridge.

Marion didn't want Konig to touch her. She shoved him away. "*What did you do?*"

"Did leaving Sheol screw up your hearing?"

"I heard you say that you're rescuing me, but that's not what it seems like!" Marion was barely coherent with her teeth chattering so hard. "I was almost to the Canope!"

"Seth's going to get it," Konig said dismissively.

Seth. Seth had seen Konig taking her, and he hadn't tried to fight. He'd just watched.

The goodbye had been obvious without needing to speak a single word.

"You—you colluded against me! Since when are you and Seth friends?" Marion asked, backing away quickly when Konig tried to take her hand again. She stumbled and fell into the snow.

"Stop being stupid and let me take you to Niflheimr," Konig said.

Anger sent magic shooting down her arms. Electricity lifted her hair around her shoulders. "Stupid? *Stupid?*"

"You were dying in Sheol. You should be thanking me."

"Thanking you for taking me further away

from my memories?" Her skin glowed white with ethereal power as she crawled out of the snow again. "*Why*?"

"Come on, princess," Konig said. "Can we at least talk about this somewhere warm?"

"No! You *will* take me back to Duat, and you'll do it right now!"

"If I take you back to Sheol, Seth is going to kill you."

Marion's magic sputtered. "What?"

"Oh, princess. I hadn't wanted to tell you, but..." He shrugged. The glow was returning to his skin as well, now that they were back in the Middle Worlds. "Seth confessed to me that Genesis gave him a killing urge, which is manifesting in the desire to kill you. He asked that I remove you from Sheol before he acted on it. Your safety is always my highest priority. That's why I dragged you back to the ley lines."

Her magic flickered one more time and then went out. The cold struck Marion anew, like knives buried in her flesh. "You're lying."

"When have I ever lied to you?" Konig asked.

"Oh, let's see. Like in the last two weeks, when you told me that Seth wanted a reward for saving my life?"

"He told you that was a lie? And you *believed* him?" He took Marion by the elbows, cradling her gently. She didn't pull away again. "Princess, Seth has lied to you about *so* many things. He wants you dead, but he can't risk killing you before you talk to the gods for him."

Marion couldn't bring herself to argue with Konig.

Seth had been acting strangely toward her for days. Ever since he'd returned to her for help after the summit, he'd been acting as though he couldn't bear to look at her most of the time.

He wanted Marion dead.

She was so distracted by the realization dawning that she didn't even notice when Konig gripped her arms.

"To Niflheimr," he said.

The world bent around them. The black trees swayed.

With a *pop*, they vanished from the hilltop.

Nori Harper had grown accustomed to being uncomfortable in the service of the sidhe. The Autumn Court's temperatures ranged from "standing in front of an air conditioner on full" to "taking an ice bath while eating a snow cone," and she'd learned to compensate for that in order to disguise herself as an unseelie servant, one of the gentry. A glamour here, fashionable fur coat there, fine.

The Winter Court was ice-bath cold at its best moments, and few of its moments were good without its steward within the dimension.

"The spells have failed again," reported Cyprian, standing from the altar he'd been examining. He stuffed his hands into fleece-lined gloves again. When even the unseelie were bundling up against the cold, it was bad.

"What can I do about it?" Nori asked, tensing her jaw so that her teeth would stop chattering.

"You? Nothing. These are tied by soul links to whoever rules the Winter Court."

"So I need Marion," she said.

"The sidhe ruler," Cyprian said. "These spells are sidhe. Advanced stuff."

Which meant that even Marion's return to Niflheimr would only do so much...until Marion and Konig married.

"Thanks, Cyprian," Nori said.

"Anything."

They began trudging up the bridge into Niflheimr again, where at least the walls would shield them from the wind. "How are the girls adjusting to life in the palace?" she asked.

"They love it," Cyprian said. "I haven't seen them smile this much in years. It's not just the stable environment, either. They're getting along fantastically with Ymir."

"That's wonderful to hear," Nori said. And it was a wonderful reminder of why she was suffering in this cold—for real people, with real problems.

She left Cyprian in the thinning refugee camp. They'd been relocating families as quickly as they could identify rooms that were structurally sound. A good third of them had already been moved. Cyprian had been offered one of the first rooms since he had children, but he'd declined in order to remain with Ymir.

The frost giant brightened to see Cyprian approaching. Nori lingered long enough to watch them meet, smiling through her shivers.

Then she retreated to the throne room—now the warmest, safest room in the palace, though that wasn't saying much. It was the difference between temperatures at freezing and so far below freezing that eyelids froze shut. She still couldn't shed any of her furs.

More of the Onyx Queen's personal touch had appeared in the throne room. It looked like the icier version of the Autumn Court's throne room now, from the hand-carved vases to the plush furniture. No number of tapestries depicting frolicking wood nymphs could conceal the room's chill, though.

Nori was on her way to her quarters when she realized that the looking glass in the back was glowing.

She had never seen the mirror as anything but a dull, flat sheet that barely reflected the throne room from its dusty corner. Now she could see her face in it clearly, picked out in sharp relief. It poured silvery light across the floor.

She touched the frame gently. Magic buzzed against her fingertips.

Another face appeared in the mirror. This one belonged to a woman with round features and short, spiky hair that was a washed-out shade of blue. "Hey," said the new woman. "Where's

Marion?"

Nori startled, stepping back. "Who are you?"

"The name's Dana McIntyre. Marion's expecting a call from me."

"Through the looking glass?"

"That's how you call someone in the Winter Court." Dana rolled her eyes and heaved a sigh. "Look, I'm Marion's sister. She'll want to hear from me."

Dana McIntyre looked less like Marion than literally anyone else on the planet. Marion was long and lean with olive skin. Dana was stocky, muscled, almost spherical in form, with ruddy cheeks.

But who'd lie about information so easily checked?

"She's not here," Nori said.

Dana looked relieved. "Then you tell her what I found." Her hand thrust through the looking glass, appearing in the Winter Court clutching a fistful of paper. Wisps of steam drifted from her warm flesh. "She'll want these."

Nori took the papers and the hand retreated. She was surprised to find that two of them were drawings she'd given to Seth—pictures of people who had tried to assassinate Marion. The backs of each page were covered in messy, square handwriting that surely must have belonged to Dana.

"Only one of the men was a triadist," Dana said. "His name was Oliver Machado. He was found dead outside Ransom Falls, California a few days ago. The other two men are well-known mercenaries named Geoff Samuelson and Vasicek —just Vasicek. Werewolf and megaira. Vasicek is dead. Geoff was never found. I wrote down more details on the pages."

Dana was right. This was all information Marion was going to want—she'd want it quite a lot. "Thank you," Nori said.

Dana didn't stick around. She vanished before the second word had come from Nori's lips.

An instant later, the doors banged open.

"Don't follow me!" Marion blew into the throne room with a gust of snow. Nori had to clutch the papers to her chest to keep them from getting ripped out of her hands.

Relief flooded Nori. "Oh, Marion, thank the gods!" She hurried away from the looking glass. "Did you find everything? Are your memories back?"

"Don't talk to me right now," Marion snapped before whirling on Konig, who was only a few feet behind her. She crackled with magic. Nori hadn't seen Marion glow with power like that in weeks. "You have no right to drag me around! I'm not an object!"

"I have every right to protect my future bride," Konig said.

Nori backpedaled, eyes widening. She shouldn't have been privy to the argument. The magic lashing between them was making the whole throne room tremble.

Marion jabbed a finger into his chest. "See,

that's the problem. You're so damn *presumptive*. First you think you can drag me back to the Winter Court from Sheol—"

"Seth told me to take you!"

"And you listened to him, rather than asking my opinion!" Marion shoved Konig. "You made up your mind about how to resolve the problems with the angels. You followed me to Sheol, even though I've made it perfectly clear I know what I'm doing. You talked to Seth and then dragged me to the Winter Court. Now you demand that I marry you without the slightest consideration for what I might want! What about *me*, Konig?"

"I thought you'd want to marry me." Konig's tone was frostier than the towers of Niflheimr.

"You haven't *asked*."

"I did. In Sheol."

"For the love of the gods, Konig! This isn't the time. I couldn't possibly consider marriage until I get my memories back, which you've endangered by ripping me out of Duat!"

"Seth will take care of it," Konig said.

The mention of his name made Marion waver, but only for an instant. "Will he? Or will he be hurt —killed—because he has no help left in Duat? I'm meant to be there with him. He's only one man."

"A demon."

"We don't know that," Marion hissed. "He *needs* me!"

Konig stalked away from her, and then paced back, as though searching for an outlet for his frenetic energy. "This isn't about the Canope. This isn't about your memories. This about the fact that you don't want to marry me, after all I've done for you!"

"You're right about that," Marion snapped. "There's no chance in the Middle Worlds, the Nether Worlds, or *anywhere else* that I will marry someone who treats me like this!"

A frightening calm settled over Konig's face. "You're rejecting me."

"You earned it," she snapped. And then, more frighteningly, Marion rounded on Nori. "Take me back! I need to get back to Sheol right this moment!"

Nori hesitated. She glanced at Konig.

That glance was enough to make Marion completely lose it. She gave a frustrated scream and the icy roof of the throne room cracked.

Marion stalked toward the hallway leading toward the bedrooms. "Stay the hell away from me!" she screamed over her shoulder.

When she slammed the door, frost showered around Nori.

Oh my gods.

It wasn't the first time Nori had seen Konig and Marion fight like that, but it was the first time since Marion had woken up without her memories— and the first time they'd had such a fight in a palace made completely of ice.

"Yes, go ahead and leave!" Konig shouted at the door that Marion had slammed. He ripped a giant sword off of his back and jabbed it into the air, as though piercing the heart of an imaginary Marion.

"Leave! I don't need the likes of *you*!"

He hurled the sword into the wall. The point embedded into the ice so deep that a foot of its blade vanished.

Nori flinched. She couldn't help but squeal a little, too.

The tiny sound made Konig whip around to glare at her. "What are you doing here?"

"I was inspecting the wards on the towers. It's been so cold...and...and..." He wouldn't care about that. She thought about telling him of Dana McIntyre's call, but she doubted that Konig would be interested in that, either. "I'm sorry. I'll check in on the refugees."

She made it halfway to the doors before Konig said, "No."

He stalked toward her. It took all of Nori's strength not to move or meet his eyes. It was dangerous to meet the prince's eyes when he was in a mood like that. He'd had his servants tossed into the dungeons for less.

"I saved her life, and this is what she does to me," Konig said. "It's insane. It's irrational!"

"I agree," Nori said.

"Marion doesn't care about saving the Winter Court from war. All those refugees—she would see them dead before she'd let her memories slip from her fingers! And why? Because she wants to remember, or because the pursuit of that moronic Canope gives her the opportunity to be with Seth?"

Nori was holding Dana's papers so hard that

they crumpled.

She didn't know what to say.

"I'm looking for answers, Nori," Konig said savagely. "Speak to me!"

After a deep breath, Nori managed to speak. "Marion has always been selfish. I don't know what she wants this time, but...it's all about her needs, not the needs of the court." Her stomach flipped. "She doesn't deserve you."

Something shifted in Konig's face. "No. She doesn't."

Time held still between them. She stared up at him and he stared down at her, as though seeing Nori—again—for the first time. It wasn't only admiration for her evolving thought processes in his expression now. He wasn't thinking about how smart Nori was.

His thoughts were much more animal.

"She has no idea how many ways she could die in Sheol," Konig said. "I'm the one who defeated Arawn. I'm the one who killed dozens of demons to free her from the tower."

"She should be grateful," Nori said.

"She should, but she's not." He clutched at her shoulders, gripping so hard that Nori was nearly wrenched off of her feet. She was short for someone of ethereal descent, and shorter still compared to Konig. "You're grateful, aren't you?"

Nori only had to nod.

He dragged her against his chest, and his lips crashed into hers, icy cold and desperate. Dana McIntyre's papers tumbled from her arms. She wrapped herself around him—arms around neck, legs around hips. He lifted her effortlessly. She was giddy at his touch, dizzy with the promise of it.

A prince. A sidhe prince.

Of all the times that Nori had participated in Autumn Court parties, she had never joined with a sidhe who made her skin ache like Konig did.

She also hadn't joined with a sidhe who was involved in an exclusive relationship with her cousin.

"Wait," Nori said, breaking the kiss.

And he said, "No. It's been too long. I won't wait longer."

The throne room bent around them, bowing from the position where the two of them stood. Konig jerked both of them through the ley lines into the bedroom he'd chosen for himself. He all but tossed Nori onto the bed and then collapsed atop her, his weight suspended on his elbows.

He bit at her neck. "Tell me you want me."

"I want you," Nori said. She'd never said anything truer in her life.

"Tell me you need me," Konig said.

Nori wasn't sure *that* was true, but she would tell him anything to get him to continue kissing her like that. "I need you, Konig—Prince ErlKonig of the Autumn Court."

He made a savage, needy noise deep in his throat, and together, they rolled across the bed.

In the king's bedchamber, the cold couldn't touch Nori.

Cast in Hellfire

Nori had never seen a body as glorious as that of Prince ErlKonig's, and never one in such a lush setting as the oiled skins and furs of the king's bed. The prince was lying back on the pillows, head propped up on one arm as he languorously blew fog into the air, his hot breath creating billows above his face.

Sculptures dangled over the massive bed, like an elaborate chandelier made of icicles. Nori and Konig's combined body heat was making them melt so that they slowly, steadily dripped chilly water onto her naked back.

She rested her chin on his chest, stroking along the lines of his pectorals with a fingernail. His skin still glistened with sweat and magic.

And it was hers. All hers.

At some point in the near future, Nori was going to have to think of a way to break this to Marion. She'd have to think about the implications that it would have for her relationship with the Autumn Court, the ethereal delegation, and Marion herself.

For now, she only wanted to rest on Konig and admire him.

"What are you thinking about?" Nori asked, tracing a circle on his ribcage.

"Marion," he said.

Nori sat up, tugging the furs into her naked lap to try to stave off the chill. "Me too."

"If you have any ideas of how to make her see reason, I'm all ears," Konig said.

She laughed uneasily. "Reason? About what?"

"Marriage, of course."

The warmth of the afterglow was gone so quickly that she physically shivered. "But...we just..."

"Yes, we made love, and it doesn't change anything." Konig pushed up on his elbows, gazing at her with violet eyes that seemed more like sapphires in the icy bedroom. "You don't think that I'd endanger the Winter Court for this, do you?"

It seemed a hell of a lot like that was exactly what he'd done.

Nori slid out of bed. Her underwear was ruined, so she pulled her slacks on without them. "I suppose I assumed—"

"I'm unseelie," he said. "Sex is only an avenue to magic, which you provided excellently. Thank you. I feel much better. It's otherwise meaningless."

"I wonder if Marion would agree," Nori said.

"You're not going to tell her. Pull the stick out of your ethereal ass, Nori. It's only sex." He rolled onto his belly, resting his chin on his hands. "Besides, you're the one who pointed out that Marion and I needed to get married."

But that was before Konig had done things to Nori that no man had done before—at least, not in those particular ways. She burned with humiliation to have thought it was special. Nori had hooked up with several sidhe in the Autumn

Court without making that mistake. Why was it different with Konig? Especially when the stakes were so high.

She pulled her shirt on over her head. She was composed again by the time her head popped out. "You're right."

He was an asshole, but he was right.

"It's a shame you're not the steward," Konig said as he watched her dress. "You're so much more reasonable than Marion." Nori wrapped herself in furs, pulling them around her chin to conceal her blushing. "My princess and I are lucky we'll have you as our lead advisor when we rule together."

Advisor to the rulers of the Winter Court? Well, there were worse things than that.

Better things too.

But she didn't have better things. She didn't have Konig, with the long line of his muscular back leading into his well-shaped posterior, which she had been admiring ever since she'd started working for the Autumn Court.

"I'll talk to Marion," Nori said. "I'm sure she'll come to her senses."

Konig swept the hair out of his face, shooting a smile at her that was pure sex. "Come here."

Hesitantly, she obeyed, bending over the bed to reach him. Konig's kiss sparked electricity over her lips. When she started to draw back, he held her in place with a hand on her throat.

"Thank you, Nori," he murmured against her lips.

Her heart was pounding when he released her.

Nori wasn't sure how she made it out of the king's bedroom, and she wasn't sure if anyone saw her leaving. Minutes later, she found herself in front of Marion's door unaware of how she'd gotten there and too numb to feel when she knocked.

Marion's voice echoed from within. "Enter."

Nori edged into the room.

Konig had selected one of the smaller bedrooms for Marion—not a set of royal rooms, but a special apartment where seelie children had once lived. It was the one place where trees could grow, and the air was at least twenty degrees.

The mage girl was sitting under one of those magicked trees, knees hugged to her chest, her hair frizzed from the moisture in the air.

Nori stood a few feet away, waiting to see if Marion would know what had happened. Marion had read Nori's mind more than once in the past.

Yet Marion seemed barely aware of Nori's presence, much less interested in her thoughts. "Gods, Nori," Marion said into her knees. "I'm so stupid. I'm so, so stupid."

Nori sat beside her. There was a time that Marion would have recoiled at having an ethereal Gray so close, but this lobotomized version of the steward leaned into Nori's touch.

Marion still wasn't herself. She wasn't the

woman that the Winter Court needed—or the woman that Konig needed, for that matter.

Nori took Marion's hand, trying to rub warmth into her chilly fingers. "Marion..."

She should have been talking Marion into wedding Konig.

It had been Nori's idea in the first place, after all. And she'd promised Konig she would help convince Marion. Even now, Nori believed that getting Konig on the throne beside Marion was best for everyone.

So why was it so hard to speak?

Marion lifted her head. Her eyes were puffy, cheeks wet. "Did you know that Seth wants to kill me?"

That wasn't remotely the direction that Nori had expected the conversation to take. "Are we talking metaphorically or literally?"

"Very, very literally," Marion said. "Genesis changed him, and it's given him these killing urges, which seem to be fixated on me. That's why he's so desperate to talk to the gods."

"So he's been using you," Nori said.

"No. That's the thing. He wouldn't even *tell* me what he needed. He's been keeping it a secret to try to protect me."

"Protect you from...him?"

"From whatever the stupid gods did to him," she said. "Why do you think he wouldn't have told me what he was struggling with?"

Nori imagined that was a rhetorical question, but she ventured a guess anyway, erring on righteous indignation on Marion's behalf. "Because he doesn't trust you?"

"It's not his fault. He's been alone for so long— he doesn't know how to trust anymore." She lifted the statuette she had been using to contact Nori. "Look at what I've been working on."

The statuette had changed. It no longer glowed with magic that spoke directly to Nori. It audibly hummed, glittering as though its surface had caught starlight.

"You changed the summoning spell," Nori said, startled. "I thought you didn't remember magic that complex."

"I don't, but the gods are guiding me," Marion said. "This statuette—it won't do anything from here, in the Winter Court. But if I get back to Sheol, I can use this to bring me here again. To my bedroom, specifically."

"How do you know that?"

Marion shook her head. "I just *do*. I'm meant to be with Seth in Sheol." She hurled her robe onto the bed and fumbled to grab her quiver. "If Konig won't take me back, I'll find someone who will."

"I'll take you," Nori said.

Marion's eyes filled with such hopeful light that it physically pained Nori. "You will?"

"Of course. I'm your assistant." She smiled tremulously. "I live to serve."

"Gods, you're the best." Marion slung her bow over her shoulders and crammed a pair of slender-armed spectacles onto the bridge of her nose. "But what about Konig?"

"Don't worry," Nori said. "I'll take care of *everything.*"

SIXTEEN

Seth's path through Duat was clear.

He walked on streets of crumbled obsidian, passing between buildings with empty windows. He sensed demons everywhere: behind the narrow alleys, within structures that might represent a marketplace, and lurking in the shadows beneath iron trees.

Duat had been recently filled with life. Trash blew through the streets, and lights extinguished in windows when he got near. The residents were hiding from Seth.

From the corner of his eye, he caught flashes of white. Every time he tried to focus, though, he didn't see anything.

The only white things he'd seen near Duat were the Hounds.

They were following Seth.

Hunting.

None attacked or even approached.

They *wanted* him to reach the temple, and the Canope within.

The Hounds and demons weren't the only ones who wanted Seth to reach the temple. He felt as though invisible hands were holding his shoulders. They pushed him ever forward, ensuring he couldn't change his mind and go back.

It was destiny propelling him onward.

He was meant to be there, in that moment, walking that exact path.

The fact that the dark environment felt so familiar to Seth was more disturbing than the spindly arches of the demon architecture. He'd never been to Hell before Genesis, and he certainly hadn't been to Sheol since. Seth had never specialized in demons. He'd been a werewolf hunter, and, eventually, a werewolf guardian.

Sheol should have been frightening.

It shouldn't have felt like a quiet homecoming.

The only problem was how lonely he felt. Destiny was satisfied to have him there, but he shouldn't have been on his own. Marion should have been locked to his side. Yin and yang, positive and negative, half-angel and...whatever Seth had become in Genesis.

But he didn't regret sending her away.

None of Duat's residents disturbed Seth on his long, winding path through the ghost town. Not until he reached the base of the temple.

There were seemingly thousands of crumbling

black steps bridging the distance between street and temple, but he couldn't start climbing. A figure stood in his path.

It was the gondolier again.

She lifted her hood, exposing a skull from which two curved horns grew. Shining opals dangled from the tips. Without the shadow of her hood, he could see that she had opals embedded along her cheekbones, too. A necklace of metal bones glimmered on chains looped around her neck.

He could now see her the way she may have looked in earlier days, before the illusion of a human form rotted away and left her a skeleton. She would have been a beautiful and noble demon.

Now she was a husk.

"Nyx, I take it," Seth said. She was the other Lord of Sheol that Arawn had been talking to on his palantír, and she'd been following Seth around ever since he'd entered the Nether Worlds.

"Goddess of Night, Lord of Sheol, Daughter of Phlegethon," Nyx said. "I am she. I've slept so long in wait for you."

Seth imagined that news should have surprised him, but he could still feel the pounding of fate within his veins.

Everything was predestined and nothing was unexpected.

"This is your final opportunity, Seth," Nyx said. "Turn back and leave. Leave the Canope. Forget its existence."

"I can't," he said.

Nyx drifted from the stairs, settling on the ground before him with a wave of smoke billowing out from her robe. She flashed bony legs as she glided forward. "I'll allow you to save the revenant if you leave the Canope."

"You will? Isn't Charity your prisoner?"

"She belongs to Arawn. My only interest in her is using the revenant as leverage to drive you from Sheol," Nyx said. "You must trust me when I say you should leave the Canope for your own good. I have your best interests at heart, Seth."

His name again.

It was like she knew him.

"Who *are* you?" he asked.

She flowed around him with the scent of brimstone. "You should ask who you are, not who I am. In the grand scheme, I am nothing."

"You know what happened to me in Genesis. You have answers."

"You wouldn't be satisfied to know them. You'll live in despair when you know the truth, lost in darkness deeper than any other within the Nether Worlds." Her bony fingers slid down his shoulders, her left horn brushing his hair as she bent closer to whisper in his ear. "You don't need to know the truth. You don't need the Canope. Leave and be satisfied knowing ignorance is best."

But then Marion would never have her memories back. She wouldn't be whole again.

"Would that be terrible?" Nyx asked, swimming behind him to whisper in the opposite ear. Her breath was the heat of a forge lit by magma.

Seth didn't think he'd spoken aloud. She was reading his thoughts in some way.

A powerful demon. Too powerful to trust.

He couldn't help but wonder, though. He'd been wondering it ever since they'd left Dana McIntyre's condo.

Would it be terrible to leave Marion without her memories?

He shook his head. "I need the Canope. It wouldn't be fair to leave her like this. She isn't herself." He turned to survey Nyx. Up close, he could see himself reflected in the gems in her skull.

Seth didn't fear her in the slightest.

In fact, strange feelings were stirring deep in his gut that resembled affection.

"I'm going to take Charity and the Canope to the Winter Court. It's a Middle World in eternal darkness," he said. "You might be able to survive there, if you wanted me to free you from Sheol."

She recoiled an inch. Even without facial muscles, he could tell she was surprised. "You think I need to be freed?"

"Don't you?"

"Sometimes I think I do." Her bony fingers traced a line down his cheek. "You've always been too kind a heart for the soul you've been given."

"You keep talking like you know me."

"But I do," Nyx said. "Surely you must wonder what became of us in the eternity of Genesis."

"Genesis was a moment." Seth knew she would argue with him, so he didn't give her the opportunity. "Come with me to the Winter Court."

Nyx seemed to consider the option. At least, it took her a long time to say, "No. It's too late, and I'm too old, for that to happen. But I'll show you to your friend. May she have the sense to avoid the Canope that you do not."

She turned and drifted away.

Seth followed.

The halls of Duat's temple weren't tall by sidhe standards, but compared to the rest of Sheol's structures, they towered. Seth's footfalls echoed throughout the rafters even though Nyx didn't make a sound. She had no feet to strike against the ground.

He practically bored holes into Nyx's back staring at her, trying to figure out how he could have known her.

Seth wasn't missing memories like Marion. He *wasn't*.

He'd been born to a werewolf hunter twenty-some years before Genesis. He'd grown up learning his father's business. Killed a couple werewolves before he started needing to shave. Dedicated his teen years to his werewolf girlfriend's ranch, and then gone to college for a pre-med degree.

There were no gaps in those memories, nor were there in the painful years that had followed his return from college. That was when Abel and Rylie had fallen in love, after all.

And then he had died.

Every memory since his return after Genesis was intact, too—painfully so. Seth didn't forget things the way he used to. He had no trouble recalling the most inane details of medical school and job-hunting while pretending to be Lucas Flynn.

Nyx was nowhere in those memories.

The only blank spot in his mind was that year between the Breaking and Genesis. But nothing had happened then. He'd been dead.

And Genesis had been only a moment.

Nyx led Seth to a door in the hallway. The arching frame had stone horns at its peak. "He's put her in here," she said, slithering backward to allow Seth to push the door open.

Inside, he found a spacious but empty room of stone. The walls were covered in murals depicting the Hounds.

Seth stopped inside the door. The only creature inside that room was tall, lanky, demonic-looking—a hideous thing facing the windows.

It turned at the sound of him. Though the features were frightening, he knew them, just as he knew the glasses that were tucked into the neck of the revenant's shirt.

That was no demon.

"Charity," Seth said.

"Oh gods, Seth." Charity fell onto him, embracing him so tightly that he could barely breathe. It was nothing to do with revenant strength and everything to do with his relief at finding her whole. He'd expected to find her on a meat hook by that point.

"Are you okay?" he asked, holding her at arm's length to study her vampiric form. "Did he hurt you?"

She shook her head over and over again. It was strange to see such a nervous gesture from such a monstrous creature. "I don't think he ever planned on it. You shouldn't have come for me."

"I couldn't leave you here," Seth said. "Get the glamour on and let's go."

Charity's monstrous face fell. "Put the glamour *on*? Why?"

She looked so crestfallen that he instantly felt guilty. "I mean...we're going to the Winter Court the instant we've got our hands on the Canope. You're not subtle like this."

"Maybe I don't want to be subtle anymore," Charity said.

Seth had seen her like this before, and there had still been no bracing himself for her appearance. People who didn't expect it would most likely scream and run. That was what everyone had done after seeing her outside of the United Nations, after all. She hadn't even had to attack to cause a stampede in the crowd.

Even so, the Winter Court would be better equipped to deal with it than the mundane world.

"Okay, it's fine," Seth said. "We'll talk about this later. Let's go."

"There isn't anything to talk about," Charity said.

That was up for debate, but a debate he didn't want to deal with at the moment. He pulled her toward the door.

Charity stopped when she saw Nyx.

Seth rubbed Charity's arm comfortingly. "It's okay. She's on our side—kind of. She wants me to get you out of here."

Nyx remained floating silently in the hallway, watching them expectantly.

"But?" Charity asked without taking another step to the door.

"She doesn't want me to have the Canope," Seth said. "And she's hoping you'll agree with her."

"The Canope is a trap," Nyx finally said.

"Yeah," Charity said, "it is."

Which was when the trap sprung.

"Look at what we've got here." Arawn emerged from the opposite side of the room, sauntering out of the shadows. He had changed into a corset cinching his body tight from underarms to hips, which Seth imagined must have been holding his shredded body together. He dragged a long leather train behind him, walking on boots with six-inch platforms. "You weren't going to leave me, were you, Charity?"

Seth pushed the revenant behind his back. "We don't have to fight, Arawn. I'm happy to leave peacefully."

"You don't leave at all," Arawn said. "Not with her. She's *mine*." The demon surveyed Seth with opaque eyes. "You still haven't gone for the Canope. Why not? It's not far."

"I brought him to save his friend." Nyx slid in from the hallway.

What little good humor had been in Arawn's face vanished when he saw her. "Are you such a miserable, petty asshole that you have to fight me every step of the way?" He turned to Charity. "And you—I thought we were getting somewhere."

It was weird for Seth to have a revenant even taller than he was trying to cower behind his back. "You kidnapped me," Charity said.

The demon lord's face spasmed. "But..."

Rage came over him like starlight after nightfall. Arawn's switchblade appeared in his hand.

He hurled himself at Seth.

Nyx billowed through the room, blocking both Seth and Charity from Arawn's attack. Through her semitransparent body, Seth saw Arawn's arm, knife and all, get caught in her ribs.

"You won't hurt him," Nyx said.

"Watch me," Arawn said.

He wrenched his arm free and stabbed again. Nyx evaded the blow a second time, wrapping herself around Arawn so that he was consumed in shadow.

Seth was tempted to leave while they were distracted. But Nyx registered actual pain when Arawn stabbed her. She wasn't merely an incorporeal puff of smoke. She was a demon who had been nothing but kind to Seth, and she was struggling.

But the two Lords of Sheol were only growing

in power. For the first time, Seth glimpsed the true depth of Arawn's abilities. He'd hidden them fighting Konig to humor the sidhe rules, but against Nyx, after such a long grudge, he held nothing back.

White flame crashed against shadow. Arawn's presence erupted from his body, and it quickly became even more massive than Nyx's. Seth recognized the shape of it: the long, spindly legs, the arching neck, the red-tipped ears. At his core, Arawn was the biggest of the Hounds, and his maw was filled with endless teeth.

The entire temple shivered. Obsidian groaned. Distant bells chimed discordantly, making the floor roll underneath Seth's feet. He staggered and almost fell.

"You won't control me ever again!" Arawn roared through a mouth bigger than the temple, bigger than the universe.

His jaw yawned wider, exposing the tunnel to his stomach. He bowed over Nyx.

And he began to swallow.

Seth struggled to reach Nyx's side. He didn't know what he could do—he didn't think his guns would work against Arawn any more than they had worked against the Hounds. But he had to do something. *Anything*.

Nyx's hollow eyes met Seth's through the ghost of Arawn's Hound form.

"Don't," she said. Despite Arawn's growling, which was so loud that it drowned out even the bells, Seth heard her voice clearly. It was as though she spoke from within him. "Leave without the Canope."

Those were her final words.

She stopped struggling.

Arawn's mouth snapped shut on Nyx.

In a blink, the giant Hound vanished, and Arawn stood in the center of an empty room. He looked like a man once more.

Arawn lifted his black eyes slowly to Charity and Seth, wiping the blood off of his bottom lip with the back of his hand. "So," Arawn said, "what were we talking about before Nyx interrupted us?"

SEVENTEEN

The Canope was a ceramic jar so nondescript that Seth wouldn't have looked at it twice were it not the most mundane-looking thing in the Temple of Duat. Statues of long-legged dogs were posed on either side of it, staring at the jar with blank-eyed wonder. The air around the Canope buzzed enough to make the wall beyond seem blurry.

The pedestal was the crowning feature of the hypostyle hall, filled by stylized columns fashioned like trees, mountains, and clouds as imagined by a tormented artist. The reliefs on the walls depicted wailing demons. Everything was jagged and black—except for that jar.

Death is Death, Nyx had said.

Seth could easily imagine some kind of death god ruling from that temple.

The Canope was an obvious mismatch, not

only in visual styling, but also in its energy. Seth could smell a faint hint of burning oak and lavender. It was Marion's distinctive scent.

What the jar held was clearly ethereal in origin, not infernal.

"Is this what you wanted?" Arawn asked, wandering along the edge of the room with visible amusement.

He'd readily led them to the innermost sanctum of the temple. Nyx's body had barely begun to cool when Arawn had happily shown Seth and Charity the path.

"This is such a trap," Charity muttered from behind Seth.

Seth didn't need to be told so many times. It was true.

That didn't change one damn thing about the situation.

"I'm going to take it," Seth said.

Arawn yawned. "Oh no, please don't."

Seth mounted the stairs leading toward the altar. The air became thicker as he drew closer, as though the Canope were pushing back at him, begging him in the voice of Nyx not to touch it.

It was a trap. He *knew* it was a trap, and he still pushed through, reaching his hands toward the jar.

"Don't," Charity whimpered from behind him.

The jar was a hundred miles away yet only inches from his fingertips.

The temple faded and Marion's memories swirled around Seth. Everything she had forgotten flashed like fireworks as wispy knowledge flitted through his mind. He understood magic on a level that he had never understood before—on a level no witch but Marion could.

For a few seconds, Seth thought he might even understand French.

He pushed through the torrent of memory and kept pushing until his fingertips brushed hardened clay. It was heavy—so very heavy, heavier than anything else he'd tried to move before, as though it were affixed to that exact point in the universe and couldn't be broken free.

But Seth hadn't come that far to be stopped.

He wrapped his hands around the body of the jar and pulled.

The universe shifted like it had every time he'd touched Marion's skin.

Destiny smashed through Duat. He felt it in every atom of his bones and every hair on his body.

Time was changing. Every single world was changing.

Seth hugged the jar to his chest as he fell, tumbling through eons of existence. He saw the garden that Marion had talked about—the one with the big trees and the blue light. He saw a brown-skinned boy with curly hair and a friendly smile. He saw Marion knocking on doors, and he saw those doors opening to reveal worlds Seth hadn't been able to imagine until that moment.

He fell. He kept falling.

There was no bottom.

He saw the time that Marion had gotten shot in the ribs with an arrow by one of Konig's guards. He felt her excitement at the wound. Her exhilaration.

He saw Marion soaring through the clouds, riding an ultra-light airplane that glittered with magic, and her laugh of joy swelled within Seth's chest.

All of the faces that Marion had seen in her life sparked on the edges of Seth's vision, too. Family members, like Dana and Nori. Politicians who had been subjected to Marion's teenage whims. Friends from the werewolf sanctuary.

And the Alpha, Rylie Gresham.

Even in Marion's memories, Rylie was a shy, radiant woman. But there was mistrust in her eyes, which Rylie had never once directed toward Seth.

Rylie didn't like Marion. And Marion had known that.

It was no secret to Marion that she was widely loathed.

Seth kept falling down the stairs, but he never let go of the Canope, even when it heated to a thousand degrees within his arms and shook so hard that he thought his bones would break.

If the jar shattered, Marion would be lost—all of her memories and the answers that went along with them.

But holding on to it was a struggle. Her magic was endless. She was so much more powerful than he ever could've dreamed.

It was easy to see why everyone hated her. That much power had made her a god on Earth, without any of the wisdom one would hope a god to possess. As a mage, Marion had the ability to reach out and change anything that she wanted.

And she had.

She had influenced elections, ordered world leaders to do her bidding, made a sidhe prince fall in love with her.

It was all in the Canope. Every last instant of it.

After a hundred years, Seth slammed into the floor at Arawn's feet.

Joy filled the demon's face. Even his black eyes didn't seem to be quite as flat as they'd been until that moment. "Here comes the sun," he said softly.

Seth frowned up at him, confused. "What?"

Dogs howled.

Their cries drifted through the temple, echoing off of the walls and rattling throughout Seth's mind.

"The Hounds are coming," Arawn said, backing away. "They're tied to the Canope. You stole it, and they'll want you dead." He was almost giddy, his words closer to song than speech. "You're almost dead, and then...they'll take me. They'll let me go to Earth."

"What have you done?" Charity asked.

Arawn extended his hand toward her. "I've cleared my path to sunlight. Join me."

She shook her head slowly as the yipping of the Hounds grew.

They were coming for Seth. He needed to run.

Seth staggered to his feet, and Arawn stood back to let him get up. The Lord of Sheol didn't need to attack. A white dog had appeared at the entrance to the hallway, and its eyes were fixed on the Canope within Seth's arm.

Seth grabbed Charity. "Run!"

They bolted out the back door of the temple. Seth didn't drop his grip on the revenant's elbow. He clung to her and focused on Earth, on sunlight and rain and actual, living grass that was touched by the brush of time, and he tried to teleport.

But nothing happened.

He still couldn't leave Sheol.

"What are you doing?" Charity cried desperately. "We need to leave!"

"I'm trying!"

Seth refocused. If they couldn't get all the way back to Earth with the Canope, then he could at least teleport to the hive, where the Hounds wouldn't be able to reach them.

Reality twisted around them.

They disappeared from the temple's hallway and reappeared a few feet down.

He couldn't leave Duat.

By the time Seth realized what had happened, the Hounds had appeared at the doorway, only a dozen feet behind them. There were six of them now that he could see.

Charity all but yanked Seth off of his feet. "Don't stop!"

They raced through the darkness of the temple and broke out above Duat.

The city was no longer empty.

Shadowy demons packed the streets, as though they'd sensed Nyx's defeat. They came in a thousand forms: some huge, some small, some little more than smoke, some multi-legged and frightening. They crashed toward the temple in a black tide.

They were going to block Seth's exit from the temple.

"How do we get out?" he asked.

Charity looked around. "That way!"

She wrenched him down another hall, toward the back of the temple where demons had yet to reach.

The Canope jostled in his arms. Some of Marion's essence hummed out of the jar.

For an instant, Seth was trapped in the mage's memory, looking through her eyes. In the memory, Marion had been confronting her half-sister, Elise. The woman who had once been known as Godslayer, but had now become God. "I won't do it," Marion had said.

Elise had glared at her half-sister. "You want to rethink your answer?"

"No. If a man doesn't want to be found, it's for good reason. You disrespect him by refusing to acknowledge his wishes." Marion had been at peak form, drenched in her own arrogance.

"You can't side with him," Elise said. "You don't even know him. I'm family and you do what I tell you."

"Just as you always did what Isaac told you?"

Elise had slapped Marion. Hard. Right across the face.

The contact had been physical, though Elise's form had not. She'd been an imaginary figure standing in a garden that drifted among the stars —god stuff that Seth's mortal mind couldn't begin to interpret. But the pain of the slap had been very, very real.

It had only been the beginning.

"You little shit," Elise had said.

Pain jolted through Seth's physical body, dragging him out of Marion's memory. His toe had caught on an uneven tile at the edge of a staircase in Duat. He tripped, stumbled, and rolled down the stairs.

He stopped at the bottom, surrounded by shadowy demons. They receded from him and the Canope he clutched.

No, not from Seth—but from the Hounds that chased him.

Charity descended upon him. "Doctor!"

Seth shoved the Canope into Charity's arms. "Get it out of Duat. I'll divert the Hounds."

She clung to the Canope, despair twisting her features. "But Seth—"

"Run! For the love of God, *run!*"

Charity didn't need to be told again. She left.

And when Seth ran in the other direction, taking a path perpendicular to the temple's entrance, the Hounds followed him.

He was the thief. The one that the trap had been set for.

They wanted *him.*

As Nyx had said, that was the whole point.

Seth couldn't run fast enough like this, not when he could barely teleport more than a few feet at a time. He felt sluggish and weak.

Worse, even he could feel Marion's memories rattling around inside of him.

"Hit me all you want," Marion had said with blood trickling down her lip, glaring in defiance at the god known as Elise. "If this Seth Wilder guy doesn't want you to find him, then I won't help you look! You're deities. That doesn't mean you have to be assholes."

Elise had said, "If you won't choose to do it, I can make you."

"I'd like to see you try," Marion had said.

And Elise had.

Damn it all, Elise had *forced* Marion to find Seth Wilder.

She'd stripped away Marion's memories, leaving nothing behind but Seth's name. And then Elise had given all that she took away to Dana McIntyre along with the instructions to deliver that essence unto Sheol.

The Canope was a trap so much worse than Seth could have imagined, because it had been set by the gods.

For some reason, Elise wanted Seth dead.

He was beyond screwed.

Seth leaped behind an old apartment building, hoping that the path would be narrow enough to keep the Hounds from following. It didn't work. The Hounds were behind him. They were white ghosts in the darkness, flashes of light.

He couldn't run as fast as them. They were ideas, and he was only a man.

Somehow, he managed to reach the walls of Duat before they did. The Bronze Gates were still open. Mnemosyne waited on the other side.

He raced between the two layers of walls protecting Duat. The warlock runes hadn't been reset, so there was nothing to set fire to the Hounds who chased him.

When he reached the grass, he hurled himself down the hill.

Seth struck Mnemosyne with a splash.

The waters of the river were impossibly cold compared to the muggy warmth of the rest of Sheol. They swallowed him whole, flooding his nose and ears, weighing down his clothes. He clamped his jaw shut to make sure he swallowed nothing.

Through the fluctuating surface of the river, he could see the white forms of the Hounds stopping on the bank.

They wouldn't follow him into the water.

Seth sank and kept on sinking.

Swim, dammit. Swim.

His feet connected with something firm. He pushed off, pumping his arms in long strokes. He kicked off his shoes as he went. They only weighed him down.

He surfaced long enough to gasp air, and then submerged again.

It had only taken a few moments for Nyx to cross the river in her gondola. Seth felt like he was swimming for days. His muscles burned with exhaustion—which was strange, because he couldn't remember the last time he'd been tired in such a way. The changes that Genesis had forced upon him seemed to have left him preternaturally energized.

Mnemosyne was preternatural too. It was deep and wide and immense in dimensions Seth couldn't fathom.

His foot struck something solid again, and again. He was too high in the river for it to be the bottom.

Seth looked down.

There was no riverbed. Only bodies layered upon bodies, all of them preserved in the icy water, gaping up at him with eyes rolled back to show the whites.

Their arms drifted above them, as though reaching for Seth.

He'd accidentally kicked one in the head.

Seth's mouth opened in a silent cry of shock. A bubble escaped him, and water rushed in.

The instant he tasted it, he was struck by memories.

These didn't originate from Marion's essence in the Canope—wherever the hell that had ended up. They originated from some murky, forgotten place within Seth, shadowier than the Dead Forest and more remote than Duat.

He remembered standing on the edge of the Pit of Souls. It was a chasm so broad that he couldn't see the other side and so deep there was no sign of the bottom. If Seth had fallen into it, he'd have had miles to tumble.

Nyx stood beside him in this memory. He knew it was Nyx even though skin covered her skull. She looked like an older woman with stringy gray hair, which had been arranged into an artful bun between her gem-decorated horns.

Death is Death, Nyx had said. *Arawn can only inherit the Pit of Souls if Death steps down.*

And Seth had said, *Or if Death disappears.*

He shocked out of the strange vision of the Pit of Souls when his body washed against the ground.

Had he reached the opposite shore of Mnemosyne?

Seth barely had enough time to push himself up onto his hands before he realized he'd gone the wrong way. He hadn't reached the Dead Forest. He hadn't even left Duat's hill. He'd only managed to end up a few hundred yards down the river.

He vomited cascades of water out of his stomach, but it was too late to clear the river's influence from his system. He had already drunk from Mnemosyne—the river of memory, he now recalled—and he was beginning to reach memories he hadn't realized he had lost.

Death is Death.

Nyx had been truly beautiful before she had withered away.

Seth tried to stand and failed. He needed to run before the Hounds located him again.

You are Death, Seth.

A projectile slammed into him from behind. Seth was driven face-first into the dry grass.

The Hounds were on him.

He rolled over. Heavy paws weighed against his ribs, his spine. Jaws opened wide to reveal so many teeth.

No matter how hard he swung his fists, no matter how much he kicked his feet, the Hounds didn't react. They dug in to devour his mortal flesh and strip it from his bones.

Seth was dying, and the gods were satisfied.

Nori dropped Marion inside the twin walls of the Bronze Gates.

Neither of them took the transition into the Nether Worlds well. They arrived gasping, lungs burning, flesh boiling.

Marion spent the first several seconds on the ground with her eyes shut, struggling to remember how to breathe. Her chest burned. Inhaling hurt. The lingering remnants of Arawn's potions continued to race through her veins, but it wasn't enough. Not anymore.

"Go back," Marion gasped.

Nori shook her head. Her eyes were watering and a line of blood trickled out of her left nostril. She had angel blood, just as Marion did, and she hadn't had any of the potion.

She would die within minutes.

"I'm sorry," Nori said.

She blinked out of Sheol.

Marion forced herself onto her feet, clutching the statuette. It hummed with the power she had borrowed. The magic was reassuring. It was her ticket to return safely to the Winter Court, where she would be able to breathe.

But not until she found Seth.

It took a moment to orient herself and realize that guards were rushing toward Marion's position. She had materialized not far from the place Konig had taken her. She could see the temple where the Canope had been hidden atop the hill.

She jammed the statuette into her pocket.

A pair of guards reached her. The left one yelled, "Stop!"

"No," Marion said.

She nocked an arrow quickly, drew the fletchings back to her cheek, and released.

The arrow flew true.

It punched into the left-hand demon's throat and passed through. He fell, clutching at the new hole underneath his chin. He gurgled as blood dribbled between his fingers.

Before he'd hit the ground, Marion had drawn and fired another arrow.

The second guard dropped.

Still, they kept coming. Marion backed up as she continued to shoot, targeting throats and chests and even foreheads. It was different shooting arrows at living creatures rather than the targets at the Autumn Court. These things were moving and breathing. They wailed when she struck them.

Marion reached for another arrow, but the quiver was empty. She hadn't brought enough.

Yet more guards were coming.

"Don't kill her!" said one demon to his companion. "Arawn wants her."

Marion lifted her hands. "Tell him to get me himself." Electricity rippled down her arms and lightning arced between her fingertips.

Ethereal magic was dull in the Nether Worlds, where it wasn't meant to function. But even her dull magic was far brighter than Konig's. It flowed from her in waves.

She shoved the guards away with lightning and wind. They flew off of their feet. Both of them punched into a building, and the force made it collapse.

Marion whirled on the guards who were coming from another street. There were crowds of demons beyond them, gathered near the temple like maggots on a corpse. She flung lightning at them too. It burned a path up the road, clearing a route to the temple.

It was amazing what magic Marion could perform once she knew she needed to get back to Seth. The desperation was a special kind of motivation. She didn't require memories when she had driving, powerful *need*.

When another creature ran at her, she prepared more bolts of lightning.

"Marion, wait!"

The demons shouldn't have known her name.

She dropped her hands, and as the light from

her magic dimmed, her eyes adjusted. Something resembling a gangly corpse ran toward her.

"Charity?" Marion asked. "Where's Seth?"

The revenant unfolded her arms. "I lost him. I'm sorry," she said as a large ceramic jar was revealed, a plain, clay-colored thing that was shaped like a lidded vase. "Seth gave it to me and told me to run."

Marion reached for the Canope reflexively, but drew her hands back. The Canope didn't belong to her. It *was* her. Everything trapped inside those ceramic walls was something that had come out of Marion's soul. She was entitled to it in the way that she was entitled to her own body.

Yet she feared the way it tugged at her. As soon as her eyes rested on it, Marion knew that the Canope was what had been calling to ever since she'd arrived in Duat.

She wasn't sure she was ready to become who she used to be.

Charity drew back an inch, keeping Marion from touching the Canope. "Arawn's Hounds are tied to this thing. They're chasing Seth because he stole it. I don't know what they'll do if you try to take the Canope back."

"The Hounds are chasing Seth?" Marion's hesitation evaporated. She yanked the Canope away from Charity. "Where is he?"

She'd barely gotten the words out when the power overwhelmed her.

The magic of the jar was more immense than any other Marion had experienced. Touching it was physically painful.

Marion was inside the jar, outside the jar.

The Canope was everything.

It took a miracle of willpower not to fling the jar away from herself.

Only Dana's warning—that if the Canope broke, then Marion's essence would evaporate—kept her gripping it, even when it made her palms feel like they were burning off.

"Seth and I split paths at the temple," Charity said. "I don't know where he is now. The Hounds —"

"I'll find him," Marion said. She shifted the Canope into one arm so that she could take the statuette out of her pocket. She gave it to Charity. "Use this to go to the Winter Court. Tell Konig and Nori what happened. Tell them..." What? That Marion had left again, chasing the doctor into Sheol? Konig would be thrilled to hear *that*. "I need Konig's help."

"How do I use it?" Charity asked, clutching the statuette in both fists.

Marion rested her hands atop Charity's. She shut her eyes and focused.

Magic jolted between them.

Once Marion opened her eyes again, Charity was gone, and she was alone with the shimmering Canope.

She lifted the jar to study it. The lid was affixed firmly to the top, as though it had been baked into one solid piece. Marion was certain that couldn't be the case. The Canope was a thing of magic, and there would be a magical way to open it.

There was no time to figure it out at the moment. Marion could battle with magical artifacts and her sudden reluctance to restore her memories later.

Seth needed her.

Marion flung her magic into Duat, searching for his presence. He wasn't within the Bronze Gates. She kept reaching out with fingers of power. She mentally leaped over the warlock runes between the walls and combed the world beyond.

That was where she felt him. He was on the shore of Mnemosyne.

"I'm coming," she said, knowing he wouldn't be able to hear.

Marion raced through the Bronze Gates. She traveled safely between the two doorways, since no one had relaid the incendiary warlock runes since her first arrival, and erupted onto the hillside breathing hard.

Mnemosyne frothed at the edge of the grass. It had been so calm when Marion had last seen it, but now it looked like it was on the brink of flooding.

She couldn't see Seth anywhere.

Marion was certain she had felt him outside the Bronze Gates.

The sound of dogs yipping echoed from around the corner. Her heart leaped, but the sounds weren't growing closer—the Hounds weren't hunting her. They weren't even on the move.

They'd already caught their prey.

Marion slid down the embankment to see a dozen white Hounds digging into some hapless prey animal, something mutilated and dead. She clutched the Canope tighter to her chest. She took two steps back.

Then one of the dogs shifted, and she saw a sodden foot between its legs. Once she saw it, she instinctively reached out with her magic again, searching for Seth. And she felt him.

A ragged cry ripped from Marion's chest.

That piece of meat—that raw, bloodied body—was Seth. The doctor. The man who'd saved her a thousand times.

He was dying.

But he wasn't quite dead. If he had been, Marion wouldn't have been able to feel him anymore.

"Stop!" Marion cried to the Hounds.

They didn't hear her, or else they simply didn't care.

She lifted the Canope above her head. "I told you to *stop!*"

The motion made one of the Hounds look at her briefly before returning its attention to mauling Seth.

Marion didn't even consider the risks. She didn't weigh her life against Seth's, or whether or not her plan would work, or what she would be losing. She didn't wonder if she'd even be able to survive without her memories.

She hurled the Canope to the ground.

It shattered into a hundred pieces, and kept shattering. A thousand fragments, and then a million, a billion—they sprayed across the grass in diamond shards before dissipating.

The Hounds stopped mauling Seth. They all lifted their heads as one, jaws stained by his blood.

Marion felt the weight of two dozen haunting canine eyes on her.

Charity had warned Marion that the Hounds were tied to the Canope. They had hunted Seth because he'd stolen it. What would they do to the woman who had destroyed the thing?

"Come and get me," she whispered.

And they did.

EIGHTEEN

Seth was dying, and it hurt. Few things had hurt in the last thirteen years.

It hadn't hurt when he'd gotten a tattoo of a caduceus right above his hipbone. That had been little more than a numb tickling.

It hadn't hurt when a drunken patient had attacked him, unleashing werewolf power on Seth in the Mercy Hospital emergency department.

It hadn't even hurt when he'd accidentally rested a hand on an active burner on the stove at home. He hadn't healed with preternatural speed because there'd been nothing to heal.

Nothing hurt.

That was another of the weird symptoms demonstrating that he'd changed after Genesis, similar to teleportation or the inability to age. Seth didn't hurt anymore. He didn't hurt, he didn't love, he didn't feel *anything*.

But Arawn's Hounds ripping him apart hurt. It hurt a lot.

Their teeth shredding into his skin, shattering his bones, gnawing on the meat...

It hurt.

Seth hadn't been in that much pain in a long time, and he didn't know how to deal with it anymore. All he could do was scream and scream and scream. He loosed his agony into the universe because it was so much easier than trying to trap it inside.

Teeth scraped against his liver.

Pain.

Yet there was another level to that pain.

Every pinch of a nerve, every tearing scrap of flesh, felt like it was unlocking something within his skull.

One Hound snapped its head back with a chunk of flesh so large that it included Seth's bellybutton. He could see into the dog's brain as though fur and flesh had turned transparent. He knew that the Hound was a living thing, and he knew that it was going to die in exactly seven minutes and twenty-eight seconds.

The Hound's death loomed like the Genesis void.

Seven minutes and twenty-one seconds.

Tick-tock.

Another Hound clamped its jaws on one of Seth's small ribs. With a vicious twist of its head, the bone snapped free of his spine.

That Hound was not due to die for years to come.

It would be killed by an archer. A woman hunting with a bow. The arrow would plunge into its heart, and it would fall among the roots of the Dead Forest, immediately consumed by the hungry fingers of the foliage.

His mind continued to expand as the pain swelled.

Seth was dying, and in his death, he saw every other death in the universe.

The Hounds were nearest, so he saw what would happen to all of them. Every death was ugly. Brutal. Some were within minutes or days, others were within years or even centuries. Regardless of when it would happen, he knew that it *would* happen, as certainly as he knew that the sun would rise on Earth the next morning.

Seth's mind brushed against a watching soul.

His eyes rolled in his skull. He focused on a human figure standing atop the hill near the Bronze Gates.

She was tall, slender, graceful. She had a heart-shaped face framed by brown curls and eerily bright eyes that might have been mistaken for blue.

It can't be Marion.

Seth had told Konig to take her back to the Winter Court, where she would be safe. Where the harsh environment of the Nether Worlds couldn't damage her purer ethereal system.

Yet he *felt* her. The Hounds stripped his skin

286

away to expose his organs and Seth felt that Marion was real—that she had returned, that she was alive for the moment, although Death was on the horizon of her existence.

She was clutching the Canope against her chest.

"Stop!" she cried, her voice echoing off of grassy planes.

Seth wanted to tell her something similar.

Stop. Leave. Run away.

The Hounds weren't interested in her presence, even though Seth was so painfully aware of Marion's nearness that it overrode the sensation of being eaten. The whole universe could have been coming apart at the seams and he still would have been able to feel Marion there.

The Hounds didn't care. They had what they wanted.

But what they wanted wasn't what Seth had expected.

He was dying, yes. But Seth's death was only the erosion of a mortal form. When he lifted his head an inch to look down at himself, he realized that the dogs were exposing a lot more than anonymous human meat, like the bodies dangling from Arawn's hooks.

They were exposing Seth's truth.

His energy.

There was so much more to Seth than a human body. That physical form was no more than a prison of flesh containing his essence, just as the Canope contained Marion.

He wasn't dying. He was transcending.

That wasn't what Marion seemed to be seeing. Her beautiful face was twisted with horror.

She lifted the Canope above her head.

Seth opened his mouth to tell her to stop, but he couldn't speak. One of the Hounds was gnawing on his diaphragm.

Marion hurled the Canope to the ground.

It shattered.

The magic binding the Hounds to the Canope activated again. Not because it had been stolen this time, but because it had been destroyed.

Their protective instinct flared to life. Every single one of those red-eared heads lifted to focus on Marion.

Through his hazy vision, Seth could see Marion's defiant despair. She was crying. "Come and get me," she said so softly that her voice barely reached his ears.

No. Don't. Stop.

The Hounds leaped for her.

Marion tried to run, to her credit—but she must have known that it wasn't going to work. She'd seen how quickly the Hounds could move.

She only made it a handful of steps before they descended on her.

For all that being mauled had hurt him, watching them rip Marion apart was even worse.

No...

Seth's muscles had been pulled apart fiber by fiber, half of his guts swallowed by Arawn's hounds, with so much blood dribbling into

Mnemosyne that his heart shouldn't have been able to beat. Yet the frailty of his human form didn't seem to matter. He rolled onto his hands and knees, and the pain receded, growing more distant.

Strength of body had been replaced by strength of soul.

Marion's screaming shook the trees.

"No," he said, this time aloud.

He got to his feet. Seth's organs dangled from the cavity that the Hounds had dug below his breastbone. Shredded large intestine dangled over his right thigh, but it didn't matter. The waterfalls of blood didn't matter. The missing spleen didn't matter.

Marion's death hovered as her screaming became strangled. A Hound began to drag her body away, teeth digging into her delicate wrist, where once her pulse had beat so strongly.

He stepped forward. One foot after another.

"Get away from her," he said.

The Hounds reacted to his voice the way they'd reacted to nothing but the Canope, shying away from Marion's body as he approached. They cowered. Heads tilted, legs bowed, tails tucked. Seth had spent enough time around werewolves to recognize signs of submission.

Seth stretched his hands out the way that he had reached for the Canope to seize it. His fingertips brushed the wiry white fur of the nearest dog.

Its skin peeled open. Jaws split. Eyes burst.

In an instant, it was dead. It hadn't required a single thought from Seth. Merely the faint desire to save Marion.

The rest of the Hounds fled.

Even the idea of mortality that they represented couldn't stand up to Death himself.

And then Seth was alone with what remained of Marion.

Even in the confusing, better-than-mortal state that Seth had entered, he was horrified. "Marion," he said, falling to his knees beside her. The name was uttered in a thousand dimensions, across every world that existed.

Her heart was beating every few seconds now. Her right eye was shut. Her left eye had been torn free.

"No. *No.*" Seth pulled her into his lap, even though his medical training told him that was one of the worst things he could do. One of the Hounds had been gnawing on her spine after she crumpled. It had snapped her neck. Moving her would only cause more damage.

What did that matter now? Seth could see the end all over Marion.

She was on the precipice of oblivion, but regardless of whatever powers Seth was assuming, he couldn't heal.

Marion was going to die.

He cradled her in his arms—her fragile mortal body, tall and lean, gushing crimson from the wound in her throat—and bowed over her body, pressing his lips to her hair. She smelled like the smoke of distant campfires drifting over the mountains, all tangled up with pine and sun-warmed grapes and lavender.

This was his last chance to smell it.

"Take her soul."

Seth's head snapped up. Nyx stood over him, even more translucent than she'd been before. She was little more than the idea of a ghost.

"You're dead," Seth said.

"So are you," Nyx said. "Take her soul to the other side. End her suffering as she once ended the suffering of Elena Eiderman."

Seth was so wracked with despair that it took him a moment to understand. Mrs. Eiderman had been a patient in Ransom Falls—his last patient. She'd been an old woman dying of lycanthropy. It had been slow and painful until Marion eased the end with her ethereal magic.

The magic had been beautiful, but it had been a distinct ending. Elena Eiderman was gone. And Nyx wanted Seth to end Marion in that same way.

"Help me save her," he said. "Please."

"That's beyond my ken," Nyx said. "My only power is in death, and even that is a mere shadow of what you do. You have to walk her to the other side."

Marion's heart wasn't beating.

The power lurking within him wanted her to die, but he was more than the infernal forces that had seized him. He was Seth Wilder: the only human man to ever run a werewolf pack; a doctor with an oath to heal, not harm; friend to Marion

Garin, a helpless and hopeless innocent.

"I won't do it," Seth said.

"Neither of us needs to take action. Once it's time for her to walk, she'll walk," Nyx said gently. "We can only make it easier."

He intended to ask what Nyx meant by "walk," since it was clear that Marion wasn't going anywhere. She was utterly limp in his lap.

But then fog lifted from her chest. It pooled in the air above her nose and mouth.

Her soul was going to walk to the other side.

Nyx touched his shoulder so lightly that he could barely feel the tap of bone upon his injured flesh. Her demon mind connected to his. He saw what it would take to guide someone into death: how simple it was to open pathways between life and oblivion.

"Take her through the Dead Forest," Nyx said.

Was that all he could do for Marion now? Make it easier to die?

Seth stood with Marion hanging from his arms. At least, some part of him stood—not his shattered body, which remained hugged around Marion's equally broken form, but his soul tangled with hers. Power reaching for power. Life with life.

He stood and Marion flitted away.

"Wait," he said.

The ghost of the girl smiled at him with eyes vacant of understanding, and she ran across Mnemosyne without her feet ever contacting water. She disappeared through the trees.

"Take her," Nyx urged.

When Seth turned to the demon, he was shocked to see that the shrouded, skeletal creature had been replaced by a beautiful woman of human features. She was even more beautiful than he had remembered when they had stood at the edge of the Pit of Souls together. Diamonds studded fleshy cheeks. Plump lips curved into a loving bow. Her black eyes were filled with as much compassion as there was chaos.

Nyx was a black woman with gnarly curls that sprayed in every direction, enhancing a noble jaw, strong shoulders, a tiny waist. Filmy veils flowed from her hips.

She was a Lord of Sheol as much as Arawn, but she was the kind of lord that anyone would have bowed to in relieved submission, knowing that they were in maternal hands. She represented the tragic mirror image of birth. Everyone who was born had to die, and Nyx attended with love.

The demon gestured toward Marion's retreating form, and said again, "Don't let her be alone."

Alarm clawed within Seth. "I won't let her go at all."

He tossed aside all that was physical and chased her.

After all, in his glimpses of Marion's memories whilst he bore the Canope, he had seen the truth.

Elise had wanted Marion to seek out Seth. Why had Seth been hiding from her in the first place? He didn't know. The particulars were neither relevant nor surprising. Before Genesis,

Seth's relationship with Elise had never been better than fraught.

Marion hadn't known Seth at the time, but she had defended him from Elise. The Voice of God had tried to protect Seth from the intervention of deities.

Now that Seth was bleeding his life onto the ground of the Dead Forest without actually dying, he thought he could guess as to why. Elise had changed him, and she'd wanted to possess him, like Dr. Frankenstein with her monster.

But Marion had protected Seth—more than once now.

Dammit, she deserved better than death.

Seth raced into the trees.

"Marion!"

There was power behind her name for the first time, and she stopped when she heard him. He'd reached her just in time. The ghost of Marion had somehow found a doorway among the trees, and her hand was already lifted to knock on the frame.

He hadn't seen the door before, but he recognized it deep within his soul.

"What is it?" Marion asked. Her lips didn't move, but her eyes never fell from his.

"Don't go through that door," Seth said. "That's the last door you'd ever go through."

"But this is what I'm meant to do, isn't it?"

"You're meant for so much more than this. You aren't done, goddammit."

"Why stay?" Her voice cracked. "What remains for me here? I destroyed the Canope, and most of my spirit along with it. My memories are gone. I'll never know who I was, what I wanted, or the things I've done. I'm a ghost of myself in life or death."

Seth risked a step toward her, and Marion didn't yet move.

"Even if you've left the past behind, there's still a future," he said.

Marion swayed. "What rests in my future? Political marriage?"

"What are you talking about?"

"Konig wants me to marry him," she said. "It would give us an avenue to protect the Winter Court from the angels. That would be the end of my life as surely as that door."

"You love Konig," Seth said.

"I do," Marion agreed. The way that she looked at him might as well have been a very distinct "but," suggesting so many more things to be said.

But Marion didn't want to marry for politics.

But she wasn't certain she wanted to be with Konig.

He took another step.

Marion did, too.

She was only inches from the door now— inches from abandoning a tumultuous, confusing life that had been foisted upon her by gods who didn't care about what she wanted.

"Don't go in there," Seth said. "I can still save you."

"You don't know that."

"I won't ever know if you don't let me try."

Marion wavered again. "Seth..." She shook her head. Her ghostly hair swam around her shoulders as though she were one of the bodies submerged in Mnemosyne. "I know your secret, Seth. I know that you've been thinking about killing me. And you're so noble, such a hero, that you've been fighting against it although you don't even like me. Once this is over, you won't need to fight anymore."

Seth stared at her. "I like you."

"Do you?" she asked. "*Really*?"

God, how was he supposed to respond to that?

Charity was lurking in the back of his mind. *Tell her the truth.* That was what the revenant had been urging the entire time, and Seth had continually resisted. The truth was too much.

Now they were on the threshold of a doorway into death.

There was no more damage for the truth to do to Seth or Marion.

"I care about you a lot more than I should," he said carefully. "You said that there's something between us...and you were right, Marion. I've felt it, too."

"A connection," she said.

Seth clenched his hands into fists. "Chemistry."

Her whited-out eyes shimmered. She flickered where she stood. "What are you saying?"

Being careful wasn't enough. The door was still dragging her closer. Even though she hadn't taken a single step, she was inches nearer the threshold than she had been moments earlier.

Marion was still dying.

"I'm not ready for you to leave." Seth drew in a long breath—or what would have been a breath if the two of them hadn't been spirits wandering through a Dead Forest that was more metaphor than physical. "Don't leave, Marion. Please."

He held his hand out, and he waited.

The truth was that Seth wouldn't have fought to protect her so hard if he didn't like her.

A lot more than like her, actually.

Seth felt things for Marion that he hadn't let himself feel in years—and certainly not toward *her*. The half-sister of the god who'd ruined his life, and also happened to have a boyfriend, for fuck's sake. He'd sworn off fighting over women. He'd sworn off women altogether.

But most women weren't Marion.

"Please," Seth said again.

She stepped away from the door. "I don't want to leave you."

Her fingers settled against his.

There were no boundaries left between them. Not skin or bone or magic.

Seth and Marion were one, mind and voice.

The forest blurred around them as he pulled her toward him. The doorway flickered.

He saw nothing but Marion, stripped of all her power and pretense. She was nothing but a woman. Magical, powerful, fiery, and entirely mortal in spirit. Her arrogance was merely a feature. It didn't conceal the compassion at her core.

Seth *would* ensure she survived. Whatever that

took.

"Stay with me," he said, drawing her toward their bodies on the banks of Mnemosyne. "Don't let go."

Marion surrendered. They drifted.

Nyx was waiting beside their physical forms, faded away to nothing but a scrap of herself. There was a door waiting for her, too. "You shouldn't be capable of sparing the girl. It isn't possible."

"Then watch me do the impossible," Seth said, tugging Marion toward her body.

"But the gods have said—"

"Screw the gods," he said forcefully.

Marion nestled against his chest, head bowed to his heart. "Let's go back."

They folded into their bodies.

For the first time in minutes—eons—both of them inhaled.

NINETEEN

"Well, well, well. Look at what we have *here*."

The angel Suzume hopped over the counter in the Winter Court's meeting room. She had absolutely none of the usual grace of an angel; she flopped over, head down and butt up, and grabbed alcohol from the bottommost shelf.

She hopped back to her feet with a triumphant smile.

"Pixie vodka, Jibril!" She shook the bottle. "When's the last time you had some of this tasty stuff?"

Jibril folded his arms, his face immobile even as he radiated palpable disapproval. "Yes. Pixie vodka. With pixies who have been trapped for a good five years."

"Or more," Suzume said. She uncorked the bottle with a thumb and took a long swig. Then she wiped her hand over the back of her mouth. "Ahh. That's the stuff! *Now* we can talk politics." Suzume rounded on Nori. "Where's the steward this time?"

Nori backed away, swallowing hard. "Um."

She hadn't been expecting to explain Marion's absence to the angels yet again. When she'd returned Marion to Sheol with promises that she could handle "everything," her thoughts had been primarily oriented on distracting Konig, not on the politics that might unravel in Marion's absence.

Except that Nori had extended an olive branch to the angels after the last disastrous meeting, assuring them that they would have Marion's attention if they came again.

And when Nori had returned to the Winter Court, she had found that guests were waiting for her.

Jibril and Suzume had come back to mend fences with Marion.

The problem was that Marion was gone.

Again.

It was harder to tell with Suzume, but even the good-natured angel was starting to look annoyed.

"Here's the thing," Nori said. "Marion's had a lead on her memories, so she's trying to get them back. She simply could not wait to resolve that issue." There. That was a perfectly good explanation for her absence. As long as Nori didn't explain that other people were fully capable of retrieving Marion's memories, then it would be fine.

Jibril's expression didn't change, though. "Her memories seemed to be perfectly intact at the summit. She was collected enough to ensure our race didn't get the Winter Court."

"It was momentary," Nori said.

Jibril laughed bitterly. "How convenient. I'm supposed to believe this nonsense?"

"You know, it's funny," Suzume said, walking around the meeting room with the vodka bottle. She was tiny in comparison to the oversized ice sculptures twisting across the walls and arching over the ceiling. "Jibril came back to me the other day and he said, 'Suzy, I think we're going to war.' And I said to him, I said, 'No way, that'll never happen. Marion's going to find a way around it. Let me talk to her so I can fix things.'" She turned to face Nori, framed by a sheet of ice. "But Marion's still not here. Maybe Jibril wasn't wrong."

"He *was* wrong," Nori said. "We're working on a way to handle the alliance on the sidhe end. All you need to worry about is making sure that Leliel isn't a problem, and we'll have nesting space for the angels in no time."

"Leliel! Ha ha." Suzume rolled her eyes dramatically. "Yeah, *Leliel* is totally the problem."

Nori struggled for words. "It's not Marion's fault."

"I'm not interested in assigning blame," Jibril said. "If I were, though, I'd be inclined to agree with you, daughter of Azazel. This isn't Marion's fault." Nori only had an instant to feel relief before he stalked toward her, wings snapping wide at his back. "It's yours. We assigned you to smooth relations between sidhe and angel, not ruin them."

There was no way he could know what she'd done with Konig. "But—"

"There has been nothing but tumult since we gave your assignment to you. You're utterly incapable of performing the smallest diplomatic tasks." Jibril shook his fists at her. "Don't you realize the stakes we're dealing with? The death of our *entire species?*"

"Of course I do," Nori said.

"Don't speak to me," he growled.

Jibril vanished.

In his absence, there was nothing but silence.

Nori's anxieties rushed to fill the void.

She hadn't had a clue that the angels were planning to visit again. If she'd known, she could have facilitated a meeting with at least Konig, if not Marion.

No. Nothing she'd done could have kept Marion in the Winter Court.

Maybe they were right. Maybe this was all her fault.

"This is it, isn't it?" she asked dully, numb from the crown of her head to the tips of her toes. "This is what will initiate war."

"This vodka's not right for my mood. I need beer," Suzume said.

How could she think of alcohol at a time like this? "Shouldn't you get back to Dilmun before we start fighting?"

Suzume rolled her eyes. "Chill out. The death

of our species isn't worth this much drama."

"But war," Nori whispered.

"There's not going to be any goddamn war." Suzume plopped onto the edge of the bar and reached over to scoop another bottle from behind it. "You've been to Dilmun. You've seen how empty it is. There's like, three and a half of us."

In fact, there were twenty-eight angels who drifted in and out of the capital city of the Ethereal Levant. And that counted Nori, who was only half-blooded and served as a go-between for the angels and the sidhe.

"So what?" Nori asked.

"So there's no chance we'd survive war against four fucking courts in the Middle Worlds," Suzume said.

"Leliel said—"

"She's suicidal. I'm not. I'm immortal! I'd rather live alone for eternity than kill myself swinging my dick around trying to teach people a lesson." The angel emptied a beer bottle into her frosted glass. "If anyone goes to war, it will be Leliel alone. She'll drop dead and the rest of us will die peacefully one by one in the centuries to come."

Nori hadn't been drinking, but her head was still buzzing as if she'd been tossing back shots for hours.

The threats of war from the angels had been little more than grandstanding. Jibril was angry, but not angry enough to kill himself. Leliel was probably serious about attacking, but she had no backing.

War wasn't going to happen.

Most importantly, Konig didn't need to wed Marion to forge an alliance with the EL.

"If Leliel attacks again, you know everyone's going to take that as an act of war from all of us," Nori said. "Rylie Gresham in particular won't take that well. She could have President Peterson punch in the nuclear codes and flatten Dilmun."

"It won't happen," Suzume said.

"You sound confident."

"Hell yeah I do. Jibril will calm down. He's cool. And once he's levelheaded, the two of us will take care of Leliel. Like I said, I plan on living a long goddamn time."

Suzume tossed her head back, and her throat worked as she swallowed the alcohol down. Her eyes were watering when she dropped the glass.

"It sucks, getting to be an angel in Genesis only to watch my species die off," Suzume said. "Whatever. I'm going back to Dilmun. We've got the strong stuff there. *Way* better than pixie vodka. Wanna come?"

Nori shook her head numbly.

"Suit yourself," Suzume said.

The angel's wings extended. Her wingspan was impressive for a woman of her size—broader even than that of Leliel or Jibril—and her wings shone with even more light.

Suzume took off through one of the ballroom's open windows.

She vanished.

Nori tossed the empty beer bottle into the

recycling bin, and then put the glass into the sink. She was still numb when she walked through the hallways of Niflheimr to search for Konig.

He was in the south wing, with the refugees. At present, he was talking with Cyprian, the unseelie sidhe who had been helping Nori figure out the wards. They seemed to be arguing rather intensely about how to best protect Niflheimr from assault.

Konig's violet eyes brightened when he spotted Nori's approach.

"Excuse me," he said.

Cyprian nodded, taking the stairs down to the courtyard, where the other refugees were waiting.

Nori joined Konig on the mezzanine.

"The ethereal delegation was here," Nori said.

His face fell. "Why didn't you get me?"

"There wasn't time." She swallowed hard. "When Marion didn't show up—"

"Where's Marion?"

Nori clenched her fists so hard that her fingernails bit into her palms. "She didn't come." Let Konig infer that Marion was still locked in her bedroom, throwing a temper tantrum.

"Gods," Konig breathed.

"Jibril was pissed, but Suzume said there's no chance we'll go to war over this. Only Leliel's crazy enough to pick a fight with the sidhe over nesting space in the Winter Court. And the angels aren't going to let her do it." Nori's heart beat faster as she spoke, until she felt like she was on the brink of giggling. "You don't have to worry about an alliance with the angels. You and Marion don't have to get married!"

She'd expected that to be like dropping a bomb on Konig. Certainly, hearing it from Suzume had felt like that for Marion.

But the prince's face didn't change.

"I still want to get married to Marion," Konig said.

Nori struggled for words. The only thing she could manage to ask was, "Why?"

"I love her. You know that." He took her hands. "Nori, precious, I'm not going to wait for my immortal parents to die before becoming king. I'm going to have an extraordinary queen like Marion, who is truly one of a kind. And I'm going to cement one hell of a legacy." He shrugged. "'Father of a new ethereal race' sounds like a great note in the history books."

Distilling Marion's significance to a novelty—a highlight in the memoirs he imagined writing—stung almost as much as the realization that nothing would change. That Nori wasn't going to be with Konig. At least, not publicly. Not the way that she wanted.

And he wasn't going to let everything with the angels slide, either.

She stared at him wonderingly. This whole time, she'd believed Konig was struggling to perform damage control, when he'd really been playing a longer game. He had never feared war with the angels. He'd wanted to use them.

It was frightening.

And a little sexy.

"Think of it," he said softly. His knuckles stroked down her cheek. "Think of how much influence I'll have as a king who's restoring the ethereal race against all odds. And think of how much influence my advisors will have. Think of what this could do for *you*."

Nori couldn't stop shaking, and she didn't think it was the cold.

But she did think of it.

It would have been hard not to.

Konig couldn't become King of the Autumn Court until his parents stepped aside or died, and an ethereal Gray like Nori couldn't have any power in the Ethereal Levant on her own, either.

If they worked together, on the other hand…

A whole race. They could remake angels together, from a mere two-dozen to a booming species that would owe everything they had to the likes of Konig—and Nori, at his side.

Her trembling subsided. She took a few deep breaths.

"I see," she said.

Konig tugged her against him. His lips were cold when they kissed. Very, very cold. "I knew you would," he murmured.

When Charity used Marion's statuette, it felt like she had been squeezed through a meat grinder. It hurt so much that she couldn't help but cry out.

Then she appeared in the Winter Court.

She tumbled to the ground on a bed of moss, which grew inside a bedroom that was otherwise carved of ice. It was obviously sidhe magic allowing there to be spring among winter, and so it was no surprise to realize that it was Marion's bedroom—an unusual home for an unusual leader. Everything reeked of the mage girl, from the woody scent of her skin lingering in the air to the gold-trimmed contact lens case on the vanity.

Charity leaped to her feet, tossed the statuette aside, and burst from the room.

The hallway outside was empty.

Konig. Nori. I need to find them.

Marion's plea rattled within her mind.

Her glasses bounced on her chest, the arm still tucked into the neck of her shirt. She could have donned her glamour in order to make sure she'd look less alarming to the residents of the Winter Court. But there was no time for that. She couldn't waste a moment before finding the assistance that Marion so desperately needed.

Seth and Marion were trapped in Sheol with the Canope, and Charity needed to find the unseelie prince.

She ran down the hall to the throne room. It was freezing cold in the Winter Court—cold enough that the temperature burrowed its way into her revenant flesh. The throne room was no exception to that.

Disoriented, confused, Charity spun within the center of the empty hall, searching for signs of life.

"Konig?" she called.

Nobody responded. A mirror glowed faintly, dully, from the corner. The liquid light it poured was the only motion within the walls.

Voices echoed from the opposite side of the room.

Charity ran toward the other hallway.

"Konig?"

She exploded onto a mezzanine overlooking a courtyard. It was filled with tents, cots, and people, who Charity assumed must have been unseelie sidhe. It was strange to see so many of them milling in a single area. She'd assumed that the Winter Court would be empty after the civil wars that had wracked the plane for the last several years. They must have been refugees.

Prince ErlKonig stood on the other end of the mezzanine. Charity almost approached him until she realized what he was doing.

His arms were wrapped around Nori—delicate Nori with her straw-colored hair chopped to jaw length, who passed for a sidhe far better than she did an ethereal Gray. And Nori was wrapped around him, too. They were tangled up in each other in a way that could never be construed as anything but sexual.

Konig lifted his lips from Nori's. His eyes locked on to Charity, and his nose wrinkled with disgust at the sight of her revenant form, too ugly to stand among the stark beauty of Niflheimr.

"What are *you* doing here?" he asked.

"Marion's in Sheol and she...uh...she told me

that she wanted help, but..." Were her words even making sense? And would Marion want Konig's help if he was cheating with Nori?

His tone sharpened. "She's in Sheol?" He strode toward the doors, and then he seemed to remember that Charity had seen him kissing Nori. He stopped dead at the end of the hallway. He turned to face her slowly, a dangerous calm settling over him.

What would he do to Charity to keep things quiet?

She was pretty sure he was wondering the same thing.

Neither of them got the chance to come to a conclusion.

Acid gushed over the mezzanine, spraying from a pinhole in midair. It blasted a gash into the icy palace floor. Charity leaped away to keep her feet from getting burned, hand clapped over her mouth with shock.

The flow gentled as the pinhole stretched. It extended to be eight feet tall, like a bolt of black lightning that had frozen into existence atop Niflheimr.

A torrent of demons followed once the acid had waned, blasting forth in a whirling mass. Limbs flashed. Insect wings buzzed. One after another, they erupted into the air and tore across Niflheimr.

The screams followed a moment later, coming from the encampment below.

"No!" Nori only got a few steps toward the

stairs before Konig restrained her.

"I'll take care of this." He lifted a hand into the air. Shimmering light resolved into a sword—not the impressive demon blade he'd used in Sheol, but a proper sidhe weapon summoned through the walls of the Middle Worlds.

Charity wasn't confident it would help. Not against this attack. Even a big sword was a sole weapon, and hundreds of demons had poured through—enough to blanket the camp in utter darkness.

Sidhe scattered, racing away, too slow to fend off an unexpected assault.

The portal wasn't done producing demons, either. A human-like leg slid through the gash between dimensions, followed by a shoulder, and a striking face with glossy black eyes.

Arawn emerged from Sheol, and he didn't look happy.

TWENTY

Marion came back to life reclining on a bed of dead grass, colorless and dried, to the point where a single spark might have made all of it catch fire. A bronze wall towered over her.

Then the pain registered.

It wasn't the throbbing ache of having been attacked by the Hounds earlier. This wound was new. Ongoing.

There were teeth currently sunk into her throat.

Marion tried to pull away. She wasn't in command of her body—not her arms or legs or any other part. Mind and soul had disconnected on the brink of death. It took every ounce of her strength to even rest her hands on the shoulders of the man who gripped her.

She couldn't push him away.

The bridge of a nose pressed against her jaw. Lips were clamped to her throat.

Someone was drinking her blood.

She'd returned to life, but she was still fading.

"Stop," she rasped.

The sound of her voice was as much a shock to the creature that attacked her as it was to Marion.

Teeth released from her throat.

Seth lifted his head, gazing down at her in confusion that slowly shifted into horror. He looked like he'd recently returned to his body, too. His spirit had chased hers into the Dead Forest, and he'd lost his sense of reality as much as she had.

They'd come back to Seth drinking her blood.

She felt so faint.

"Seth," she whispered.

Her trembling hand lifted to his cheek, pressing against the side of his face. His lips were coated in her blood.

"Oh my God," he said.

Marion wanted to make a joke about that— saying "oh my God" as though it were some kind of expletive instead of something very literal and very relevant. She was so exhausted that she could only sink against him.

"No," Seth said, clutching her tighter. "Wait."

Marion let her eyes slide shut. She pressed her temple to his chest. There was a heart beating under his breastbone, strong and steady, sending the blood he'd devoured coursing through his body.

Seth gathered her into his arms. She felt herself come off of the grass, which must have meant that he was picking her up. She couldn't feel much aside from pain.

Marion peeled her eyes open. Seth was as injured as she was. He was dribbling blood from gashes carved into his throat and chest.

Yet he was standing.

"Hang on, Marion." Eyes as black as the night bored deep into her skull.

He changed.

Seth filled the Dead Forest with an energy that exceeded any mortal form. He was beyond human, beyond doctor, beyond demon. Smoke peeled from the wounds on his torso and drifted into the night.

Blood dribbled from his chest, and every drop that departed his body seemed to make space for more power.

In his arms, Marion could see all of Sheol: the complexity of the hive tunnels, Duat's temple, the dust that had once been the Canope. A million demons. A dozen rivers. So many trees. So much blood.

Seth expanded and kept growing.

Marion recognized what was happening—the extension of Seth's form out of the boundaries of the Nether Worlds, reaching to the Winter Court with little more than a thought. It wasn't teleportation, but something very much like ripping open the walls between dimensions so that he could slither between them.

She hadn't experienced that kind of energy since waking up in Ransom Falls. But she had done it before.

It was the kind of effortless disregard for reality only a god could have.

Marion snapped back into human form in the Winter Court.

The Dead Forest was gone. She was no longer held by arms, but resting on the bed in her rooms, stretched out under the canopy of trees that crowded her bed.

Seth didn't exactly stand in her room. He stood within it, and without. He existed within the Winter Court while also existing on every other plane.

She couldn't quite make out his face, because there was no face.

Only essence.

"You're going to be fine, Marion," Seth said. "Damn it, you're going to survive, whatever that takes." His voice wasn't something she heard with her ears, but within her skull.

Marion couldn't remember ever hearing his voice quite like that, but she'd heard voices like it before.

God voices.

"You're the third," Marion said. "You're like they are—like Elise and James."

Seth reared above her, outside of rational existence, yet radiating utter horror. "No."

"You're the third god of the triad," she said. "That's what they did to you. That's why you're different."

And he said again, "*No.*"

His denial was meaningless. The word itself carried throughout Sheol and the Winter Court. It rippled onto Earth.

No, no, no...

Marion reached toward him, hands lifted in a gesture resembling prayer.

"Seth," she said.

But he disappeared before she could make contact.

Demons crashed over Niflheimr's refugee camp in a tidal wave of suffering. Nori was frozen by shock, unable to do anything but stare as a hundred creatures from the Nether Worlds destroyed everything she had spent days trying to build. They ripped through tents, smashed supply crates, and tore sidhe apart.

And Nori could only watch.

Her mind raced as her body remained immobile.

Niflheimr should have had safeguards against invasion. That was part of the reason that civil war had been devastating, after all. It had murdered most seelie sidhe who had come in from the Summer Court. And they were almost the same species. Demons should have been creamed the instant they set tentacle on the ice.

But they hadn't been able to activate the wards on Niflheimr—not without a ruling sidhe to control them.

There was no way to stop the demons. Not until they decided to retreat or froze to death.

"Arawn, *stop*!" Charity Ballard raced toward the last demon to step through the portal.

Nori drew back, a strangled cry caught in her throat. She'd seen what Charity could do when she was angry, and she was currently in her revenant form—a thing of pure terror.

But Charity only clung to Arawn, and he clung back.

"Back off," he said with shocking restraint. "I'm not here for you."

Konig marched toward them, sword drawn. "Then talk to me."

"Where is she?" Arawn roared, spinning in place to search the mezzanine with wild eyes. "Where's that damn angel-spawn?"

Nori was certain he wasn't talking about her.

"How did you get here?" Konig asked. "You can't survive outside the Nether Worlds!"

"I can't survive in sunlight," Arawn snarled. "There's no such thing in the Winter Court, and I have as many planeswalkers among my people as you do."

"Get out of my palace!" Konig seized Arawn by the suspenders. Charity took a step toward them, and then stopped, as though she wasn't sure what to do.

Arawn suffered from no such confusion. He

gripped Konig's wrists, digging his fingers in. "I'm not going anywhere until I get satisfaction. She didn't take her memories back, and that means I don't get to go to Earth! Give me that damn mage!"

"What are you even talking about?"

"I agreed to hold on to the Canope, lure Seth Wilder to my position, and restore Marion Garin's memories," Arawn said. "I *told* them I would do it, but only because they were going to make me immune to sunlight!"

Konig released the suspenders. "Who told you that?"

"Those cursed gods!" Arawn screamed it to the sky, as though trying to get their attention. "But she shattered the damn Canope, and now they're gone—along with the promises they made!"

Refugees scrambled up the stairs, trying to escape the carnage below. Nori recognized Cyprian drenched in blood, cradling Ymir in his arms, with no sign of his daughters. They must have been lost among the camp.

Nori reflexively moved toward him to help, but the motion was a mistake. It drew Arawn's attention.

And he got to Cyprian first.

Arawn's fist slammed into the sidhe's belly. He was holding a switchblade that Nori hadn't noticed before, and it sliced right through the sidhe's gut.

Cyprian fell with a gurgling cry, dropping Ymir.

Nori screamed. She screamed, but nothing changed. Nothing got better. Cyprian was dead, along with dozens of the refugees. Their cries mingled with hers and echoed through all of Niflheimr.

Arawn yanked the child off of the ground. "What's your name, boy?"

"Ymir," he croaked.

"Put him down," Konig commanded, lifting his sidhe sword and stepping forward.

He stopped when Arawn shook the little frost giant.

"I'll kill Ymir if you don't let me have the mage!"

It was obviously a desperate move. There was no way that Arawn could think that some refugee child would be worthy of trading for Marion. But Konig looked alarmed.

Nori understood. Marion had taken a special interest in Ymir. A refugee child might not have meant anything to Konig, but to the woman he planned to have as bride...?

"Arawn, *please.*" It was strange to see such an earnest plea coming from Charity when she was in her revenant form. The ache in her gaze should have humanized her. She somehow managed to look even more frightening.

Arawn didn't waver.

"If the Canope is broken, you won't be able to give Marion her memories," Konig said. "It doesn't make sense to take her. It won't get you anything you want."

Arawn dragged the blade down the side of Ymir's throat, pressing hard enough to draw a thin line that bled. The child cried. "Then I'll just kill him!"

"Why not take something better?" Konig asked.

"There is nothing better! *Nothing!* Not when the sunlight has been stripped from me!"

Danger glimmered in Konig's eyes. "You don't need sun to have light in your life." He flashed across the mezzanine, using his unseelie power to leap several feet and reappear behind Arawn.

He seized the back of Charity's skull. Sidhe magic gushed over her.

The revenant didn't have time to react before her eyes went blank. She collapsed.

Nori smothered a pained squeal behind both hands.

"Take Charity," Konig said. "Leave Ymir."

Now Arawn was faltering. He gazed at Charity's unconscious form with adoration—not only unbothered by her monstrousness, but tempted by it.

Nori stepped toward him to save Charity. Konig shot a warning look at her. "She's the only witness," he said softly. This was how he would keep Marion from learning what Charity had seen. They'd all be protected from the fallout of the revelation.

But giving Charity to a demon?

Was that the best way to protect Nori and Konig from Marion's wrath?

Arawn dropped Ymir. He scooped Charity's limp body into his arms, stroking the scraggly hair back from her bulging forehead. "Yes," he said slowly. "Yes, I think that will work."

He snapped his fingers. The remaining swarm of demons vanished from the courtyard.

"You can't," Nori whispered. She was too afraid to say it any louder, even though she was screaming inside.

Arawn carried Charity into the portal that one of his planeswalkers had opened. It slammed shut, and there was nothing left in Niflheimr but silence.

After what felt like many years of calm, Marion jolted awake again.

She found herself in bed in the Winter Court, resting under clean sheets, surrounded by a tangle of vines and blossoms. Konig sat beside her, head tipped back against the wall. He stirred when she sat up.

"You're awake," he said, pushing shining black hair out of his face. "Thank the gods."

"What happened?" She remembered being injured—mutilated, really, pouring her blood out on the floor of the Dead Forest. She'd seen the Hounds shredding her flesh. Damn it all, she'd felt them *eating* her, and she should have been dead.

"I healed you," Konig said. "Again."

That was the second time he'd had to intercede with magic to save Marion from potentially life-threatening wounds. Or was it the third? She was losing track.

"What was wrong?" Marion asked.

"It looked like you got caught by the Hounds when you returned to Sheol."

The rest of her memories came rushing back: her run through the Dead Forest, approaching the doorway among the trees, and then Seth.

Seth.

She scrambled over Konig's legs to try to get out of bed. She was so much stronger than she had ever been in Sheol. "Have you seen Seth around?"

"He was gone by the time I came to help," Konig said. "He'd abandoned you to die."

She shivered hard, hugging her arms around herself. "That's because..." She didn't really have a way to finish the sentence. Because Seth was afraid to talk about what had happened in the Dead Forest? Or because he didn't want to explain why he'd been drinking her blood?

Marion's hand flew to her throat. There was no sign of the bite wound that he'd delivered.

Konig had truly healed everything.

"Charity said that the Canope was destroyed." The prince stroked his hand over her curls. "Marion, I'm so sorry."

She suspected that she should have been sorry, too. She should have been mourning for the memories she'd lost and the personhood that would never be restored. Everything that had made Marion who she was before waking up in Ransom Falls had vanished the instant that she had chosen to shatter the Canope.

For the moment, she felt nothing.

"I'd like to talk to Charity," Marion said. The

revenant had seen things in Sheol. She might know if Marion had witnessed Seth becoming what she thought, or if Marion was going completely crazy from having her essence destroyed.

"I'm afraid that won't be possible," Konig said. "The news keeps getting worse, princess. While you were gone..." He sighed. "I'll have to show you."

Her heart jumped. "Show me what?"

"Come," he said.

Konig wrapped furs around Marion and helped her down the hallway toward the courtyard where the refugee camp had been erected. She stepped onto the mezzanine.

Nori was there, and she stiffened at the sight of Marion. Her eyes darted between Marion and Konig.

"Thank the gods you're okay," Nori said hesitantly.

Marion grimaced. "Please don't do that."

"Do what?"

"Thank the gods."

Nori obviously didn't understand, but she nodded. "Anything."

Marion had to lean heavily on Konig as they walked toward the mezzanine's railing together. It was so quiet in the courtyard. She could hear only the wind.

Her foot caught on a furrow in the icy floor. She nearly tripped. "What happened there?" Marion asked.

"This," Konig said, resting her against the railing.

The camp below was decimated. Every single bed and tent was shredded, and the wreckage was so severe that it took Marion a moment to realize that not all of it was inorganic.

Those splashes of blue weren't potions, but the strange, gem-colored blood of unseelie sidhe.

The cloth wasn't entirely canvas, but clothing.

The refugees were dead.

"No," Marion whispered.

She staggered down the spiral stairs, bundling the furs around herself so that she wouldn't trip on them.

"Wait," Konig said. He hurried to catch up, and he reached Marion just in time, because her knees buckled on the bottommost stairs.

"What happened?" she asked, clinging to his arm. "Where is everyone?"

"There was only one survivor," he said.

Ymir was sitting on the very bottom step of the stairs, tousled white hair stuck to his forehead with blood. His cheeks and throat had been scratched. He gazed at Marion with haunted, hollow eyes and then dropped his head to his arms again.

"Are you okay?" she asked.

He wouldn't speak. He hugged his legs to his chest, bowed his face to his knees, and rocked in place without saying a word.

Her relief at seeing the little frost giant was quickly overwhelmed by grief and horror.

There was no motion in the camp. Just a lot of

dismembered bodies that were getting rapidly covered by snow.

"Cyprian?" Marion whispered, turning her eyes toward Nori at the top of the stairs.

The other half-angel only shook her head.

Marion tried to move out into the camp to search for survivors. She only made it two steps away from the stairs before her legs buckled again. This time, Konig let her fall. The icy cold that seeped through her shredded jeans was only fractionally worse than the cold spreading within her heart.

"Charity tried to save everyone, but she just ended up being taken," Konig said. His hand rested on her shoulder.

"Who did this?" Marion asked. It shocked her how calm she sounded. The frigidity had entered her soul.

"It was Leliel," Konig said. "She was infuriated that you missed another meeting, and she decided to retaliate."

Tears burned in Marion's eyes. "By killing helpless refugees?"

"I tried to save them, but...there's only so much I could do against the might of an angel." Konig swallowed audibly. His eyes shimmered, though it looked like he was blinking back tears of anger, not sadness. "We could have stopped this, Marion."

He was right. If she hadn't run into Sheol to chase her memories, she'd have been able to negotiate with the angels.

Marion picked up the remnants of a fur cloak.

It was stained with the sparkling blood of sidhe.

"I should never have left," she whispered. Not the first time, or the second time, or...any time at all.

The Winter Court had needed her. The steward.

She had failed them all.

"Don't blame yourself for that," Konig said. "You did what you needed to do to restore your memories. You had to go. But..." He looked away without finishing the sentence, and Marion appreciated his momentary discretion.

He didn't need to say anything else. Even if Marion hadn't been there for the meetings, they could have brokered peace another way.

She could have agreed to marry Konig when he'd proposed to her.

"What will happen next?" she asked, letting the cloak fall from her hands.

"We should fix our relationship with the EL," Konig said. "We need to make it clear that we're on the same side. If this is what one angel did to Niflheimr, think of what a concerted attack could do to the Autumn Court."

Marion could imagine it far too clearly.

All those dead bodies. All that blood spilled.

And many more orphaned children, just like Ymir.

Marion was too late to save the refugees, but she could protect Konig's family, his court, and his kingdom. "Ask me again," she said, barely able to speak through the tears. She stood up and locked her knees. She wouldn't fall again. She wouldn't be weak anymore.

He touched her hand. "Ask you what, princess?"

"Ask me to marry you."

Konig's eyes widened. "You were right when you said it shouldn't be like that. When we marry, we should do it for love."

Seth's expression in the Dead Forest swam to the forefront of Marion's mind.

Chemistry, he had said.

There was chemistry between them.

But this? This was so much more than whatever she felt for Seth.

"This *is* about love," Marion said. "Love for the people we can save by going over Leliel's head and making a real, proper alliance with the angels."

"Princess..." Konig's Adam's apple bobbed when he swallowed hard. "I wish I had a ring, or— it will just have to be like this, won't it? Marion Garin, my princess...will you marry me?"

She clutched Konig's hand, standing among the dead with their blood on her fingers.

She looked at poor little Ymir, alone again in her shattered palace.

And Marion said what she should have said long before.

"Yes."

Seth appeared on Earth.

When he'd fled from Marion's bedroom in the Winter Court, he hadn't been aiming for anywhere in particular. His only thought had been to get *away*.

He'd gotten away. So far away that he found himself in desert that was unmistakably Nevadan, most likely outside of Las Vegas, and distant enough that the city's lights barely lightened the horizon. He was kneeling on packed desert soil and surrounded by sagebrush.

Seth was also bleeding.

"Oh shit," he groaned, clutching at his stomach.

The bite wounds that the Hounds had inflicted upon him had hurt again. It turned out that he wasn't immune to pain after all—as long as the pain was the sort that came from one's intestines flopping out of the abdominal cavity.

He clumsily tried to stuff everything back where it belonged, but it was like trying to pile spaghetti noodles into fishnet. It all kept flopping out again.

I should be dead.

People didn't survive these kinds of wounds. Newborns could live through something similar. It was called gastroschisis, when they were born with their internal organs bulging through the navel, and was best resolved by covering the intestines until they naturally reduced into the stomach cavity. But adults, no. Never adults. Not when everything was perforated and dribbling onto the desert.

Seth wasn't exactly an ordinary adult, though.

The night weighed heavily on him as he wrapped his arms around his body. Large intestine slithered through his fingers like giant earthworms. The warm desert air stung inside of him, biting at places that never should have been exposed, even as the moon bore upon his flesh.

He could still taste Mnemosyne on his tongue, lingering underneath the flavor of Marion's blood.

That was the worst of it. The fact that he had bowed his head to Marion's throat and drank from her when she was most vulnerable.

She would never forgive him.

Hell, Seth would never forgive himself.

The more that he struggled against himself, the more wounded he seemed to become. Despite his lucidity, he was still distinctly dying. The skin was peeling away. Blood was gushing out of him.

He pressed a hand to his chest.

His heart wasn't beating.

"I can't," he whispered. He wasn't sure how that sentence was supposed to end, but those two words summed up all of his feelings about the situation.

I can't be alive right now.

I can't be what Marion thinks I am.

I can't be a god.

Headlights fell on him, so bright that they blinded. He flung a bloody arm in front of his eyes to shield them.

For a wild instant, he thought that it was the

Office of Preternatural Affairs seeking retribution for his attack on their detention center. Las Vegas wasn't all that far from their facility in the Mojave. There were surely security cameras that had caught sight of his face.

Then the off-road vehicle's lights angled away, allowing Seth to see that it was covered in leopard print. That wasn't the OPA's style.

A door on the side of the ATV opened and shut again. Sagebrush rustled.

Seth fumbled to draw a gun, but his underarm holster had been destroyed by the Hounds, and the Beretta was gone. He was still patting his body in search of a weapon when a woman stepped into the beams of light.

It was a stocky, square-faced woman with spiky hair and stone gauntlets. She was checking the time on her phone.

"*Finally*," Dana McIntyre said, shoving her cell into her back pocket. "What took you so long?"

Seth gaped at her. "I was—I mean—you know I had been in Sheol. How did you find me?"

"I was told where you'd show up."

"By who?" he asked.

Dana didn't answer the question.

She didn't need to. Seth already knew.

"I have two things to say to you. First thing: you better have brought my map back like you promised. Second thing: Elise says that she hopes you're done being a little bitch because it's time for you to go back to the garden. She misses your punk ass. And it's time for you to be God again."

www.ingramcontent.com/pod-product-compliance
Lightning Source LLC
Chambersburg PA
CBHW051332250626
47155CB00007B/2568